A Clean Pair of Hands

A Clean Pair of Hands

Oscar Reynard

Rev. date: 06/19/2013

To order additional copies of this book, contact:
Xlibris Corporation
0-800-644-6988
www.Xlibrispublishing.co.uk
Orders@Xlibrispublishing.co.uk
306175

Contents

COVER ILLUSTRATION

The painting by Eugène Delacroix, *Liberty Leading the People*, portrays the July 1830 French Revolution in which Charles X of France was deposed and replaced by his cousin Louis-Philippe.

One interpretation of the image is that it encapsulates the forces of people wanting liberty and the battle the people went through to gain freedom and equality. Liberty, herself, is no ordinary woman; she is a lone revolutionary goddess depicting power and even supernatural strength in her leadership of men. Since liberty is part of the French motto—Liberté, égalité, fraternité—this painting has become a primary symbol of the French Republic, and its message is still valid today, as we will discover.

DEDICATION

This book is dedicated to Thérèse, an unrecognised character, who by her lucidity, romanticism, and cool, logical observation overcame the difficulties of putting sometimes passionate events into words.

FOREWORD

Every man has two countries, his own and France.

(Thomas Jefferson)

France is the most visited tourist destination in the world, with over seventy-nine million arrivals in 2011. These tourists expect to enjoy a closer view and sample a country known the world over for its gastronomy, sophisticated Paris fashions and luxury goods, adult fun, quaint rustic communities living in golden-stone medieval villages, Provence under sunny skies, chateaux proudly proclaiming an illustrious past, art in all its forms, the Tour de France, and occasional accordion music.

France is a meeting point for the northern and southern European cultures, and this is evident in the ongoing confrontation between the population and authority, a fight that takes the form of brazenly challenging rules and by high levels of assertiveness when working around any obstacles that confront people in their daily lives.

What most tourists may not appreciate is the level of deep-rooted distrust that the French have towards their government and authorities, which explains their individualistic reaction to rules and constraints imposed by their leadership.

What lies behind this distrust? Probity in public life is low on the French achievements' list, for although successive governments proclaim themselves to be 'open and transparently democratic', this is far from the truth. According to the Transparency International Corruption Index for 2011, France ranked twenty-fifth in the world. But, before anybody thinks this is merely a finger-pointing exercise, the USA was twenty-fourth, Ireland nineteenth, and Great Britain sixteenth.

We all have a long way to go, but Canada, who ranked tenth, Australia, eighth, and above all, New Zealand, first, show that reasonable levels of probity in public life can be achieved. In a modern society, it is increasingly harder to keep dirty secrets and knowledge of corruption in public life trickles down to every individual, so one could assume that if it is known about and tolerated, it must be OK. But how does that situation affect public attitudes? What can the electorate do to reorientate their leaders?

The lyrics of a French song by Jacques Dutronc derisively articulate the irony:

Madame L'Existence
Je voudrais m'acheter une démocratie
Je voudrais m'acheter le meilleur d'une vie
Je voudrais m'acheter de la liberté
Et puis un peu de fraternité.
On n'a pas ce genre d'articles
Vous vous trompez de boutique
Ici c'est pas la république.[sic]

Translation:
'Lady Life
I'd like to buy myself a democracy
I'd like to buy the best of life
I'd like to buy some liberty
And then a bit of fraternity.
But we don't have those kinds of things in stock
You are in the wrong shop
This is not the republic.'

(Jacques Dutronc, French singer and songwriter, 2003)

This story recounts how members of one modern French family carve out their individual lives, with dramatic consequences. For families and presidents who live dangerously close to an edge where they may lose control, those consequences are not always direct or immediate. They can strike suddenly, unexpectedly, and, in many cases, retrospectively.

PREFACE

A Break-In, December 1998

I have never believed in the absolute power of truth by itself. But it's important to recognise that when the energy on both sides of the balance is equal, truth will win over lies.

(Albert Camus)

The four cyclists parked their bicycles carefully and used them to climb over the high wall. The last man handed up a backpack and they quickly crossed the lawn and disappeared into shadows at the back of the house.

There was a break-in at Michel and Charlotte Bodin's home at Maisons-Laffitte, in the Yvelines, to the north-west of Paris. Charlotte phoned her aunt, Thérèse Milton, a few days later to tell her that some masked men had broken in, beaten up Michel, and locked her in a cupboard. She had been terrified but was unhurt. Michel was recovering from bruises and had been very withdrawn ever since.

Thérèse expressed concern before asking, 'What did they take?'

'Nothing much. Just some small items of jewellery and alcohol. There was no money in the house for them to take. They kept asking where the money was kept, but in the end, they left with almost nothing of value.'

'Have the police caught anybody?' probed Thérèse.

'So far they haven't. Nobody saw anything.'

It seemed an odd story, but in the absence of further information, Thérèse and her husband George Milton had no alternative but to be relieved that nothing worse had happened and to speculate on the rationale behind such an apparently pointless intrusion. They knew that their nephew, Michel, usually carried a large roll of banknotes with him. Why had the raiders not found that? Perhaps, they had. And why had Charlotte said there was no money in the house? There was no explanation.

Later, on the Sunday morning of the break-in, at around 4 a.m., Annick Bodin the eldest of three daughters, returned to her parents' home with two of her friends who intended to sleep over. They had a drink in the kitchen and quietly retired to Annick's bedroom so as not to wake her parents.

At around ten thirty, when Annick eventually began to move towards the kitchen, she was thinking that her parents usually went to bed late and slept in, especially on a Sunday morning when there was no housekeeper, but she still wondered why there were no sounds of anyone moving about. She tapped on their bedroom door, entered, and found them, much as the intruders had left them.

When the police arrived, Annick opened the front door to find an unfit-looking man and a woman, probably in her mid-thirties, both with glum faces. Annick's first impression was confused. The man wore a dark overcoat over a rumpled suit, with trousers that were too long, and a white shirt. His sticky black hair hung below his collar. The woman had unevenly dyed, short blonde hair, long brown leather boots over dark jeans, and a multi-coloured knitted top with a generous loose collar which fell away from her neck. They introduced themselves as Francis and Paula, and Annick was seriously wondering if they might be journalists until she saw the police markings on their car and the man described himself as 'head of crime'. She let them in, and as they entered, Charlotte came to meet them in the hall, wrapping her dressing gown closer and led them to the kitchen where Michel was staring into a large cup of coffee, holding an icepack to the side of his head. Annick took up a position standing with her back to the sink and folded her arms nervously across her chest.

There was no circumlocution. No customer-care scripted sympathy. The officers drew up chairs, sat at the table, opened notebooks, and the man asked what had happened.

According to Charlotte, some men, probably four, had broken in through the garden room door, beaten up her husband, and demanded to know where the money was kept. She had seen very little of what happened after that because they had thrown her into a cupboard and locked the door.

'Was there any money or a safe in the house?'

'Little money, and there is no safe.'

'So what did they take?'

'Two new bottles of whisky that were on the bar.' She gestured in the direction of the salon. 'We haven't looked around the rest of the house yet.'

'What sort of whisky?'

Michel raised his head. 'One bottle of Chivas Regal and one bottle of Glenfiddich.'

The officer attempted a glacial smile for the first time. 'So you are saying that four masked men broke into your house to steal two bottles of whisky?'

'They took some cash from my wallet but left the credit cards,' added Michel.

'How much?'

'About five thousand francs.'

'So not exactly a big haul. Can you describe the men in more detail? Did you hear them speak? How do you know they were men?'

Neither of the victims could add to the description of four masked people in black. None of them spoke, and there were no identifying marks.

'I thought you said they asked where the money was kept.' There was a pause. Michel's eyes flickered momentarily towards Charlotte.

'Yes, they did,' she responded.

'One of them or several?'

'One of them.'

'Was it a French or a foreign accent?'

'Maybe a slight foreign accent.'

'Go on,' the officer encouraged Charlotte to say more.

'I don't know for sure, but it might have been North African.' Charlotte slowly raised her handkerchief to dab a teary eye. She sniffed.

'When you heard them speak, were you already locked in the cupboard?'

'No, they shouted when they first came into the bedroom and then put me in the cupboard.'

'Can either of you explain why it took from around 2 a.m., when we think the men left, till nearly ten thirty this morning before your daughter discovered you?'

They shook their heads and remained silent.

The officer continued, 'I know your mouths were taped, but did either of you make a noise so she might hear you?'

'I tried to bounce the chair and make a noise on the floor,' said Michel, 'but I was too weak to lift it.'

'And you, madame?' He turned to Charlotte. 'Did you bang on the cupboard door or try to force the lock?'

'No, I was too frightened. I wasn't sure if it was my daughter or the intruders looking around. I was aware of several people in the house, so I stayed quiet.'

The policeman continued, 'During this period, when you were alone, did you try to communicate with each other?'

'No, I didn't know where my wife was. I didn't see her being put in the cupboard. It was on the landing outside the bedroom,' Michel explained.

'Madame Bodin, did you try to make a noise or communicate with your husband?'

'No, as I said, I was worried the men might still be in the house.'

'So even this morning, until your daughter found you, you believed that the burglars were still here?'

'I must have dozed off. I can't remember. It was dark in the cupboard.'

Turning to Annick, the policeman asked, 'Do you have anything to add, mademoiselle? Did you notice anything unusual when you arrived with your friends?'

'No, nothing special. I was tired and I didn't look around.'

'And where are your friends now?'

'They left when I called you. I had to go next door to make the call,' Annick responded.

'Can you give us their names and addresses?' She did so with the minimum of words and became silent again.

The two police officers diligently completed their notes and then raised their heads 'Do you mind if we look around now?'

'Go ahead. Would you like me to come with you?' offered Michel.

'No, that won't be necessary. I'd prefer you to stay here.'

The officers opened a large, dark briefcase, took out a camera, and put on rubber gloves and blue plastic overshoes. They went first to the garden room door. It was a double door, single glazed, each side with fourteen panes of glass in two columns by seven high. One pane next to the lock had been pushed or levered out of the glazing bars. This must have made a small noise when it fell on the carpet. The male officer opened the door carefully and closed it again several times, moving it with one finger. It moved smoothly and quietly but bumped lightly against a rubber stop fixed to the wall. That might have been audible upstairs, but it would have been easy to prevent the door swinging so far. The glass on the floor was in one piece, having fallen on to the thick carpet. It had been placed against the skirting board as if someone wanted to avoid treading on it.

Then they went to the main bedroom and saw silver duct tape still adhering to the chair and plenty more at the foot of the bed and on the outer bedposts. The woman officer took photographs as they proceeded.

When they came downstairs, Michel asked the police officers if they intended to have a forensic examination carried out.

'We'd like to ask you some more questions first if you don't mind,' said the woman officer. She summarised, 'As we understand it, four men, we'll call them "men" for the time being, entered your house by removing a glass pane and turning the key which had been left in the lock. Do you always leave the key in the lock?'

Charlotte answered, 'Not normally, but sometimes we forget.'

'So this time you forgot. The men make a small noise, perhaps when the glass fell or when banging the door open, and when they hear movement upstairs, they wait for someone to come down, render him semi-conscious and grab you at the top of the stairs. They ask for money, but after throwing you in a cupboard and tying your husband to a chair, they leave with a few thousand in cash and just two bottles of whisky. They appear to be efficient, professional burglars with identity disguise and protective wear. It doesn't sound like an opportunist robbery attempt. Have we understood that correctly so far?'

'Yes, that's about right,' said Charlotte in a flat voice.

'That's it as far as we know,' added Michel.

'Did they look around the house?' enquired the male officer.

'They did in the bedroom, but we couldn't see what they did in the rest of the house.'

'Well, it looks as though they were very tidy people because there is no sign of what burglars typically do when making a quick search for valuables, especially money, and they left your credit cards I believe.'

'Yes,' mumbled Michel, his head hanging forward above the coffee cup.

'It's strange,' said the woman officer reflectively, creasing her face in puzzlement and pushing her glasses up her nose, 'because there is usually a pattern to these things, and there have been no reported incidents of this kind in the area. Can you think of anybody who would do something like this to embarrass or frighten you?'

They both shook their heads.

'Where were your other two daughters this weekend?'

'Our middle daughter is studying at an international college in Spain. She comes home only a couple of times a year. And the youngest is on her way to stay with relatives in Ireland until Christmas. Only our eldest daughter, Annick, was staying here,' Charlotte informed them, nodding towards Annick.

'And, mademoiselle Annick, how did you call the police. We noticed that the phone cable was torn out upstairs?'

'Yes, and they did the same to the downstairs phone. As I said before, I had to go next door to our neighbours to make the call,' replied Annick.

'Your call was timed at eleven thirty-eight. That's quite a long time after you discovered your parents, isn't it?'

'Well, I had to see to my parents first, and they were both suffering from shock, so I dealt with them as a priority. There was nothing more anybody else could do by then.'

The woman turned to the male officer enquiringly and then back to the Bodins.

'Well, I don't think we can do much more here today, but if you remember any other details, however small, please call us on this number.' She handed a card to Michel.

'Are you going to make any more enquiries?' asked Michel.

'Yes, we will talk to the neighbours to check if anybody heard or saw anything unusual, such as any strange vehicles parked on the road. And we would like to take a statement from you, mademoiselle, and from your friends down at the station on Monday morning, so please let them know. We would also like to interview your sister when she is back from Ireland, so please ask her to come and see us as soon as she returns.' She smiled a cheerful but business-like smile, beaming it at each of the Bodins in turn.

Then to the parents she said, 'We will also need you to come to the station to sign statements to the effect that we have registered all your testimonies correctly and that you swear to the completeness and truthfulness of your statements. We will let you know when they are ready.'

That was it. The police shook hands all round and left, easing themselves into their tiny Peugeot car and drove away, leaving Michel, Charlotte, and Annick with their thoughts.

In the car, the officers agreed that the couple were lying, or in the case of Annick, possibly concealing something to protect her parents.

'You saw the tape on the bed, Francis?' asked the woman. 'It looked to me as though someone had been bound to it.'

'Yes, and you could see that they both had tape marks on their faces and their wrists.'

'Why would they not want to discuss that?' she asked.

'For the moment, they are in denial, but we'll see how it evolves. I think this was done to frighten or warn them. You can't ignore the fact that it was so easy for the burglars.'

'Do you think the daughters could be behind it?'

'It's unlikely but possible, but we don't have enough to go on yet.'

'Why would they do something like that?'

'I don't know, Paula. An alternative scenario is that Bodin could have organised it himself. It's just that in all the similar cases that I know about. The motives were to profit from an insurance claim or have someone killed and make it look as though it was part of a robbery. There was no attempt here to do much more than enter and leave.'

'They are not claiming sex as a possible reason. Madame Bodin is very attractive.'

'No, they haven't said so, but sometimes, victims are too ashamed to admit it. But in any case, you don't normally have four professional burglars entering a house to rape a woman. That is not the modus operandi of a sex maniac.'

'So were they perhaps after something else, which they took, and Bodin can't say because it was something illegal? Or at least something he can't admit in front of his wife.' suggested the woman.

'That's a possibility. When I said I would come with you today, it was because a number of unrelated reports have mentioned this address, and I wanted to meet monsieur Bodin. I'll ask for some more background on him and have the earlier reports reviewed to find out if he's in contact with something murky. Some businessmen get drawn into crime financing because they have an honest front and clean cash to invest. Once they start doing something dirty, however minor, they are in the hands of the criminals. I don't think this is something we need to investigate as a crime because I believe it was more a disciplinary matter, but it gives us some information to add to what we have.' He slid his hand across to Paula's knee, and they drove back to the office in silence to file their reports.

After the police interview, Michel Bodin climbed slowly back upstairs, feeling increasingly stiff after his ordeal. He planned to take a hot bath and soak for a long time. When he opened a drawer of the chest in the bedroom to take a clean towel, he saw to his amazement a brown envelope he recognised. It had been resealed with thick tape. He tore it open. Inside was a wad of twenty, five hundred Franc notes with their images of Pierre and Marie Curie and smelling of fresh oil from the printing press. He quickly hid the envelope under his dressing gown and then on second thought, put it on the top shelf of the wardrobe where he knew Charlotte could not reach it. He was sweating profusely, and his head was banging. He really needed that bath.

CHAPTER ONE

Introduction 1950s-1970s

I was very young when it came to my mind that morality consisted of proving to men that after all else, to be happy, there was nothing better to do in this world than to be virtuous.

Immediately I started to meditate on this question and I still am meditating on it.

(Denis Diderot, philosopher and author, 1713-1784)

Michel Bodin grew up in Paris in the 1950s and 1960s. His mother Huguette was to be the major influencer of his life, during the early years as a mentor, and long into adulthood as a strong competitor. She had left home at seventeen to escape paternal discipline and improve her prospects and married first, briefly, a young man who shared her taste for excitement, but once the whirl of dance halls and laughter had subsided, Huguette realised that her husband's modest intellect and vision left him with little prospect of wealth acquisition; so for the foreseeable future, she was faced with a daily reality of living in a tiny second-floor apartment above a shop in an unfashionable Paris suburb, with a downstairs outside toilet. She could see no way forward and became increasingly frustrated with her narrow existence. She was not someone who would obediently endure.

There had to be a way forward or out. Huguette was a talented singer and dancer and, as a child, had hopes of becoming a star. At the age of seven, she had won a scholarship to the Paris Opera Ballet School, but her family's limited resources meant there was no question of taking up the opportunity even with a partial sponsorship. Now, twenty and married, she was already too old for all that, but the idea lingered that she might try to get into show business. She had good looks, vivacity, and enough determination to succeed as an actress, so she continued to dream of getting into a drama school at the earliest opportunity. Meanwhile, her husband's succession of small business ventures, financed by his parents, all ended inconsequentially, but at least, the experience she gained within their small-scale commerce demonstrated Huguette's innate business sense and a facility with figures. If it wasn't for the fact that her husband was less capable than her, slower on the uptake, and unwilling to let her take control, the results may have been better. Their ensuing arguments, mostly about lack of money, were loud and sometimes violent.

After nearly two years of married life, Huguette felt like a trapped tigress. All her plans were blocked, but she was determined to regain control of her life somehow, so at this point, she swallowed her pride, went back to her parents, and found a job at a local hardware and paint shop. There, she showed the young owner how to expand his business by offering decorating services to local shops, and from the success of that basic idea, she developed a wider range of services, including refitting local shops, bakeries, and bars that had been neglected since the Second World War, engaging teams of artisans to carry out the work under her direction. François Bodin, the young owner of the business, which he had inherited from his father, was impressed by the ideas and by the woman herself, and soon after Huguette got a divorce, the pair married. Huguette's theatrical dream was replaced by a more accessible new vision—success in business.

Huguette's marriage to François Bodin brought her fulfilment on several levels. François appreciated her flair for commerce, combined with toughness and ambition, which when teamed with his energy, enthusiasm, and creative skills as a designer, boosted their business substantially. He was happy to involve her fully as an equal partner, though his male pride demanded that when he told the story, he tended to take full credit.

The fruits of their partnership included an only son, Michel, who was born soon after they were married, and the money the business brought in enabled Huguette, her husband, and their son to enjoy a celebrity lifestyle. Thus, in his teenage years, Michel could enjoy the madness of a *blouson doré*, a description applied to the spoilt children of wealthy and indulgent French families.

Michel's mother wanted him to miss out on nothing, so as she was heavily committed to building the business with her husband, she expressed her love for Michel through generous allowances and by turning a blind eye to his increasingly loose morals.

Michel later described his life at that time as a lust for experience, to a point of wanting to kill himself. During his early teenage years, he was one of a gang of youths who, on warm summer evenings, gathered to drive around quiet suburbs on small-engined, but ear-shatteringly noisy, mopeds that only the French seem to tolerate and for which no driving licence was required. Later, he drove his increasingly powerful motorcycles faster and faster, racing friends around Paris until one of them hit a traffic sign and subsequently died. Another jumped a red light as part of their games and was seriously injured in a crash with a lorry. Girls were attracted to the little band of high-spending youths, and sex was a commodity that required no relationship beyond sharing a ride on a motorbike as a prelude.

Many acres of print have been published about violent political extremist groups that sprouted in the late 1960s across Europe, a time when horrendous crimes were committed by young people who were simply floating aimlessly and seeking excitement. That could have been where Michel was headed next. However, just as he was beginning to tire of the easy life and was wondering where to find further stimulation, he was called up for compulsory military service.

Although army generals wanted infantrymen and were not concerned about the future career prospects of their temporary charges, there was a steady undercurrent of unofficial negotiation in which wealthy parents could obtain favoured postings for their offspring. Clearly Huguette and François Bodin knew somebody with a lot of influence because Michel was posted to the island of La Réunion, to the East of Madagascar, in the Indian Ocean. It wasn't the most useful posting from a career-development or character-building perspective because he spent most of his time guarding the military airbase by walking the perimeter with a dog, but it was safe, and there was an attraction to offset the boredom. He was followed by a besotted girlfriend, Charlotte, and together they spent all of his free time in a thatched cabin or beachcombing for magnificent tropical seashells, which formed the central attractions of a collection that Michel brought back to France.

Once his military service was over, Michel found that his dissolute school years and consequent absence of educational qualifications left him little alternative but to settle into the family business; for in France, academic qualification is the only recognised key to career opportunities in the public and private sectors. One could say that he pursued the only career that nature fitted him for, but it turned out to be an excellent move for him and for the business. He shared his mother's drive and ambition, and he had the wit and charm to channel it in ways which added significantly to the company assets once he had learned from practical experience how the business worked and especially how it depended on good personal relations with the clients, an art that he soon mastered.

Huguette and François Bodin were in many ways a dream team. They were intelligent fighters who would do what was necessary to achieve success. They were powered by acquisitiveness, and their frenzy for visible wealth was amply rewarded. One might have expected a clash of Titans from time to time, but although François was an archetypal alpha male, he adored Huguette and always gave way to her. Michel noted this and later commented that his father was a sheep, rather than a wolf. He said this about his father although their relationship was, on the surface, always respectful. But it was his mother's outrageous ostentation that Michel admired and copied, and he was determined that he would show he was her equal. He also learned from his mother that once you were locked on to making money as your first priority in life, other sentiments could take a back seat. You could always be generous with money as a substitute for affection.

Charlotte had been in love with Michel since the age of fourteen, and having followed him to the other side of the world, it was hardly surprising that once established in his new job, Michel married her, and by their late twenties, they had three daughters, Annick, Estelle, and Lydia.

With time and experience, Michel proved capable of taking further responsibilities for the business, but his parents were not yet ready to relinquish absolute control, which built up friction from time to time, especially between Michel and his mother. By now, they were effectively rivals. Their differences came to the surface because, whilst like most people running small businesses in France, Huguette considered the French tax authorities to be public enemy number one, and therefore to be out-played at every opportunity, she had very strict ideas about ethics in the context of dealing with clients, an area where Michel tended to have a more flexible attitude. Later, as his parents moved towards early retirement to pursue other interests, they handed control of the business to Michel and Charlotte, and it took another forward leap under the impetus of Michel's new initiatives, which included exploring beyond some of his parents' ethical constraints.

CHAPTER TWO

The Cash Machine, 1980s

The first source of happiness is health.

Then a loving family life, and friendships, together with a fulfilling job.

In summary, health, love and work are the three keys to happiness.

Money is a means to acquire some of the essentials, but it plays a secondary role.

(Ernst Fehr, born 1956, Austrian economist and psychologist)

The François Mitterrand Presidency, which came to power in 1981, established itself as the flag bearer for a culture that pervaded and has continued to pervade French life. It flourished in an environment of inequality, self-interest, and cheating and set up its own framework for fraud on a massive scale, based on an earlier communist model. It demonstrated how a government can quite overtly exploit ways of playing beyond the limits of its own rules to tip the odds in favour of staying in power and acquire whatever financial resources are necessary to secure support and influence election results. In short, it was a kleptocracy. So how did French taxpayers respond?

They felt under threat from their own government, so just as in ancient times, those who had the means built their own citadels to protect them. The modern equivalent of a stone fortress and private army is to set up contact networks of influence and protection along the lines of the socialist government's own model.

Tax evasion in France is founded and justified in the belief that the level and form of taxation is onerous, unfair, and inefficient, so evasion has become a national sport. Knowing this, the tax authorities assume that taxpayers will under-declare, so for business tax assessment, inspectors arbitrarily increase declared benefits or reduce offsetting losses before calculating taxes—thus inciting taxpayers to be even more determined to beat the system. Anybody who raises objections to the treatment is likely to be subjected to invasive tax inspections over a long period.

The owners of the Bodin family business conscientiously practiced the national sport and did whatever was necessary to wage war on the taxman as part of their mission, whilst still considering that their business was run on entirely ethical lines. During their period at the helm, Huguette and François were able to encourage some of the smaller customers to pay cash, thus reducing their value added tax (VAT) bill, but Huguette Bodin baulked at one of her son Michel's suggestions that they should over-order materials that could be reused on their own projects whilst charged to client accounts, though, because they employed three teams of builders and tradesmen, she did allow any idle labour time to be used on projects for the family, their friends, or for 'marketing purposes'.

Once the younger Bodins entered the period when they controlled the direction and style of the business, their ideas were unbridled. Michel's motivation, at first, was to prove to his mother that he was even more capable than her and that his newer, expansive ideas could generate greater wealth for them all. He was about to demonstrate over a period of years that in his business and private life, his motivation to achieve could overcome all obstacles or constraints. He and Charlotte expanded the business into new market segments, and one of their most successful initiatives was a change of emphasis from shop-fitting mainly for big luxury retailers, a sector that was becoming more competitive and favoured larger suppliers, to renovating the multitude of bars and restaurants for which Paris is noted. The owners of these establishments were a breed apart of mostly independent entrepreneurs, a no-holds-barred community, partly from the regions of France but also from other European states, including Eastern Europe. It proved to be a turning point in the company's fortunes, and Michel's relationship with this market fostered a broad relaxation of corporate and personal ethical constraints. The clients' businesses dealt mainly in cash which they hugely under-declared, so they were able to pay at least partly in cash for significant building works. A single transformation project was worth hundreds of thousands, and the contracts went to the supplier who was most accommodating in a number of ways, including tax avoidance, but who could also fulfil some of the most private and secret desires of the owners.

Michel quickly got to know the preferences and sensitivities of his clients, and a measure of his success was that he and Charlotte could afford to live in a palatial house which they built in the park of an old film star's residence in the elegant and wealthy suburb of St Cloud, to the West of Paris. They took time off to travel the world in a quest to satisfy Michel's lust for knowledge and culture, taking on deserts, mountains, and jungles. Charlotte was always his willing partner in business and social life, adding glamour and sound advice to Michel's enthusiasms. They were seen by family and friends to be an ideal couple. Michel brimmed with relentless energy and a sensual curiosity which filled Charlotte with admiration and delectation. She didn't question what was happening in the business and where it might lead. She wanted it to last.

CHAPTER THREE

Family Reunion, 1982

It was Charlotte who thought it was time to seek out members of the family who, for various reasons, had drifted away to a social perimeter to run their own lives, so she made some initial contacts and encouraged selected relatives to renew close relations with her, Michel, and their three daughters. Thérèse Milton, François Bodin's much-younger sister, had been a favourite aunt in Michel's childhood, and because she was only nine years older than him, she bridged a gap between two generations. She was now happily married to George Milton and living in Northern Ireland.

Michel had attended Thérèse and George's wedding in Paris when he was fourteen, and that was the last he saw of them for a long time. When Thérèse married, she moved from her parents' home in Paris to Ireland, tearing herself away from her parents for the first time beyond holidays, and she had to make a new life in a new country in a new language. There were lots of other demands for her attention over the next fifteen years, and the Miltons could only afford the time and cost of travel to France to join Thérèse's parents in Paris once a year, usually at Christmas. Holiday entitlements for George and Thérèse, at that time, were only two weeks per year, so communication with Michel and Charlotte was limited to fleeting moments over the holiday period, during family meetings at the parents' or grandparents' homes, and maybe a phone call every six months.

The first opportunity for Thérèse and George Milton to spend time alone with Michel and Charlotte Bodin was during one of their visits to Paris for Christmas and the New Year, which they were able to extend by a few days. They had responded enthusiastically and with some curiosity to an invitation to dinner at the house that Michel and Charlotte had built near the racecourse at St Cloud, one of the wealthiest residential areas, to the west of Paris.

It was a truly stunning place.

The electric wrought iron front gates opened on to a vast park of mature cedars set in carefully swept and manicured lawns bordered by well-pruned shrubs. It was dark when the Miltons arrived, but as they drove their car forward between stately pillars topped by large stone pineapples, hidden projectors lit up the park, illuminating the massive trunks and swooping lower branches of the trees and spreading pools of light randomly across the smooth lawns to the walls of the house. From the outside, the house was undistinguished, apart from its great size, which was comparable with other residences in the area, but once the heavy wooden front door with its prominent ironwork and studding was opened, the full effect of a fantasy world took over the senses, starting with a wide and open flag-stone-floored entrance hall, bordered on two sides by a massive curving stone staircase, and with tall double doors leading off to reveal a high, hammer-beam ceiling in the main reception hall. Like a huge wooden sailing ship built upside down, thought George Milton.

The first impression was the antithesis of a family home. It was ostentatious in Hollywood style, like a film set for a gothic period movie. An imaginative visitor could easily picture Christopher Lee, Vincent Price, and Peter Cushing sitting by the blazing wood fire in the monumental chimney of the great hall, discussing the next supernatural threat to mankind.

A tour around the house gave no respite from the grandiose scale. The bedrooms were enormous, furnished with original but perfectly renovated four poster beds from the sixteenth century. A Templar's 'armoire', in dark wood at least eight feet high, must have been dismantled to pass through even these large, ornate-panelled, double doors. Charlotte's clothes room was on the scale of a high-street boutique and similarly equipped with clothes racks and walls of drawers. Life-size marble statues and bronzes gazed across the polished wooden floors from their vantage points. Charlotte explained that Michel was an avid buyer at auctions, and he had acquired these genuine, rare pieces at a fraction of their retail value at provincial auctions where chateaux were being stripped of their contents.

'It's like a museum,' whispered George to Thérèse.

Dinner for four was served by efficient and polite caterers at one end of what looked like a monastery dining table that could have seated twenty-four monks, surrounded by high-backed carved chairs in dark wood with deep-red velvet cushions. The table was lit by gothic iron candelabra and decorated with spectacularly hand-painted Limoges porcelain. The cutlery was ornate and heavy-handled, and George soon found that it easily fell off the scalloped plate edges if you weren't careful. Thick, heavy-based antique stem glasses completed the table display. The food was excellent, the Aloxe Corton 1970 Burgundy wine, dark, delicious and copious, and by the end of the evening, the visitors were not only impressed, they were concerned as to how they could possibly reciprocate and more than a little curious as to how a family building and shop-fitting business could generate enough to pay for such a lavish lifestyle.

Despite their disparity of wealth, over the following years, the Miltons drew closer to the Bodins, and as their travel budget and holiday entitlements increased, they found more occasions to get together in France or less frequently in Ireland. Visits and attendance at anniversary celebrations became so frequent that there could be no doubt that for Thérèse and George the rapprochement was welcome. The two couples were closer in age and had more in common than other older members of the wider family, and as the years passed and as the age gap became less noticeable, they developed a genuine loving friendship. The newfound intimacy was based on mutual trust and respect, together with shared hopes and fears, and they seized new opportunities to reconnect with enthusiasm. There was good humour rather than envy. The Miltons were truly happy to enjoy the Bodins' success and took pride in their achievements.

Most of the immediate Bodin family and other more distant relatives were also happy with the renewed relationship and reciprocated the Bodin's apparent joy at their rediscovery of an extended family. As the initial contact developed into a more relaxed and regular dialogue and as Thérèse and George observed and learned more about Michel and Charlotte, Michel's approach to life and his obvious success became a regular subject of conversation in the family. Sure, he had started from a foundation of business success established by his parents, but he was so forceful, energetic, and just like his father, had such an easy, engaging way with people that it was unsurprising that he should be doing so well. He was lucky that the economy in France was buzzing and Paris was the hub where internal renewal of catering outlets and new or retro-style changes of decor were essential to attract and retain customers.

In those early days, Michel was easily able to demonstrate to potential clients that a direct relationship existed between investment in interior and exterior styling, and increased turnover, so customers followed each other in a competitive race. Once he knew who was competing with whom, it was relatively easy for Michel to clean up groups of businesses in a neighbourhood as each tried to outdo the others.

Between the Bodins and the Miltons, family stories and business experiences were shared, especially as Thérèse and George had recently launched their own business in Ireland and could therefore exchange thoughts and ideas on a par with Michel and Charlotte. The two couples appeared to share a sense of what they wanted from life and a common feel for subjects to be treated with humour or seriousness. They discussed business problems and opportunities, and those discussions tended to confirm their affinity, though under the surface, there was always a marked difference in the scale of commitment to wealth acquisition, levels of risk they were willing to take, and, once wealth was achieved, the degree of flourish in displaying the results.

Thérèse and George Milton did not often have to worry about signing cheques for whatever they wanted; the funds were usually accessible, but either they were happy with less than the Bodins considered normal, or it was simply that their budget didn't extend so far, but whatever the reason, there was a visible contrast in the level of wealth sought and displayed by the two families. The Miltons were happy to share their success with friends and family, but were more discreet about it, and as they were to discover later, they were more conventional in their means to achieve it.

The Miltons' existence was largely regimented by their small business, which was demanding of their own professional input in addition to the cares that went with management of others who sometimes took advantage of employment protection legislation. As a result, although they developed a professional-contacts network, there was little time for private socialising. Their business commitments encroached on the time they had to maintain regular contact with friends and family, with the exception of a few long-standing friends. Their business was deeply affected by economic cycles, and there were worrying times when it lost money for long periods. The trick was to know when and how much to cut back and how to regenerate business quickly after a recession. They believed that success in business, as in other endeavours, consisted of getting up one more time than you fall.

With no children to force them into contact with schools and other parents, the Miltons devoted most of their social space to family, and as older members died, their relationship with the Bodins assumed greater importance.

CHAPTER FOUR

A Closer View, 1983

A celebrated people lose their dignity upon a closer view.

(Napoleon Bonaparte)

Apart from a few glitches, the wheel of fortune turned around very well for Michel Bodin over the next few years. Anybody looking in on the Bodin family would conclude that he was the epitome of a happy family man, with a beautiful and adoring wife, three children growing up, and a successful business. He could afford to be generous with those around him who suffered setbacks from time to time; for example, he could hand out cheques and advice to his wife's sisters when they experienced on-going marital or financial difficulties, or he would comfort them when they needed a shoulder to cry on.

One of those to benefit from Michel's generosity was Charlotte's sister Catherine, who was married to Aldo, a handsome and charming Italian marine broker specialising in luxury yachts. The couple led a jet-set lifestyle following the very wealthy wherever their yachts took them. They had lived successively in Italy, Monte Carlo, and then Florida, where it all came unstuck.

Aldo had taken a big gamble by acquiring a motor yacht for which he paid $4 million and expected to sell it after some renovation work for around $8 million. His calculations were not unreasonable. He knew the business well and probably had some prospective buyers lined up before he bought the boat. If successful, it would have been quite a coup. What Aldo didn't anticipate was that while the refitting was taking place, the bottom would fall out of the luxury yachts' market. That is what happened, and he could not offload the yacht at any price. He was left to continue paying the marine mortgage and settle repair bills that proved to be more costly than budgeted. Catherine and Aldo's living collapsed. They had no money to pay off their debts including the mortgage, so they had to sell their home in the United States at a time when resale prices were low. Although Aldo did manage to sell the yacht two years later, he could barely cover his costs. By then, Catherine was suffering from myalgic encephalomyelitis (ME) though they didn't know it at the time.

Aldo brought Catherine back to France, and Michel and Charlotte took charge of her when Aldo returned to the US. They installed Catherine in a small apartment that Michel bought for her, and for months she did very little. But eventually, though still mainly confined to her bedroom, she began to experience short periods of self-reliance, and despite her continuing weakness, Michel's visits made her smile, the only time she did so.

Before long, Michel was visiting her frequently and becoming more and more interested in his sister-in-law. As Charlotte was busy with her daughters and managing business operations and accounts, Catherine saw Michel more and more. The relationship reached a point where Michel was planning to make love to her as soon as she recovered sufficiently, and not only to put the colour back in her cheeks.

Michel was always driven by sentiments and impulses even beyond those he imagined. He was sure these weeks of intimacy close to this defenceless stretched-out body had ignited desire in both of them. Michel didn't admit this openly to Catherine. He wanted to provoke her into making the first move, and Catherine proved to be just as vulnerable to Michel's humour and compliments as his other women contacts. She realised that her marriage to Aldo was over. When he last phoned her from Florida, she found out during the conversation that he was staying with a friend whom Catherine knew—a woman who was kept by a very wealthy American media owner but who was free to pursue any part-time relationships so long as she was available for him. Aldo fitted in perfectly with this configuration, and from his point of view, the temporary accommodation at the friend's private apartment was welcome.

As the months went by, the rest of the family began to think that Catherine's illness was either psychosomatic or a caprice. Michel, on the other hand, was increasing the number of his visits, and he found her more attractive each day. She was able to sit up, and they were hugging each other ferociously. Michel's head was spinning. He had dreamed so much of these moments that sometimes he had almost lost hope, but he never gave up completely. Now he felt freed from the heavy burden of uncertainty. He needed all his faculties to think about his incredible liaison with the two sisters. He realised it was a transgression, and he had never imagined he could commit such treachery against Charlotte. But there could be no doubt that the sexual *frénésie* he felt for Catherine was mutual, and it was putting life back into her tortured body and mind.

As Catherine recovered and started making her own way in life again, she still turned to Michel for advice and comfort and made every effort to thank him for the help and support he had given when she needed it most. He continued to be generous financially. His rationale for this heated liaison and erotic fling was that if Charlotte loved her sisters, why should he not do the same in his own way?

CHAPTER FIVE

Sex and Money, 1985

The cockerel is an animal dear to the French. Nature has given it several of the worst faults shared by men: Self-satisfaction, a taste for polygamy, and the disturbing habit of telling everybody who is sleeping that he is awake.

(Anne-Marie Carrière, 1925-2003, actress, humourist, and author)

Thérèse Milton put it this way, 'French men like the role of godfather and don't take kindly to anything they see as a challenge to their position.'

Anyone who has watched French television will be aware that eroticism and, in particular, naked women are used routinely in advertisements.

French radio applies a similarly liberal policy, for example, local radio stations carry advertising for sex shops—'sexy centres', and more generally, you can hear women with baby voices singing sexually explicit songs on the radio at any hour of the day. At a time when UK BBC 4 listeners are hearing yet another repeat of *The Archers*; one state radio programme runs a radio series on erotic literature where no detail is spared, including such advice as 'How to Contemplate a Virgin' and an episode in a revered series on psychology is entitled, 'The Psychology of the Penis, A Life of Anguish'.

It is within this media environment that many French men consider it normal to stimulate their ego by freely and systematically exploiting women in the home, the workplace, and beyond. It is widely understood that for women to scale political or industrial career 'ladders', they will have to handle a few 'snakes'.

The kind of treatment of women that quite openly permeates French business and public life starts with, for example, the civil servant at the French Consulate in London who was an inveterate bottom-pincher. His interpretation of personal service was to approach women customers in a queue and feel them covertly from behind, literally helping himself. When a customer demanded to report his behaviour to the manager, he announced, 'I am the manager.'

More serious was the case of the young business graduate who, after three months with a marketing company in Paris (her dream job after months of searching), was called to her boss's office for an interview just as the office was closing. He told her she was doing well and that he had good reports of her potential, so he had decided to take a more personal interest in her career development. As a start, he invited her to join him on his next business trip to London to meet some important contacts. There was no shortage of innuendo as to the role he expected her to fulfil during the trip, and he made it clear that they would be sharing a hotel room. He asked her to give it serious thought and confirm the next day.

She politely declined the offer, welcoming his interest, but insisting that it be kept on a purely professional track. The man repeated the proposition in more detail, this time balancing the offer that if all went well, she could be managing the UK account, with the threat that if she did not comply, she would be considered incompatible with the team and should therefore expect to look elsewhere for employment, starting by joining the ranks of the unemployed, with a bad reference. Again she declined, expressing disgust that he should try this approach.

Within a week, she received a dismissal letter, giving her pay in lieu of notice. She was told to clear her desk and go immediately. The victim went to an employment adviser who warned that if she took action against the company, whether she won or lost the case, she would find it difficult to get another job. She felt she had nothing to lose, so she pursued a claim for sexual harassment and unfair dismissal, subsequently winning her claim and receiving compensation.

It was three years before she got another job. A contributory factor was that the action she took was publicised and remained available to employers checking references. In France, you blow the whistle at your peril.

The Bodins and the Miltons often exchanged confidences about money, in general, though Michel was always discreet about his sources of revenue. Once, when discussing financial matters, Michel revealed a wish to move a large sum of money out of France urgently before an anticipated government ban, so Thérèse offered to set up accounts in Jersey and the Isle of Man that he could use. Subsequently, Michel transferred the maximum possible sums to those havens. That arrangement remained in place for several years, and by the time Michel moved his reserves again, this time to Switzerland, he had made a handsome tax-free profit.

In 1985, fearing an imminent imposition of a wealth tax on large residential properties, the Bodins sold the huge house at St Cloud, which the Miltons referred to as 'Toad's baronial hall'[1], and once again built their own home, this time in a contemporary style and more modest scale, in the nearby smart neighbourhood of Maisons-Laffitte, with a large percentage of materials ordered on client accounts and with labour from their regular building contractors' teams during slack periods. The house was one of four built in the grounds of a recently demolished manor, so the park with its mature trees and old stone walls provided a backdrop similar to their previous residence but on a smaller, more human scale. The previous house had been sold for the approximate francs equivalent of two million Euros at 2012 values, yielding an excellent profit on the cost of land and building.

It was while the Miltons were staying with the Bodins at the new house that they noticed signs and symbols of the owners' lifestyle reflecting a 1980s middle-class quest to be broad-minded and modern, by a shift towards tastes that were more 'edgy'. The signs that Thérèse and George noticed now related not to their curiosity about the financing of the house and the Bodins' income but to more overt manifestations of eroticism.

One morning before breakfast, George sat on the comfortable settee in the salon, where the morning sun streamed in through the French doors, and to occupy his time before someone else came downstairs, he poured himself a coffee and reached for a pile of magazines on the nearby table. He thought it unusual that his hosts should keep a copy of *Playboy* so visibly when there were three young girls in the house, but having quickly riffled through the pages, he admired the photos and read a story about a competition between two women to see how many men they could seduce in one day. He put it down thinking that Thérèse might come down soon, and he didn't want to embarrass her or have to justify his interest. The next publication he selected was smaller, A5 size, and much more explicit. The banner title on the cover read: 'We Take on the Hottest Mothers in Your Neighbourhood and Pump Fuck Out of Them.' Below was a picture of a naked woman, bound and gagged, being worked over by at least three men. George quickly put the magazine back under *Playboy*, which now seemed on a par with a church magazine.

---

[1]   Kenneth Grahame's, *Wind in the Willows*, 1908.

The stairs leading to the bedrooms went up in two flights. The first, of only three or four steps, reached a small landing with the next longer flight to the right. The whole staircase was in light oak with a modern handrail and base rail with a decorative black-painted metal balustrade. Above the landing was a plain wall upon which hung a portrait in oils. It was about one and a half metres high and about a metre wide. It was modern, though it resembled some darker medieval works, but this was not a portrait of an ancestor. It depicted a naked man hanging by his arms with a black hood covering his head. The centre of the canvas showed his genitals in impressive detail. George had passed the painting several times during his visit, but at no time did he stop and examine it as he might have done a Monet or a Klimt, at least not while Thérèse or Charlotte were in the vicinity. George moved on with the impression that the subject was probably a small man with an unrealistically large penis or the artist's sense of perspective was defective. He concluded that it must be an aspirational work, though it almost gave him an inferiority complex.

You can tell a lot about a man by what he reads, and that is what George Milton was one day trying to do in Michel's beautifully appointed study—by looking at the books on display. It was a modest-sized room on a mezzanine next to the salon. The wooden panelling and built-in bookshelves covering the longest wall were in light oak and together with a deep red and blue oriental carpet deadened the sound. They created a light, but pleasantly, cosy atmosphere. The large desk carried a digital telephone and a computer that Michel didn't use. It was Charlotte who managed that. A couple of comfortable, soft, cream leather armchairs provided the perfect perch for book browsing.

Michel and Charlotte were avid readers, a pastime shared by George and Thérèse, who could spend hours immersed in the pleasure of just browsing books, and that was what George was doing now. The books chosen by his autodidact nephew consisted of a large proportion of reference books and travelogues, with politics, history, art, and architecture much in evidence. These were accompanied by a carnival of erotica filling a whole shelf and with several piles of homeless books spread along the front of the deep shelf. A quick glance at the titles revealed *A Guide to Female Psychology and Seductibility* The back cover summary described the contents as 'metropolitan, knowing, street-smart, very funny, and unrelieved by any notion of romantic love.'

There were plenty of novels, mostly claiming they had been recently listed for prizes, but notably absent from this collection were any books on cooking. George, at first, thought this odd for a French household where cooking is a prime subject of conversation but recalled that Michel would not attempt to cook or do anything in the house, and Charlotte seemed to live mainly on salads; any gourmet food for guests was brought in from a nearby traiteur. George found it strange that someone who worked from home had no cabinets, business books, papers, or files in the study. They must all be at the office, he thought.

One afternoon, after an excellent lunch, an example of the quality that the local *traiteur* could provide, Michel was sitting chatting with Thérèse about family history when he volunteered a comment indicating that he wasn't happy spending his life in the suburban normality, living in a tree-lined road in a quiet area where the only tragedies were purely domestic.

'People who live around here go to work, eat, sleep, and go on holiday twice a year and they don't want to change because they don't know what they would be getting into. I'm not like that. I do all those things, but I have to take a holiday from being myself to survive.'

Thérèse was not sure what had provoked this outburst, which self he wanted to escape from, or where his thoughts might be leading, but as it seemed as though Michel was happy to confide in her, she just nodded encouragingly, adding, 'Well, I can see there are more important things in life than having two or three cars.'

'Yes, I know, you see Thérèse, I have done all those normal things, and just now, I feel that I have broken up the conventional jigsaw and scattered the pieces, but I can't bring a picture together the way that I used to do. You might think I have everything, but there are some important pieces missing. One of them is freedom, not necessarily the kind of freedom I had when I was young but something else, something different. That's what I need. It's not something material. It's not about ownership or address.'

'Is it freedom from responsibility?' questioned Thérèse.

'Some kinds of responsibility, yes,' agreed Michel, 'that's why I plan to simplify the business. There are some kinds of work I am just not cut out for, so why should I do them if I can earn as much without?'

'What about family and domestic responsibilities?' asked Thérèse.

'I accept those, and I think I carry them out well. The family all benefit from the money I earn.'

'That doesn't sound very romantic or loving.'

Michel seemed to be lost in his own words and thoughts. He pursed his lips and frowned deeply for several seconds before producing his habitual jovial smile.

Thérèse thought this conversation left her with an enigma. It wasn't a particularly important enigma on its own, but it was part of a whole collection of unimportant enigmas which individually she had put out of her mind because she understood that she would never understand everything about Michel. However, if the facts didn't fit together, her intuition could fill in the gaps quite effectively, and the picture she compiled was sadly pessimistic for Michel and Charlotte.

CHAPTER SIX

Michel's View of Life, 1986

The great question that has never been answered, and which I have
not yet been able to answer, despite my thirty years of research into
the feminine soul, is 'What does a woman want?'

(Ernest Jones, *The Life and Work of Sigmund Freud.*)

During a visit to the Bodins at Maisons-Laffitte in early summer, Michel
invited George Milton to spend an afternoon at the French Open tennis
championships at the Roland Garros stadium. Michel had acquired some
tickets for business clients and had a few spare. George was not a particular
fan of professional tennis, though he was still involved in several competitive
sports, so he accepted largely to spend some private time with Michel. They
drove around the west of Paris easily and parked in a side street and then
walked to the stadium, which stands near the racecourses of Longchamps and
Auteuil, close to the Porte d'Auteuil. They settled into perfect seats at the top
of a stand and enjoyed the rest of the afternoon in weak, hazy sunshine that
was pleasantly warm without burning. Sporting entertainment was provided
in the men's singles semi-final by Boris Becker, though this time he was
defeated by Mikael Pernfors, who lost to Ivan Lendl in the final.

On that day, Boris was in full flight, thrilling the spectators with his
athleticism and unconventional shots. Pernfors played coolly and surgically,
less entertaining perhaps, but he scored the points that mattered.

Michel Bodin was in a relaxed mood, and George was a good listener,
so as the match played out, Michel opened up on a self-assessment, his

view of life, and his philosophy. It revealed an inferiority complex stemming from Michel's acute sensitivity about his lack of height, a flexible observance of any moral code that didn't suit him, and his traditional, that is to say, authoritarian stance towards women. His pursuit of material wealth was a means to an end, and that end was not just to make a mark for himself as a successful man but to enable him to exercise power over other people. Michel repeated his often-aired simple view that there were only two kinds of people in the world, wolves or sheep, and that he was determined to be a wolf.

The discussion continued with the two men, side by side, watching the tennis but relaxing into a reverie as the repetitive rhythm of the game played on.

'Charlotte understands me,' Michel proclaimed. 'I treat her well. After all, she is the mother of my children.'

'Is that all?' muttered George, facing the tennis.

Michel pulled George's shoulder towards him and growled into his ear,

'I am driven by impulses. I am a very passionate person. Charlotte knows that, and she accepts it.'

George wondered where the conversation was leading, but Michel turned his attention to the tennis, possibly detecting that George was unsympathetic to his ideas.

Later, during a pause in play, he leaned towards George advancing his chin.

'Eh, George! What do you really think of me?' he asked.

George was completely unprepared for this question,

'Why do you ask me that now?'

'I sometimes think you look down on me. You are better educated, and you Anglo-Saxons always think you are superior. I sometimes think you are being censorious towards me.'

George reflected before replying quietly, 'Well, firstly, I don't look down on anybody. It's just not my way to appoint myself a snob. As to being censorious, I don't judge you. Remember that an inferiority complex is often created by people who see themselves as victims to explain why they are the way they are. It is not always imposed on them, and you don't start life by being inferior even if each person is different. You just have to feel inferior and then that's what you become. I had no great results at school, though thanks to a bunch of teachers who took a real interest in their pupils in and out of the classroom, I learned a lot about a wide range of people, which has served me well. Since then, I have been continually pursuing my education, and like you, I believe that education never stops.'

'Yes, but what do you really think of me?' Michel insisted. 'You are used to assessing people. If I came to you for a job, what would you think?'

'I would keep an open mind until I had got into a comfortable discussion and tested the person's views from different directions.'

'He might be lying to you,' said Michel.

'Nobody tells all the truth when they are trying to impress someone. They filter their version of what they think the other person wants to hear,' acknowledged George.

'That's true. Honesty and dishonesty are relative terms. Appearance, authority, and confidence can make people seem more honest than they really are in any walk of life. These days, that's what makes politicians appear honest in the eyes of the public. They can afford to dress up. Politicians who dress down or look weird have no credibility.'

'But do you think politicians ever stop to consider whether what they do is honest?'

Michel thought about the question. 'Do you mean do they ever believe they are sincere and have any dignity?' he asked for clarification.

'Yes, that's a way of putting it,' George confirmed.

'Hmm, some politicians may really believe what they say until they find out that they have no effective legal levers to solve the main problems, and as soon as they try to take any remedial action, they are attacked by the press, denigrated by the electorate, and held responsible for almost anything that can possibly affect the uninterrupted well-being of the population. After they've discovered that, their words sound just like some of the most pompous and dogmatic statements of religious hypocrisy that shaped social and political attitudes two centuries ago and are still being trotted out today in some countries and by some religious extremists, and I mean in so-called "modern countries" in the west just as much as in totalitarian states. You know, George, you and our political classes have very different priorities. You see, a really ambitious man never puts dignity above the advantages of power.'

At that moment, the tennis started again. Sensing another question from Michel, George deferred the discussion. He shuffled in the seat. 'Look, if you really want to discuss this in depth, let's do it in private after the match.'

'OK. Let's do that,' Michel conceded.

For the rest of the afternoon, the atmosphere between them was less relaxed. Instead of concentrating on the tennis, George was thinking about what he would say and not say to Michel. He was dealing with his host, whom he respected, so he decided to go easy. He had no right to be critical.

After the match, they filtered through the departing crowds, found the car, and drove a short distance from the stadium on a wide boulevard that led towards the centre of Paris, until they came to a large bar restaurant. It was not the sort of place George would normally visit, but it suited their purpose because there was a space to park at the kerb, almost right outside, and there were plenty of seated clients, proving the popularity of the place for meeting, chatting, eating, and just observing. The outside terrace was plagued by traffic noise, so they headed for the main door. Once inside, George noted that it was a traditional brasserie, superbly fitted with carved dark wood and lots of glass, which made it warm and friendly yet classy in the style of La Belle Époch of around 1900. Michel knew the owner and explained that this was one of *his* renovations that had been carried out in the early 1980s. On hearing this, George took a greater interest and noted that it was beautifully executed in retro style with ornate pillars, etched glass, and mirrors so that wherever you sat, you were never faced with a blank wall. There were comfortable wooden chairs with curved backrests and solid, well-supported tables surrounded by a selection of elegant artefacts that looked old even if they were modern repro. Huge, opulent chandeliers carrying dozens of lamps looked as though they had been reclaimed from a theatre. There was a central, waist-high, carved wooden division between the brasserie, where all-day snacks were served, and the restaurant where the resident chef pampered serious diners between midday and midnight. Along the dividing screen were ornamental clothes racks in wood and brass, one for each table. It was exactly what a discerning foreigner would visualise as the archetypal traditional Paris brasserie where tourists go to impregnate themselves with French good taste and style.

Michel ordered beers and, as he was hungry, a croque-monsieur. George had the same. Once they were served, Michel reopened their conversation.

'So what questions would you ask me?' He checked himself. 'No, tell me what you think or know about me before you ask the questions.'

George was cautious not to reveal the limits of their common ground at this stage. 'Well, we've known each other for quite a few years now, and we share a lot of things—an interest in arts and culture, good food and drink, socialising, et cetera. It is quite easy for us to find things to do together. I appreciate your generosity towards Thérèse and me. I know the same generosity extends to the other members of the family too. I admire your energy and enthusiasm for business and your success in sales and project management. You have a great aptitude for that. Our feelings towards you are absolutely genuine. It's no effort on our part, and I know I can express my opinions freely with you, even where we may disagree. That's what makes it so satisfying.'

Michel appeared to ignore the compliments. 'Do you think the other members of the family appreciate me for what I do?' he asked. George wasn't sure which family members Michel had in mind.

'I think sometimes you overwhelm them, Michel. They are not used to such expensive manifestations of generosity. Some of your presents could be more modest and perhaps more suited to their needs. But overall, I think they are proud of your success. They welcome the recognition you give them when you remember them at birthdays, and they appreciate that you are happy to share what you have with them. I know Charlotte is the one who deals directly with family and social relations, but everybody knows you are behind it too.'

There was a long pause while Michel took in George's comments; then, staring into his glass, he said, 'I am a nobody, so I have to do whatever is necessary to succeed, and some people might not approve of what I do.'

In response to this statement, George decided to avoid asking any questions about what 'whatever is necessary' might mean. 'So what motivates you to work as hard as you do?' he asked.

'I am not looking for public recognition. That's not my scene at all. I just love to be one up on the people I deal with or meet casually, so I can say, "I may be a nobody, but I'm better off than most so-called 'celebrities'." I know that you and Thérèse are great analysts of people, and I wonder sometimes if you disapprove of me,' said Michel pensively.

'What do you think there is to disapprove of?'

'I don't know, but sometimes Thérèse is very direct. She is an investigator of my mind and pursues a line of questioning in a way that shows she doesn't believe me.'

'Should she believe everything you say? She's no fool.'

Michel was beginning to look uncomfortable. 'Look, I have a private life that I don't want to discuss with anybody, and I don't want anybody to probe into it. I want to keep it entirely separate.'

'I am not probing. It was you who invited me to ask questions. You don't have to answer them. I take people at face value. That's to say I initially believe what they tell me, but I also have eyes and ears to give me a second opinion.'

'And what do your eyes and ears tell you about me?' Michel urged.

'Nothing directly, but in the case of some of your friends and acquaintances, there are gaps in my knowledge as to the kind of relationships you have with them. I just don't know. I can't categorise what the relationship consists of.'

'Who, for example?'

This time, it was George's turn to cover-up. He smiled. 'I also have thoughts and ideas that I don't share with anybody. It's not that I have a secret life, but I prefer to be discreet about the lives of others because it's none of my business how people live and make their choices. I just observe. I don't judge,' he paused, 'but I do wonder sometimes whether you are taking a few risks that could one day backfire.'

'I adore taking risks. Don't you ever take risks?' Michel sat back in his chair and folded his arms across his chest, mentally savouring some of his own adventures.

'Of course, I have often taken personal and financial risks, sometimes unwittingly,' admitted George, 'but I'm not setting out to take the kind of risks that you are taking on a family and financial level. I guess that's because I'm happy with what I have.'

'Listen, I have always enjoyed taking risks, extreme risks. I have to. You have to take account of what it's like to work in France. Nothing is clean and transparent. Nothing is logical. It's not what you know, it's who you know and who knows you that matters most here. It's because nobody trusts anybody they don't know. You get a job by recommendation. Nepotism rules. Mayors, government ministers, and the president put their family on the payroll even if they don't work. You have to have contacts in the police so you can get your speeding tickets removed. You make an honest tax declaration and get clobbered by an extra ten per cent in case you are fiddling. So OK, mister philosopher, speak clearly. Wouldn't you do the same? Put your hand on your conscience and tell me the truth. You were not always as well off as you are today. I was the same. Now we are both big men in business. Surely you have taken risks?'

'Not so big,' George attempted to divert the discussion from the tax question.

'Ha! You've got plenty in the bank.'

'Not as much as you.'

'Well, you're still a big man, and you sleep well at night knowing that you can pay the bills. I don't sleep well. I'm always dreaming of how I could get more and do better, and I am prepared to take risks to get there.' Michel interrupted himself. 'Actually, that's a very important part of my philosophy—dreaming and implementing my dreams. If I didn't dream, I would have the same opinion on everything as everybody else.' He paused, took a deep breath, and continued, 'French people are competitive by nature, and firstly, they compete with authority.'

'You sound as though you are conducting a personal war against the state. I thought the revolution brought liberty, equality, and fraternity, so where's the fraternity and socialist community spirit we hear so much about?' asked George provocatively.

'Pwah!' Michel gesticulated dismissively. 'Unbridled liberty allows everybody to apply their own despotism. It means the state feels free to rob its people, so the people feel free to resist in whatever way they can. It's everyone for themselves here, and if any group is criticised or invited to change for the common good, they are absolutely venomous in defending themselves by launching personal attacks. There's no such thing as equality. That's just idealistic rubbish. In practice, you can either have liberty or equality but not both. Listen, Uncle George,' he leaned across the table and stared into George's face, 'I prefer refined vice dressed in silk to stupid virtue wearing animal skins.'

George ducked any immediate response to Michel's outpouring, fearing to be accused of being virtuous, oversensitive, politically correct, or merely defensive if he replied directly. Instead, he asked, 'So what is making you unhappy? You seem to have everything you could possibly need and more. What are you afraid of?'

'A dull life!' asserted Michel. 'My intention is not to settle into a routine, but to glide and experiment with alternative concepts. I glide from flavour to flavour, sensation to sensation, but I am not prepared to discuss sentiments at the edge of my comfort zone, like Thérèse wants me to do. In answer to your question though, I do worry about the future, but I have no pretentions that I can control it,' admitted Michel, 'I know I am not an eagle that can fly high. I have to make my way in the real world in which I live. You see, in France, people have given up trying to change things by voting for one party or another. They are powerless to change their own destiny. There is never any political agreement to the changes people call for because too many people are on the take or have gained a privileged position that they now perceive as normal and are unwilling to relinquish. They all think they are right because they are winning. They don't stop to ask who is paying for their privileges. So if you can't change something, what do you do? You get drawn into it. There's an English expression, isn't there? "If you can't beat them join them, and then beat them".

'My needs are mutable, and I follow my needs. I am a down-to-earth person. I look around me, and I take my positions. My decisions are based on perceived best interests. I am excellent at pantomime.'

'Is that what you call your talent for working with people? Pantomime? Is it all an act?'

'Like everybody,' continued Michel, raising his elbows and opening his palms in a gesture, 'everybody is doing their pantomime. The president takes his position with his mistresses and his racketeering. The ambitious middle-class crowd dances in whatever way the vilest politicians and judges or policeman allow them to do. You may look down on it as the pantomime of the proletariat, but what you are watching is the great impetus of the world. Do you think you have a special dispensation from it? Look around at your UK and Irish politicians and religious leaders and look at the political and business corruption in America and the way the political classes spend public money there. Tell me if you see anything different. You have old boy networks, don't you?'

George hesitated before replying. 'I agree you have to connect with people to do business. Networking is a perfectly respectable manifestation of self-promotion. It's about being curious and wanting to share knowledge. It's not a closed dealing room though. If you cease to connect by whatever means, you become isolated—you have no influence, no means to change anything or do anything, but you can't seriously think the manipulative behaviour you described is just a form of networking.'

At the end of his last outburst, Michel had dropped his chin. There were now six empty bottles of beer on the table, and the waiter had already cleared some away. George had drunk only two bottles.

Suddenly, Michel raised his head again and sat up against the chair back. 'You know the only things that can move France forward? Visibility and ridicule! When the rest of the world can see what we are like and when some of these cases of corruption and abuse are more widely reported and they embarrass our governments and privileged classes, including some groups of workers, to a point where they have to change, we might see some movement, but it will be a slow process. They are not easily embarrassed. Oh no. Look at Mitterrand as an example. How can you be proud of your country when he thinks that what he does is perfectly normal and justified for as long as he can get away with it. France is far worse than Britain in acting independently within the EU, even though we were one of the founders. You can see that even when the European Union tries to impose its pathetic standards on us, the French government continues to ignore the rules and pays the fines.'

At this point, Michel dropped his head again. He was thinking that's it. I've said it. I'm stopping now. I withdraw into my shell, and if that displeases Monsieur, my uncle George, then too bad.

'So are you saying that there is no sense of duty, no morality in France or in most of the rest of the world?' prodded George.

Michel struggled to reply, but after a long pause, he said, 'Where does morality fit? In France, you have the same extremes of good and bad as anywhere else. There are good and decent people who work hard and strive to improve the world around them, but the traditional simplistic concepts of good and evil have moved out to opposite ends of the spectrum.' With his index finger, he drew a line on the table in the pool of condensation from the cold beer and then a circle in the middle of the line. 'They have polarised, leaving a large grey area in the middle, and in that area, a lot of quite good things live alongside quite bad things without tension between them. The odious and the admirable coexist here. The political predators live alongside their prey and what they do is shout at each other, exchange insults, and carry on using public money as if it were their own.

There is still an underlying morality that binds us to a common opinion on some things. But that's what I was saying just now. It blinds us from taking a unique personal opinion and striking out against the majority's view. This applies to business and politics just as much as to individuals. You are a member of professional institutes, George. I call them old-boy networks because they are tribal. They all think the same. They pay experts to tell them what to think, so they all occupy the middle ground. I don't belong to any, not that they would have me. I want to be on my own, and I am prepared to take the risks associated with that. You're a rational person, George, and you analyse business opportunities in your way, but I just deliver what people want without constraints, and then I work out how I can benefit from them. If I looked at a rational business case, it would get in the way of what I want out of life. Actually, that's not entirely true. I would like to be a moralist, but it doesn't fit my plans for now. I speak about what pleases me. The rest is for intellectuals. They are the modern equivalent of monks. They have the time to sit and polish principles and express themselves in abstruse words.'

'So what are you trying to get out of life at the moment?' probed George.

'I want to understand moral psychology and use that understanding productively for business and pleasure. I am morally tolerant, and I am happy to live in a tolerant society. I only believe in something if it benefits me. As I said, I'm not going to argue or fight for some hypothetical principle.'

'So no constraints and no sense of social responsibility?'

'None, other than to my family.'

'Isn't that perhaps one of the reasons why you have the kind of governments you complain of?' George enquired. 'You know the saying, that if you want to change the world, first change yourself.'

'Possibly, but I'm more cynical. I think that businessmen, politicians, and workers dig in their heels to protect their interests and use the public good as a powerful argument, just as much as other individuals do when faced with change, but I think that in the case of politicians, the inertia is because the economic and social problems transcend their ability to solve them, so they have to live within the structures we have and as those structures evolve, driven by global powers beyond our control, and once having accepted that fact, they just use their time and energies to fill their own pockets. Money is probably the only thing they will take away from a lifelong career in politics.

Consider this, George—who determines morality and true facts? It's the experts or the self-appointed interpreters of truth. In some societies, where people don't or can't think for themselves, they are considered necessary, and the experts become a respected part of the culture, so it's easier for totalitarian regimes to build a following in those places. People are told what to think and do and are punished inhumanely if they don't agree, but that shouldn't happen in a modern, educated society where intelligent people can think for themselves and are left free to do so. That's the tension in France. You have the educated political aristocracy and intellectuals and a relatively uneducated mass who are being told what to think and do by a huge autocratic and bureaucratic middle class of civil servants and other leaders who have got such a good deal for themselves that they will never change voluntarily. You can see how minor civil servants can push people around unnecessarily and there isn't the same protection for, say, consumers as you have in the UK. Anyway, the end result is that I don't take other people's word for it. I take my position according to what benefits me, and I reject uncomfortable results.' Michel paused for breath.

'Well, I do start by taking some people's word for it,' George begged to differ, 'otherwise, we would all have to make our way in the world from scratch. Have you heard the expression, "Standing on the shoulders of giants"? That's how we benefit from the experience of others.'

'Yeah! Who are the giants today, George? Select your giants from among our elected leaders. Is Mitterrand a giant? That's reality. I don't like reality. Reality is relative. It depends on the angle of the view you are taking. The greatest villains on earth all justify their actions in their own eyes, and they find or create beneficiaries to follow and protect them and name streets and places after them. Our leaders are a bunch of sophisticated connivers, and I don't subscribe to these people who are considered to be culturally acceptable experts. Most of them are appointed by the people who pay most to have their interests represented,' Michel went on. 'I have instincts, needs, and desires, just like everybody, but I subject them only to my own test of acceptability.'

'So does everybody work to individual standards and morality, not accepting that there needs to be a common standard?' argued George. 'For example, you got married. When you did that, you were subscribing to a common morality weren't you?'

'I didn't seek to be married. Charlotte chased me to the ends of the earth.'

'So she showed that she was in love with you and wanted you more than anybody else. You must have wanted her too.'

There was a long pause after this, while Michel reflected on his attitude when he married Charlotte. True, he hadn't been under any pressure to marry, but it was convenient, and she was the brightest thing in his life at the time. He wasn't aware of the responsibilities that would come later and the expectations of those around him as to how he would fulfil them. He was rewriting the rule book on that. But the obstacle ahead of him now was tangible. He felt the scale and thickness of it as if it were a castle wall.

Michel steered in another direction. 'In France, we understand human passion, needs, and desires. We are a more virile society. The Anglo-Saxons are more cold-blooded and judgemental.'

'I don't see much evidence of that distinction nowadays. Let's say that if there are measures of cultural differences, then one of them might be the degree to which we dominate passions by the exercise of judgement, without which we become classical egotists.'

'Hmm, yes, and in that case, there isn't much to choose between any of the western cultures. That's where a lot of politicians in so-called "democratic countries" fail. They are supposed to exercise judgement on our behalf, but they are hopeless at it for themselves.'

'You say that, Michel, as if you were claiming some moral high ground. You say the French understand human passion, and certainly French culture appears to indulge extremes of human passion, but I believe you are subtly using tradition to justify exploitative male behaviour. Do you not think that at least some of the world has moved to a more equal society between the sexes, even if that doesn't suit French men? I'm not just referring to the way sexual inhibitions have given way to more freedoms. Most western countries have seen growing freedom for both sexes. I'm really questioning the attitudes that accompany those freedoms, deciding whether they are given freely or reluctantly, whether the law insists and is applied effectively, and whether men's behaviour has really changed. I think that France is particularly conservative and shameless in its exploitation of women, and that's putting it politely. It's more like a Mediterranean or Asian culture. You have equality at law, but men still openly exploit women wherever they have the power to do so.'

'So you think the women are victims?' responded Michel incredulously.

'In some ways they are, and there are plenty of examples of clear-cut victimisation, but in the grey areas, which you described, it's more subtle. You have examples of both extremes side by side as if both were acceptable. You have men who feel they appear more masculine by treating women as possessions, and there are women who want to make their way in the world by being more blokeish than the men, and others who play with and exploit the system to get what they want. But it's not a free choice for them. They are working within a system of inequality.'

'You are being boringly moralising but possibly right,' conceded Michel. 'We are sexist in all elements of our culture. Just look at how we translate the word "human". In French, it's *l'homme*, so from neutral to masculine. I agree there is no equality, but men and women are not the same. Sure men have certain advantages, and they want to keep them. Women are free to either maintain their independence out on a limb or fit in with the rest. We are not equal in nature.'

'So in English, we have the word "mankind",' George responded. 'That's not a big deal. It's not worth playing with words, like some politically correct people insist, if there is no change in behaviour. Michel, you complain about political privilege, exploitation, and inequality, but you are not prepared to change your own behaviour and apply self-discipline to allow more freedom to others.'

George was half expecting Michel to demand a personal example of what changes might be necessary in his case, but instead he moved on.

'Self-discipline is not the route to a happy life. They do that in monasteries. Listen, George, why do you think it's normal to sleep with one woman?'

'It's normal for some, because if you really love someone, you don't want to do anything to hurt them.'

Michel cut in, 'But what if it doesn't hurt them? What if both partners are happy to look around?'

'I agree that a lot of people these days persuade themselves or are persuaded by the media that it's possible to have their cake and eat it, but not if they are really in love and want to spend the rest of their life happily with the same person. Someone always gets hurt, even if they don't show it. You may underestimate the degree to which someone in love will try to adapt to meet the desires and match the behaviour of their partner. But that does not mean they are a willing collaborator. Maybe we differ about the price of happiness, Michel,' concluded George. 'You seem to believe you can get something for nothing and that you can have what you like without consequences. But I believe there comes a point where someone pays.'

Michel pondered on this and then asked, 'Do you think Charlotte is submissive?'

'I thought we were having a nice hypothetical conversation. I don't think I have any opinion about your relationship with Charlotte. You seem to work well together.'

'You are ducking the question, George. Do you see her as obedient and adapting to my needs? Be honest, yes or no?'

'OK, since you put me on the spot, yes, I do think she is submissive. You have established your role, preferences, and boundaries, and she fits around you. She loves you, but there is a tension there, and one day it may reach a limit.'

Michel did not rise to the implications of this. 'I believe that no two women are alike, but their role is to be submissive once you have overcome their exterior defence. That's part of the challenge.'

'Michel, do you agree that men make two mistakes with women—either they assume that women want sex with anybody, or if not, they assume that a woman is not interested in sex? How you assess a position between those two extremes may reveal the difference between us two, and it may answer your own question about Charlotte.'

'No it's not that at all,' countered Michel. 'It's really a question of whether a woman wants sex with me, and if not, then she's not interested in sex.' He smiled and closed his eyes contentedly.

A few seconds later, Michel opened a now bleary eye and placed a forefinger over his mouth, resting his chin heavily on his thumb. He gazed down at the table and took a deep breath. After a minute, the open eye closed. It had just occurred to him that maybe Charlotte was not interested in sex.

George Milton was not bothered that his question had not been answered, and he didn't comment further, thinking his interlocutor had fallen asleep. He sat quietly and thought about the elements of truth in what Michel had been saying, and as he looked around the place in which they were now sitting, it took on a darker, perhaps more sinister aspect. He felt tired after the day spent in the open air. Michel had been completely lucid when they were talking, and George appreciated the weight of his arguments. He recognised that his own background and culture harnessed him to honest work as the means of survival, but he was concerned that Michel Bodin must consider him to be a dry stick, sitting on a fence and judging others. It wasn't like that. He felt he had a moral base and his own values, and he generally knew where he stood at work and at home, so he would not be swayed by others where he felt justified in holding a line. But would he feel the same if he were living and working in France? Michel had thrown that level of honesty and set of values, in his face this evening, but George was not Michel. George was committed to what he was doing, and he worked in a very different, perhaps more decent, business environment where, he believed, high-level criminality was an exception and more likely to be punished. He had made his choices, but Michel's revelations and what he already knew about French culture caused him to make comparisons with Northern Ireland with its long-standing specific issues of intolerance, and the rest of the UK, where abuses undeniably occurred, but usually the lid would eventually be prised off and the offences made public and offenders pilloried. In France, evidence of wrongdoing seemed to circulate among the whole population without official judicial action being taken. Perhaps that was because the French president was the head of the judiciary.

George eventually got up, paid the bill, and took the car keys from a passive Michel. There was no more discussion on the way home.

CHAPTER SEVEN

Search for Solutions, 1990-2000

Does anybody who goes in search of a solution find it?

Michel was in search of 'stronger sensations' as he put it. Publicly, that hunger was fulfilled by ever more exotic adventure holidays, fast cars, and other material acquisitions. Those included BMW M3s and an M5, a red Jaguar convertible, and a silver Porsche 911 which he once said he drove from London to Paris in five hours and fifteen minutes, including stops and crossing the Channel by the new Eurotunnel.

More secretly, Michel was enjoying the freedom of movement given by his work whilst apparently working harder and longer. Because he was the commercial front man for the business, he had to meet potential customers at times when they were available, and that was increasingly at night. He would come home for a light meal and leave at around seven in the evening when the traffic in the direction of Paris was thinning out and return home at one or two in the morning, though sometimes that could extend to three or four. He was busier than ever and came and went, held meetings, and visited project sites and suppliers. He organised what he described as official and unofficial entertainment for his clients and kept the money rolling in.

After a long period of this regime, he was dead beat and feeling guilty as hell. He felt that he was betraying his wife and neglecting his family to a point of disowning them. He was spending more and more time entertaining prospective and recent clients in whatever ways they chose. That could mean expensive meals and attendance at major sports fixtures during the day or strip clubs or a visit to his friend Johnny Mendes's hotel at night. He resolved that he would try to do something about his sulking and often angry attitude in response to Charlotte's questions. She deserved better. She was a good mother to his children, an excellent assistant in the business, and she organised their family and social life efficiently. She must know that he was cheating. She couldn't fail to know. He decided he wanted to keep her, and he would look after her come what may. Nevertheless, his quest for stronger sensations left him feeling that sex was no longer erotic enough for him to enjoy it with his wife. She was willing to experiment with him at first but was quite unreceptive to some of his more exotic suggestions, and he had to admit to himself that his secret life brought greater excitement and more fulfilment with none of the questions which he resented and which made him so angry.

Charlotte was also looking for solutions, though most of her problems concerned the daily round of the social, educational, and working life of a family with three girls successively entering their teens, administering a business, and looking after a husband who took little interest in any of the above, though he enjoyed the results, and being his model-girl accessory as and when required. Charlotte had never loved anybody other than Michel, and since her teenage years, she remained just as besotted and devoted to him. She admired his strength and joie de vivre, and she shared his interest in the world around, though at times those strengths had put a lot of pressure on her to keep up. As a mother, she wanted to spend more time with the children and be there for them. To a great extent, she had succeeded, so the girls enjoyed a very close and confiding relationship with their mother. They enjoyed her company, good humour, and wise advice, and they were proud of the fact that she looked like a star when she attended their school. The relationship was particularly close with Annick, who, from an early age, had shown that she was very protective towards Charlotte.

Although equal partners in the business and although Charlotte considered herself to be an equal partner in the family, she had to play a diplomatic role shaped around Michel's ideas and impulses. So often when he came up with an idea for the business or for their domestic life, he would discuss it with her but equally often implement it whether she agreed or not. He would employ staff without consulting Charlotte. She would simply find that he had offered a job to somebody, and the contract and payroll were expected to follow. He would take on clients on terms that were based on historical costs because he didn't like to do the research which would have revealed significant increase in material prices. Instead, when Charlotte advised him about a margin shortfall, he would make up lost ground by overcharging elsewhere, and above all, he would keep going to auctions where he would buy items that were beautifully chosen, mainly light fittings and extraordinary ornaments for the restaurants, but for which the clients had not yet agreed to pay. Some clients were convinced and took the items, others declined, so that numbers of objets d'art ended up in the Bodins' home whether or not they were intended to be there. Charlotte was the sweeper for this kind of indiscipline, but did it all with a smile, accepting that it was just Michel being Michel.

There appeared to be a balance in their existence in which Michel was free to pursue his instincts, leaving Charlotte to manage the rest. She undertook the role willingly and well, and she naturally enjoyed the fruits of the business success in terms of shopping trips with an unconstrained cheque book with which to pay for beauty treatments and products and clothes for every occasion with which to impress. As the years went by, it was also noticeable that Charlotte was spending more time and money on medical treatment to overcome digestive and nervous problems which defied remedy and became chronic.

Charlotte was no dupe, and although her telephone conversations with Thérèse showed she was stoic and uncritical of Michel's strange work habits and increasing late nights, it was obvious to Thérèse that Charlotte needed someone she could rely on for a second opinion, and she could count on Thérèse to sum up the common-sense conclusion that something wasn't right. Nobody dared to put a finger on it, but the uncertainty was causing Charlotte a great deal of stress, and in the secrecy of the night, she could imagine and fear the worst.

She could not bring herself to challenge Michel directly, and every time she casually asked for clarification on his movements, there was always a reasonable explanation, though his unconcealed irritation at the questions was new and indicative of his reluctance to disclose more than necessary.

On another visit to Paris, Thérèse and George were staying at the Bodins' house at Maisons-Laffitte. The two couples were getting ready to go out to a restaurant for dinner. George and Michel were already downstairs, Charlotte was in the kitchen, and Thérèse was still in the bedroom getting ready, when the telephone rang. Michel took the call in his study. The door was open, and George, who was sitting reading on the sofa in the salon, heard one side of an intriguing and guarded conversation.

Michel: 'When are they coming?'
Caller: ************************
'I can't do anything by then.'
Caller: ************************
'So what can we do?'
Caller: ************************

'How can you take care of it?'
Caller: **************************

'Hmm! I'm just going out, but I'll rearrange and be there in ten minutes.'

Michel put the phone down and walked into the kitchen to find Charlotte. He spoke for a few minutes in a low and urgent voice that prevented George from making out what was said. When they emerged, a visibly tense Michel explained to George that something important had come up, and he had to go to the office to get some papers. Charlotte would take George and Thérèse to the restaurant, and he would join them there later.

Over drinks at the restaurant, George asked Charlotte who had phoned. She leaned forward with a knowing smile, trailing her long glossy hair on to the drinks table, and spoke quietly.

'It was Charles, one of Michel's contacts in the tax office. He told Michel that there is going to be a surprise tax inspection tomorrow, and he should remove certain documents before they arrive.'

'Can he do that?'

'In practical terms, normally not, but Charles is sending his men in this evening to take away what the authorities want to see.'

'Wow, that's influence!' marvelled George. 'You get the tax office to fix it so the tax office can't find anything.'

Privately, George and Thérèse speculated that the levels of undeclared tax must be substantial to afford this level of attention. Turning again to Charlotte, George asked, 'Doesn't allowing the tax people to take away documents mean they then have what they want?'

'No, Charles is a good friend and will see to it that they are stored safely.'

Thérèse and George could not fathom how such an obvious trick could work, but the next day, Michel announced that the inspection had taken place and the authorities had found nothing.

The four celebrated with a glass of champagne.

Some months later, long after the Miltons had returned home, there was another late call to Michel from Charles.

'Things are changing here, and I can't help you anymore. I don't think we should meet.'

'What do you think I should do?' Michel tensed. This was potentially serious.

'If I were you, I would sell the company as we discussed previously. Now is the time to do it. It won't solve all of the problems, but it would make things a little more difficult for them if you're careful,' Charles advised.

'Hmm! Thanks, Charles. I'll think it over, and we'll talk again.'

'Don't contact me at the office.'

'OK, thanks.'

The Miltons' second home at Branne, near Bordeaux, was an eighteenth-century chartreuse with three characteristically communicating main reception rooms, taking the full width of the front of the ground floor. It was a low, white smooth-stone building with tall, arched windows which filled it with light and made it immediately welcoming. The grounds were simple to maintain with a few flower beds containing magnificent irises and a string of small topiary yews in a dotted line across the coarse-grass lawn on the front approach. One evening, while the Bodins were staying there in 1990 with the Miltons, Michel announced that he was expecting a visitor from Paris next morning. He emphasised that he wanted to avoid any inconvenience to his hosts, but one of his collaborators was bringing some documents for him to sign and would return to Paris the same day. George insisted that the visitor should at least stay for lunch; so it was agreed that if there was enough time, he would stay a while and maybe take a siesta before leaving.

Next morning, as the sun was warming up, a BMW R1200 motorcycle burbled slowly up the driveway and halted just in front of the stone steps to the main door. The rider removed his helmet to greet George. George spent a few minutes admiring the motorcycle which had just covered three hundred and fifty miles in less than five hours, including fuel stops and making an average speed of seventy miles an hour, and was soon going to make the same journey in reverse after the rider had enjoyed a meal and a few glasses of wine. Then the pair went inside to find Michel. He was sitting on the back terrace, reading a book, so after greetings George left them together, wondering what it was all about.

Over lunch, Michel made an announcement to the family. He had sold his business. He had agreed to a consultancy contract for himself to train the buyers for one year, and as soon as the business transferred to the new owners' existing office, he would be able to let the vacated offices to an Indonesian bank on a long-term contract, thus guaranteeing another income for him. He had now signed all the documents for both transactions, and he was a happy man. George poured champagne for all.

The Miltons remained puzzled as to why Michel should sell such a successful business. 'That's the trick,' explained George to Thérèse. 'He's selling at the top of the market.' That indeed proved to be the case.

Two years later, in 1992, the two partners who bought Michel's business filed for bankruptcy, and the company ceased trading. Michel's non-compete agreement was thus void, and the field was reopened for him to move back into the same kind of business. He was in two minds. He had had enough of Paris and family life. He needed to revert to a more natural existence, with primitive virtues, as he had seen on his travels and read about. This was in line with his idealism and his philosophy. He shared his thoughts and plans on this subject only with his friend Johnny Mendes. Johnny could see no reason why Michel should not make a clean break. In fact, he was planning something similar himself. He invited Michel to join him and his Haitian wife Ayida the next time they went to Haiti.

Michel Bodin did not make a clean break then. Instead, he decided to launch a new business, working from home, with an underlying plan to build it up and sell it as a going concern when he was ready. He was taking it for granted that Charlotte would manage the administration as before, but as he brought together his thoughts about the exit plan, he realised that there were one or two changes he needed to make to his domestic arrangements, and those changes might take some time, and so Michel launched himself with his usual enthusiasm into the business of acquiring new customers by personal selling. This time, all building operations were subcontracted, so although he would advise the clients throughout the project, the client would effectively be the project manager, thus relieving Michel of much of the hassle and risk experienced previously. Within a few months, he had enough confidence to open a small office near the Bois de Boulogne on the western edge of Paris and had rehired some of his most competent design personnel.

Soon after the office had been set up and was operational, Michel was following up a sales lead from a previous customer. A man known as 'The Russian,' whose name was Liptov, but was probably not Russian, had stayed on in Paris after the Second World War and somehow accumulated enough money to acquire about eight bars and brasseries serving food around the eastern and northern banlieues of Paris. The neighbourhoods were unfashionable, and the premises scruffy, but they had the right sort of traditional, authentic ambience for 1950s movies, and some of the black-and-white BBC *Inspector Maigret* television series had been filmed in and around these establishments. One of the bars displayed proudly on the wall a yellowing wartime poster announcing, 'Out of Bounds to Allied Military Personnel'. The moulded plaster ceilings were tinted ochre with cigarette smoke and the trademark of the chain was the smoke-filled and coffee-plus-chicory-perfumed atmosphere, which was common to all these establishments.

According to Michel's information, Liptov must be making a fortune, and now, after nearly forty years of under-investment, he might be ready to put some of his cash into cautious upgrades. Liptov could not be approached directly. He was, to say the least, a reclusive person, so the challenge for Michel was to find a way in. He found out that Liptov had a manager at one of the brasseries in whom he had absolute confidence. Her name was

Kozi Dubois. She was believed to be Dutch, and some of Michel's contacts thought she possibly had a spell as a prostitute before joining Liptov and moving into management.

The Lion D'Or brasserie in Aubervilliers was just outside the *boulevard périphérique* on the north-east corner of Paris. It was a tough place to control, but Kozi Dubois successfully managed two attractive young women as house prostitutes and a regular clientele, some of whom were Paris taxi drivers, for whom she played the roles of platonic mistress and mother. Despite their foul-mouthed banter and frequent lewd propositions, mostly based on wishful thinking, the regulars adored her, and she always had a quorum of rough chevaliers in the bar to protect her if needed. In turn, she protected the girls from more extreme customers and sorted out any misbehaviour. There was a code of conduct extending to escorting clients, who had over-indulged, back to their homes, and nobody was robbed on the way. The credit slate could extend for long periods if a client was in genuine difficulties, but the debt would have to be settled quickly once fortunes improved. Infringement due to unemployment could be partially redeemed by unpaid labour, such as cleaning and washing up. This facility usually resolved any temporary staffing difficulties.

From her attitude and competence at handling aggressive, oafish men, who were often excited by alcohol, Kozi's customers speculated as to whether she had been trained in military service. They concluded jokingly that it must have been in the Foreign Legion. Kozi ran a tight ship in a way that some men saw as a challenge. Bets were offered as to whether certain individuals were man enough to overcome her by force if necessary, but none of the regulars would take a chance.

One day, three naive newcomers were talked into accepting the challenge and tried to have their way with her on the billiard table. Kozi left them bent double and holding their testicles as she booted them out. Most regulars thought her status as the unopposed ruler of her domain was secure from that day on, but there was a further challenge to come.

One warm summer afternoon, when the front doors were locked open and there was a lull in the normal flow of traffic in the street, two North Africans entered, walked to the till, pointed pistols, and spoke quietly to Kozi, who was seated on a stool behind the counter reading a newspaper spread on the bar top. There followed a tense silence, broken only by a fly buzzing against a window. A chair creaked, but nobody got up. The few customers turned their heads slowly and cautiously to see how Kozi would deal with this intervention. She slowly turned down a page of her newspaper, leaned forward with her head on one side, and shouted, 'You'll have to speak up. I'm deaf.'

The men stepped forward against the counter, gesticulated with their guns, and pointed meaningfully to the till. As they did, a muffled chattering sound filled the bar for a second or two. The two men started dancing like puppets, then bent double, dropped their guns, and collapsed, writhing on the floor. The customers saw smoke or dust rising from behind the bar and noticed that holes had appeared in the cream-coloured Formica fascia panel that fronted the bar. Kozi reached for the phone and called the police.

'. . . Yeah, I shot them in self-defence. I have about eight witnesses.'

All the men's wounds were below waist level. After a short enquiry, during which Kozi spent a day at the police station, it was found that she had not used excessive force to protect herself from armed robbers. Kozi showed customers the two fully automatic Uzi pistols that she kept under the bar, and the word got around. There were no further attempts to rob the brasserie or test Kozi's authority.

Despite her appearance and professional persona, Kozi Dubois was married, led a happy domestic life, and was the mother of three young children. She ran about two miles a day in the park at nearby La Courneuve and regularly worked out in the gym. Her biceps and upright military bearing showed the results.

Michel Bodin knew none of this when he sought her out, as his informant had suggested, by going to the Lion D'Or late one afternoon. He sat at one of the small round marble-topped tables on ornate cast-iron stands, ordered a beer, and asked to see the manager. The waiter asked him for what reason, and Michel explained that he had a business proposition. Michel bent over and stuffed a cigarette packet under one of the table legs to stabilise it, and when he looked up, the manager was standing next to him, dominating the seated caller. He had a shock, because apart from being told she was quite a character, nothing had prepared him for what he saw.

Kozi Dubois was six feet tall, quite masculine in her facial appearance, and with cropped, bleached, spiked hair. Her ears carried so many rings that they resembled a metal puzzle. She had a rough Paris accent, throaty voice, and was clearly not going to be a pushover. After standing to shake her powerful hand, Michel offered her a cigarette.

'Thanks. I don't.'

'Can I get you a drink?'

She called the waiter, 'Jerome, a fizzy water here, please.' She turned back amused and smiling. 'So what can I do for you?'

Michel noted the multiple piercings and speculated as to whether there might be more under cover of clothing. On this occasion, Kozi had abandoned her habitual military fatigues and wore a very short black skirt, revealing long athletic legs. Above that, she wore a white T-shirt and no underwear to prevent her nipples from showing. He could not quite work out whether they were adorned like her ears. It was hard to concentrate. Michel hesitated and lit his own cigarette to calm him down.

French business negotiations tend to follow a pattern, which to a foreigner may resemble dogs circling each other sniffing repeatedly and for an inordinate length of time before getting anywhere near the subject of discussion. Kozi betrayed the fact that she wasn't French by looking at her watch and saying that she had only a few minutes for him. Michel explained that he would like to show her some of the work his firm had done around the Paris region. He had anticipated objections on the grounds that 'The customers like it the way it is,' so he emphasised the need to retain traditional features whilst modernising some of the equipment, including the kitchen, toilets, and lighting so that it would be easier to clean and maintain. He had not anticipated her reply.

'OK, make me a proposition for the eight premises in our group. Show me what I can get out of it, and I'll take it to monsieur Liptov.' He hoped to obtain more information from Kozi before leaving, but she rose, thanked him, and left him to his beer. From then on, they spoke only on the telephone until the proposal was ready.

Michel spent the next month visiting the seven other establishments discreetly, estimated their dimensions so as not to alarm the local managers, and then developed sketches and selected colour illustrations of other completed projects. The rough initial estimate came to two million four hundred thousand francs. The portfolio he presented was enough for Kozi's purpose, and a week later, she called to say that they would go ahead subject to working out a project plan, phasing the work, and coming to an agreement for her. They discussed some tax-saving opportunities for monsieur Liptov, and as it became apparent that he was willing to pay a large part of the bill in cash, the main deal was done. They then talked in more detail about the special offers available, and Michel made some suggestions as to what could be achieved. Kozi seemed impressed at the range of choice and opted for a new kitchen for her house, so there would be nothing visible from outside.

Michel, though, had made a serious mistake by forming a fantasy that Kozi might become part of the deal. He was intrigued by her appearance and excited by the possibilities of having sex with such a tall, fit woman. She had a hypnotic allure for him. He couldn't get the image of her legs out of his mind. He anticipated that she would appreciate rough sex, and although he was only about five feet six in height, he was stocky and reckoned that overcoming any resistance would enhance the pleasure for both of them.

As the final plans and project details came together, he invited Kozi to his office so that he could show her the scale drawings and virtual videos of how the interiors would look. They agreed that this could be done only after working hours, so Michel collected her at eleven thirty one night from the Lion d'Or, in the Suzuki 4x4 that he used for business. Once again, Kozi had chosen to wear a short skirt, though this time she retained a khaki T-shirt under a short, open, suede jacket with fringes across the back and along the arms. They drove through the Paris streets to Michel's new office near the Bois de Boulogne on the opposite side of Paris and parked almost outside. The mood was companionable enough, and they spent more than an hour in discussion over the plans and drinking coffee. At one point, Michel put his hand on hers. She withdrew it slowly. Later, he stood behind her, looking over her shoulder, and at some point reaching around her, brushed against her to indicate something on the plans. She leaned back and looked up, turning her head with a smile.

'Look, if you think you are going to play with me, you are going to have to fight me for it.'

This was insufficient warning for Michel. He took it as the challenge he was expecting. It must be an invitation. The anticipation was immediate and warming. A few minutes later, while Kozi was still seated, he reached down in front of her with both hands, seized the bottom of her T-shirt, and pulled it up, revealing her breasts. Kozi arched her back as if with pleasure, slowly reached up to hold Michel's head in both hands, then after a few seconds of exquisite expectancy, jerked his head sharply sideways. Michel saw stars and fell back dazed. Kozi got up from the desk, calmly tucked in her shirt, picked up his car keys and her jacket and her bag, walked out of the office, and drove home in Michel's car.

Michel couldn't find a taxi driver willing to take him home, so he had to travel by public transport and on foot. When eventually he arrived, he explained to Charlotte that he had had a minor car accident and hurt his neck. She wanted to take him to hospital for a check-up, but he took two Paracetamol and went to bed. Later the next day, Michel found the car parked outside his office where he had left it, but with the front caved in as if it had run into a tree, though the damage was not quite severe enough to immobilise the vehicle. The car was old and would have been too expensive to repair, so the insurance company treated it as a write-off. There was no further discussion at home about the events at his office or the true fate of the car.

The Liptov project was completed to everybody's satisfaction, proving that Kozi bore no grudge. Michel made no further attempts to shift the relationship from the purely professional to the more intimate one he had earlier conceived.

During another visit to Maisons-Laffitte one September, George Milton was strolling in the garden with Michel. They stopped at a magnificent tree about four metres high, with dark green leaves and covered in large white flowers.

'I bet you a thousand francs you don't know the name of that tree,' said Michel.

'A thousand? That's a lot of money. You must be very sure to offer that much.' He paused as if reflecting very deeply. Then, 'OK, I'll accept the bet if you are serious,' said George calmly, though his pulse rate was increasing.

'I am absolutely serious,' assured Michel. 'Well, what is it?'

George paused for effect. Then as the tension mounted, he announced, 'It's a *Eucryphia* from the southern hemisphere, sometimes known as a leatherwood tree.'

Michel bent nearly double holding his knees and reared up with an expression of disbelief on his face. At first, George thought he was having a fit.

'How did you know that?' Michel stepped towards the tree to check for any labels. There was no label on it.

'We've got one in our garden at home.' George did not mention that his *Eucryphia nymansensis* was more than twice the height of this one.

Michel was as good as his word, and that evening, he slipped an envelope containing one thousand francs into George's pocket. Despite George's protests, the payment was unstoppable, though George used most of the money to fund their next restaurant outing on the top floor of a superb modern Japanese hotel overlooking the Seine.

While the two men were still in the garden, a visitor strolled in through the front gates. Patrick Mastrolli was a good friend, Michel explained to George, as he greeted his visitor enthusiastically and told him about George's incredible arboretary knowledge. Patrick admitted he didn't know the name of the tree. Michel explained that Patrick had progressed to a senior position in the French police where he spent a lot of time liaising with the Interpol. Patrick spoke good English and, like many in his profession, was a cool customer. He asked questions, but his own answers were relatively brief and discreet. Michel left the two alone while he went into the house to get something. Mastrolli gave George his card but explained that he spent much of his time abroad so was not always contactable directly. George could not quite fathom why he might need to befriend a senior French police officer, especially as he usually aimed to drive within the speed limits, but he kept the card in case of need. When Michel emerged from the house wearing his jacket, George discreetly left the pair to talk. They walked slowly back towards the entrance with Mastrolli's hand on Michel's shoulder. George wondered what they might be plotting.

Annick Bodin, the eldest daughter, did not bring friends home while Thérèse and George were staying there, but Estelle's friends were frequent visitors to the house. The two whom George saw most often were a black African from Mali, whom he knew only as Zu, and a Moroccan Arab boy called Ahmed. As they came and went, George noticed that Michel always had something to say to them. Was he just being polite? More than that, thought George, without further speculation.

Then, one afternoon, when Estelle was out, George had gone to the guest bedroom to fetch his camera. He looked out of the dormer window on to the garden and saw Michel talking earnestly to Zu near the gate. At one point, Michel took Zu by the elbow and led him away from the gate beside the outer wall, out of sight of the road, then reached into his jacket pocket, drawing out a roll of banknotes. George had already noted that the cash rolls that Michel usually carried were made up mainly of five-hundred Franc notes, so the amount he peeled off and gave to Zu must have been substantial. Later, when Michel was alone with him, George asked if Zu and Ahmed worked for him. Michel threw his head back and showed his teeth in a wide grin.

'They are my eyes and ears. They are very good boys.'

By the 1990s, Lydia, the Bodins' youngest daughter, the baby of the family, had grown into a beautiful dark-haired, slender teenager with the grace and perfection of a young deer. She was not only a stunner but proved to be extremely talented, and Michel doted on her. He had hardly noticed her in childhood and had certainly never attempted to contaminate her brain with adult thinking. She had offered him a radiant adolescence, and now he felt he was closer to Lydia than he had been to the two older girls whose passage into adulthood had been largely managed by their mother.

When Lydia was twelve, Charlotte had told Michel that Lydia was experiencing her first period. It represented an existential drama for a father who liked stability in domestic relationships, characterised by peace, confidence, and calm. Suddenly, this little girl could make him a grandfather, anytime. She may only have been twelve at that time, but he must make plans for her now so that she married in the best possible circumstances, not like some young people who left their families and lived their lives in an atmosphere of familial disapproval. He went over his thoughts again. The idea that this child could have a baby was shocking, especially as he had no concept of what life might be like as a result. Even before that happened, he had to come to terms with the fact that she might leave the house at some point in the future and that he would miss her decorative presence. That would take a substantial slice of pleasure away from his life. He would have to prepare for the future without knowing what it held. His first priority was to support Lydia in achieving a level of higher education that would give her greater independence. From then on, he took a much closer interest in her schooling. He made sure she went to the best *lycée*. If she wanted to take music lessons, she could have them. Later, Michel undertook to advance her sexual education with the help of some explicit photos from his erotic book collection, attempting to make the subject far more interesting that the more biological approach taken by schools.

As Lydia grew up and continued to excel, there was less need for Michel to participate so closely. Lydia was an avid student and kept the whole family on tenterhooks as she approached selection exams for prestigious universities, the first of the family to do so. She passed them all and chose to go to the selective and internationally famous Institut d'Etudes Politiques, universally known as Sciences Po, in Paris. According to their publicity, Sciences Po's undergraduate programme . . . 'encourages intellectual courage and the ability to face adversity and cope with complexity'. The Paris campus is at St-Germain-des-Près, close to the French government buildings. All the Bodins and extended family were very proud that Lydia had achieved recognition for her talent and marvelled at this launch pad from which she could reach for the top in whatever career she chose.

At this point, Michel Bodin couldn't resist forming an idea that he should identify an ideal husband for his daughter or at least speculate on an acceptable profile. He would not, could not, go as far as trying to arrange a marriage. His wife and daughter would laugh at him, but he would still act as a caring father and maybe make some suggestions or facilitate some introductions. When he started thinking about it, he realised that his problem was that none of his friends and acquaintances had sons who were good enough for Lydia. He consciously went through the list and dismissed them all on the grounds that Lydia would probably reject them anyway. He would have to give more thought to the matter. Meanwhile, he bought a small studio apartment near the campus so that Lydia would not have to commute daily.

As George had already heard, Michel's close friend Johnny Mendes and his Haitian wife Ayida ran a hotel in the eastern suburbs of Paris. What he didn't know then was its reputation as a hostel for what the French call 'five to seven' encounters (5 p.m. to 7 p.m.), allowing rooms to be let for a couple of hours for businessmen to entertain a partner on the way home. The French socialist government's imposition of a maximum thirty-five-hour working week in Y2000 meant that office workers could leave work earlier and that had opened up this market so much that the owners had subsequently been able to widen the range of personal services offered. This hotel was one of the places where Michel entertained his clients, and as the truth seeped out later, it revealed that Johnny's wife Ayida and their daughter Beatrice formed a part of the personal-services provision. When George once naively suggested to Estelle's friend, Zu that Beatrice would be a nice girlfriend for him, he laughed loudly. 'Oh yes,' he chuckled. 'Everybody's been there.' George stopped and reflected on this revelation, slightly piqued that he was not 'everybody'.

He had met Beatrice once as he and Thérèse were arriving at a party that Michel and Charlotte were organising in a large Paris hotel, and for some reason, Beatrice was on her way out. She was dressed conservatively in a black overcoat, dark-patterned tights, and high boots, with a colourful neck scarf offsetting her tumbling black curly hair. George thought she was a bright, stylishly turned-out girl just as you would expect from a French middle-class family. He also noticed that she was taller and more voluptuously built than her mother, and her face was quite different. It was extraordinary and quite hard not to study it to a point of embarrassment. Beatrice had large, pale grey slanting eyes, which she emphasised with make-up; high, apparent cheek bones; and a natural pout, which she used to effect. George imagined that some women would spend a fortune on cosmetic surgery to try to get their faces to look remotely like this. As she spoke, Beatrice's pout opened into a wide smile, revealing perfectly even white teeth, an opportunity to advertise what corrective dentistry could achieve, except she had it naturally, and she smiled a lot. George's conclusion was that in some cultures where it is considered normal for men to have no self-control, and where men make up the rules, this young woman would definitely be covered in a black tent or punished for disturbing the peace by raising blood pressures.

As they were reading holiday publications in their lounge one day, Michel confronted Charlotte with the decision that next time they went on holiday to the Club Med, which they usually did once a year, Johnny and Ayida Mendes would be coming with them. Charlotte subsequently intimated to Thérèse in a phone call that the holiday was not a great success. She said it had increased her distrust of Johnny and Ayida, and the feeling that they were a bad influence on her husband, but she was unable or unwilling to give details.

In fact, there was an event during that holiday which confirmed Charlotte's worst suspicions about the relationship between Michel and Johnny. Michel and Ayida had gone to the clubhouse above the beach together, and Charlotte thought Johnny was with them. She was left alone to take a long, relaxing dip in the warm sea and enjoy the sound and feel of the water. She walked back to the cabin and removed her wet bikini, showered in refreshingly cool water, and as it was still hot outside, she decided to lie down on the bed rather than dress immediately. She enjoyed smelling and feeling the warm wind passing through the windowless apertures and the luxury of being able to stretch out naked on the bed with her eyes closed. After a few minutes, she heard a creaking noise, but in her semi-conscious state took no notice as the wooden buildings sighed and groaned in the constant sea breeze. Then she became aware of more light entering the room. She opened her eyes and was shocked to see that Johnny had opened the door and was standing there looking at her. She grabbed the sheet and pulled it over herself.

'You don't need to do that, Charlotte. You are very beautiful.' Johnny's voice was calm and coaxing.

'Get out! What do you think you are doing here? Come any nearer and I will scream.'

He came nearer and slowly lowered himself on to the end of the bed. Charlotte was sitting up now, still with the sheet pulled around her.

'You know I've always wanted you, Charlotte. How about a little fun?'

'You need to know, Johnny that I despise you, and I wouldn't want you near me for anything.'

She was trembling now.

He saw this and didn't move.

'Michel will be back soon, and he will kill you,' Charlotte warned angrily.

'Michel is with Ayida, and I can assure you he will not be back for a while.'

Johnny paused to let his words take effect.

He went on. 'You don't have to like me to enjoy what I can do for you.' His hand moved under the sheet and he began stroking Charlotte's leg.

She could not speak now. Minutes passed. She closed her eyes, lay back, and thought about what she had suspected all along. Johnny slowly peeled back the sheet and stroked her belly and thighs until she began to move under his hands, pushing herself against him, keeping her eyes closed.

When Michel returned, Charlotte was dressed. There was a cool atmosphere between them. Michel attempted some small talk, but it was obvious that Charlotte had something else on her mind. She broke the silence,

'What have you been up to this afternoon?'

'I was at the clubhouse library with Ayida. I brought some books back.'

Charlotte admired the anticipation and attention to his alibi.

Michel asked, 'What did you do?'

'Nothing exciting. I went for a swim. Johnny came to me with an indecent proposition, and I kicked him out.'

'He tried to seduce you?' Michel didn't sound altogether surprised or bothered.

'Yes, probably no surprise to you though. After all, you left me alone with him.'

'What do you want *me* to do?'

Charlotte thought this was hardly the response of a jealous husband.

'Nothing. Do absolutely nothing. I can take care of myself.'

Michel was visibly embarrassed. Obviously, this attempt to initiate Charlotte into the swinger community had failed. He would have to discuss it with Johnny and find another way.

Charlotte's assessment of her husband's behaviour took another step towards distrust, and there was a growing layer of fear in her mind to add to her depression.

The close family suspected that they were only seeing or hearing about the tip of an iceberg, but they didn't dare to speculate how deep it went. Charlotte began to discuss her concerns more openly and in more detail with Thérèse over the telephone. Charlotte admitted that she was worried about Michel's health. She was concerned that his general irritation at home stemmed from the late nights and overworking or struggling with a midlife crisis. Thérèse discussed her thoughts with George. Neither believed that the work routine Charlotte described was an essential or good way of doing business, but as the sales orders continued to roll in, what was there to complain about? On reflection, Thérèse thought that Michel did appear to be having some sort of midlife crisis. He seemed to be trying to compete with his daughters, recreating his youth but in a perverse way. How could it be otherwise? He could not match them physically. They were tall, slim, cool, and attractive in different ways. Michel was a complete contrast. He seemed uncomfortable in his skin. He had taken up smoking again and was neglecting his fitness training and healthy eating so had put on a lot of weight. Nevertheless, he was going out to nightclubs with his daughters and embarrassing them by trying to impress their young friends by flaunting his wealth. It was as if to say, 'I may not look much, but I have what it takes for you to notice me.' It appeared to the Miltons that he was trying grotesquely, almost tragically, to rejuvenate himself or die in the attempt.

At this time, most of Michel's family knew nothing about the hotel run by Johnny and Ayida Mendes, nor precisely why Charlotte seemed to treat Johnny with barely concealed disgust. However often she made her feelings on the subject known to Michel he remained impervious to her arguments, and she couldn't avoid the couple. Michel invited them frequently, and they often went out together. Then Michel invited them for another joint holiday. Charlotte tried to put her foot down. She couldn't bring herself to explain further why she abhorred the arrangement, and Michel seemed insensitive to the fact that Johnny Mendes was, at the very least, propositioning his wife. As usual, he had his way. Thérèse and George thought that Charlotte's revulsion couldn't amount to much or she would not have complied, and sure enough, from this time on, Michel and Charlotte Bodin nearly always went on holiday with Johnny and Ayida Mendes, wherever they went.

During a telephone conversation with Thérèse, Michel said he no longer found his wife stimulating enough. Perhaps, not surprisingly, because Charlotte increasingly suffered chronic health problems which, along with their work routine and Michel's working hours, prevented them from enjoying a spontaneous sexual relationship. In another conversation, Charlotte disclosed to Thérèse that Michel was suffering from erectile dysfunction, and this was causing him to be mentally disturbed. He was making more and more bizarre demands on her and had taken her to a club where wives or partners were offered to other men, and their coupling could be observed through one-way mirrors. Charlotte said she had declined to be traded in this way, but George found out later that there was another side to this story.

CHAPTER EIGHT

Meet the Wider Family, 1997-1999

As their business generated more cash, Michel and Charlotte Bodin were able to buy a second home in the south of France, fifteen kilometres inland from the Côte d'Azur, close to a fashionable artistic village not far from Toulon. In 1997, they invited the Miltons to celebrate their eldest daughter's twenty-first birthday there. The Miltons stayed at a hotel nearby, and on the day of the party, they drove the few miles to the large Provencal-style estate, where Michel and Charlotte had gathered a wide circle of family and friends totalling around a hundred. The party was an informal all-day picnic in the sun where it was possible for guests to come and go as they pleased, to wander the lawns, splash in the swimming pool, and stroll in the fields leading down to a stream. It was magnificent. There were many opportunities to chat with family members and friends who had previously existed only as names and who were, after a few glasses of wine, willing to share their views on almost any subject.

The Miltons met Huguette and Thérèse's brother François for the first time in over a year and found them to be as bright and enthusiastic as ever, though now in their late-sixties. Huguette looked like a platinum blonde Hollywood film star who had paid enough visits to her plastic surgeon to keep up appearances, yet without suffering the visible effects of an overdose. François had a leathery skin cured naturally by frequent exposure to the sun. He was unlikely to need a 'curriculum vitae' because he continuously broadcasted his own publicity. Despite that, the Miltons enjoyed spending time with him and Huguette and agreed that they were both colourful and entertaining characters.

George Milton was taking a walk towards the pool when, on turning a corner of the house, he found himself among a bevy of at least ten topless women, some chatting while others lounged in the sun. Practising his peripheral vision, he noticed among them were Charlotte's sisters and a close friend Ayida Mendes, looking magnificent in her tanned nudity. George was relieved to note that at least, when she came to greet him, Charlotte was wearing the briefest bikini, an orange string revealing her buttocks completely and with a top not much wider than an elastic band which she adjusted modestly as she walked towards him. At least, it was a gesture.

In the middle of this scene from the harem sat Michel. He was wearing Bermuda shorts and dark glasses, and as he leaned forward on the lounger to read, he showed a great expanse of full belly and folds of fat on his lower back. He had put on a lot of weight since his earlier days as a jogging and gym enthusiast. After politely greeting his hosts, George decided to take a swim later and glided back to the house.

Back with the group of older relatives on the cooler side of the house, George met Gigi, an English actor and published author who was resident in France. His real name was Gilbert Tilson, and he was, in addition to his professional capabilities, a great entertainer in company. He spoke fluent French without accent, but when it suited, especially when telling a story, he would imitate the archetypal Englishman abroad. He was, not surprisingly, adept with words, and being bilingual, he could find humorous wordplay for those who understood, leaving the rest of his audience bemused.

One of Gigi's friends was an aspiring Formula One racing driver with an apartment the size of a small hotel in Monte Carlo and another home in Switzerland. When told that his friend had won a motor race, Gilbert put his hands together as if in prayer and pronounced, 'Oh great, I always knew he was a *vainqueur*.' (With exaggerated substitution of a 'w' for the 'v'.)

Today, Gigi had donned a magnificent embroidered black-and-silver silk dressing gown, which hung casually open to reveal a narrow chest covered in dark hair, above minute black swimming briefs and skinny legs. On his feet were gladiator sandals and socks and a bright pink towel hung over one shoulder to complete the style. He announced that he was on his way to the pool for a swim. The subject of the topless sunbathers came up. Gigi's eyes widened, 'So, George, what did you do?'

George admitted that he had sidled away at the earliest opportunity.

'Oh dear, this time you must come with me. I have a technique for that sort of thing.'

The two went towards the pool. On reaching the tanning colony, Gigi scanned the exposition and shouted, 'Darlings, what a fantastic display. Are you doing this just for me?' The women looked up. Some were smiling, others serious, mystified by this sexually ambivalent apparition. Gigi walked up to Ayida, who, with her back to him and one foot on a sun lounger, was languorously oiling her legs. He put his hands around her, cupping her breasts, pulled her upright, and kissed her ear. Ayida didn't resist.

'Now, darling, this is all so fantastic, so stimulating. I want a private séance this evening in your boudoir.' Ayida turned her head casually and spoke inaudibly.

'And can I bring a friend?' added Gigi. 'Oh great. George, you're on for tonight. Bye, darlings.' Gigi let go of Ayida after whispering something in her ear and, after a further loud kiss to all, led George away.

'We Brits are so inhibited when it comes to sex and nudity. You just have to confront it. Otherwise, you get a huge build-up of repressed feelings that can burst out in the most antisocial ways, don't you think?'

In the pool, George asked Gigi what Ayida had said and whether there was a real assignation scheduled for him. He was embarrassed because although he admired Ayida physically, he didn't know her enough to relax and fool around with her, as Gigi was able to do, or put her off diplomatically if necessary.

'Well, you will be relieved to hear that you are off the hook unless you decide to make a move. Do you really want to know what she said to me?'

'Yes, I do. I want to know what you are letting me in for. I need to know whether I am dealing with a woman you have just procured for me or whether she is a respectable guest.'

Gigi took a breath and slid under water. When he emerged, he wiped his eyes as if he were crying with laughter.

'My darling George, you are under no obligation that will embarrass you or your dear lady wife. What Ayida said, politely translated, was, "I love what you are doing, but I would rather be ridden by a pig than a camp poof like you".'

'You took it calmly. What did you say to her?'

'I assured her she could rely on me to find her an ideal partner at the first opportunity.' Gigi tilted his head sideways and exaggerated his grin. 'Oink, oink,' and disappeared under water again.

When he popped up for air, George grabbed him by the arm and dragged him to the side of the pool where they stood together laughing like a couple of ten-year-olds.

'You seem to be a very happy person, Gigi, but is there a moment in your life that isn't funny?' asked George.

'Conceptually no,' replied Gigi, leaning back against the poolside, rocking in the water, and looking up and feeling the warm sun on his face. 'I do try to see the funny side of everything, but that's just me. More generally, happiness is not about falling over with laughter. You can't put right the fact that most people have unrealistic expectations of life these days. However, I take the view that depression is not a good place from which to write a book.'

He sank slowly back into the water, rolled over, and swam away.

Although Thérèse had met Roger Timmonier before, George met him for the first time at this party. This was the man to whom Michel had previously referred as his role model. Michel's uncle on his mother's side of the family, Roger Timmonier, had served time in prison for an armed robbery in which a security man had been killed. Since leaving prison, Timmonier had lived a life of comfortable idleness, his only exertion being the maintenance of relations with three mistresses and a tolerant wife who brought up their son. His financial and personal needs were fully taken care of by the women in his life, and he moved from one comfortable home to another as the fancy took him.

George was introduced to Roger without further comment, and the two chatted amiably about non-controversial matters in the afternoon sunshine. Roger, who must have been around seventy at this time, was dressed in faded jeans and a washed-out pale yellow T-shirt which hung loosely in folds around his thin arms. He rolled a cigarette with yellow tobacco-stained fingers and lit it. As he spoke and smiled, he revealed teeth the same colour as his shirt, though mainly black around the gums. He had not bothered to shave for this event, emphasising the contrast in appearance with his sister, Huguette Bodin, who had turned up in a fantastic black sequined dress and heavy gold jewellery, having the poise and impact of a diva.

This being the role model that Michel had said he looked up to, George had one day, much later, asked him when they were having drinks on the terrace in Paris, what he saw to emulate in Roger Timmonier. Michel had been eating pistachios. He paused and replied by sticking his chin forward, pushing his face close to George, and presenting a set of teeth loaded with pistachio fragments.

'Roger lives life exactly the way he wants, free from any constraints and with all his needs catered for. He doesn't give a fuck what other people think.' As he said this, Michel rocked his head from side to side in an oriental way as if giving a lesson to an idiot and getting very exasperated. George did not pursue the discussion, believing that Michel was probably drunk and potentially dangerous. Instead, he leaned back in his chair, took another sip of wine, and wondered if it was Roger Timmonier who fired the fatal shot.

George had seen what Michel could be like when the two dined with their wives one warm summer evening at a smart restaurant in Bordeaux, not far from where Thérèse and George had their second home at Branne.

The atmosphere was good-humoured and relaxed. Michel ordered another bottle of Château Haut-Brion red wine (over €300 a bottle at today's values), though the others said they had had enough. George thought it was a complete waste of a good wine and only Michel drank any. At the end of the meal, he suggested to George that they should smoke a cigar. Smoking in restaurants was permitted in those days, so, as they were sitting at a table next to the open door, the two men lit up and began to enjoy the excellent Cohiba cigars that Michel had chosen. As they smoked, a group of diners passed close to the table on their way out. A man leaned over and said,

'You know, it stinks in here with all your foul smoke.'

As the man immediately moved away out of the door to the pavement, Michel jumped up from his chair and followed, challenging him. 'What did you say? I'd like you to repeat that so I can hear you.'

The man turned and repeated what he had said before, whereupon Michel swung a punch, catching the man on the side of the head. He collapsed and slumped to his knees. As Michel was lining up another punch, George leapt to his feet and intervened, grabbing Michel from behind, and encircled his arms. He spoke quietly into Michel's ear, 'What are you doing? You could have killed him. You don't know how fit he is and someone could call the police.'

He drew Michel back into the restaurant, meeting the manager coming the other way.

'It's all over. Just someone being rude. It's all sorted. We'll pay and go, please.' George was worried that someone might have already called the police, and they could all end up in the cells. Michel was not concerned.

'Fuck the police. I know them. They are all rotten. I have got what it takes to shut them up.'

George led him away, and they drove home in silence. Next day, Michel didn't mention the incident, but Thérèse asked Charlotte what had set him off.

'He gets argumentative when he drinks too much,' she replied, as though this was a regular occurrence.

Back at the twenty-first birthday party on the Côte D'Azur, George and Thérèse Milton were formally introduced to Johnny Mendes and his wife Ayida. Thérèse took an instant dislike to Johnny, though she did not explain to George whether it was something he said or just an impression. Later, she described him as a slimy character. George found Johnny to be on his best behaviour, though rather sly and ingratiating. He invited Thérèse and George to stay at his Paris hotel next time they needed accommodation there. Having already seen, if not met, Ayida at the pool with Gigi, George could now appreciate her dressed in a fine turquoise sarong. She was from a mixed race background of Haitian origin, one of eighty thousand Haitian migrants living in France. She had fine European facial features, svelte figure, hypnotic green eyes, and café au lait skin, a combination which would encourage men to give her the benefit of the doubt on any subject. Her broad smile and white teeth would finish the job of seduction.

Another guest George encountered at the party was Philippe Bouvet, the ex-husband of Sandrine, Charlotte Bodin's younger sister, with whom he had a son, also present. The two men struck up an easy conversation from the first encounter, and George did not have to ask many questions to elicit a wide and deep perspective on the family and current relationships. George remarked on the obvious big-budget lifestyle and how nice it was to share in it. Philippe agreed.

'Yes,' he said, 'Michel is a very generous person. I used to work with him.'

'I didn't know that. What did you do?'

'I was the chief designer for the shop-fitting business.'

'So what happened?'

Philippe nodded his head resignedly. 'What do you know about the business, George?'

'I know something about it. I'm in business consultancy, so I understand the process as an outsider.'

'So as an outsider, what do you think of our little family shop-fitting business?'

A cloud appeared in George's mind, which he dismissed, and he took another sip from his glass of chilled white wine. He decided to give an honestly-held opinion.

'Frankly, I don't understand how it adds up to this.' He looked around at the estate and the generous catering. Screams were coming from the swimming pool, and he wondered if some of the topless beauties were now bottomless too.

Philippe elaborated, 'It's quite clever. There are multiple levels of revenue . . .' he stopped. 'Are you involved financially in any of Michel's businesses?'

'Not in the businesses as such, though we have helped him with some investments, and he has invited us to invest in Johnny's next hotel project.'

Philippe smiled, closed his eyes, and raised his head knowingly at some secret joke. During this conversation, the two men realised they were both staying at the same hotel about five miles away, so they agreed to have dinner together before Philippe returned to Paris.

It was not practically possible for Philippe to stay another night, so when they did get together next day, it was over a light lunch outside on the hotel terrace. After the meal, Thérèse left to go back to the Bodins' house to see Charlotte, so the two men were left sitting under large parasols protecting them from the otherwise unbearable afternoon heat, and as they sipped their coffee, they watched a long grass snake cruise unhurriedly between sweet-smelling herbs growing around the flat stones a few feet away. George referred to their conversation the previous day and said he was still puzzled about the Bodins' business. Philippe picked up the subject,

'OK, there are legitimate business transactions going through the books, then there's a percentage of cash payments which are off the books and which cut down the customers' VAT bills. That's what gives Michel his spending money. The next level of income is from over-ordering materials. So for example, you have a minimum order value or minimum delivery quantity from the supplier to get the best price. That might be more than we needed for the project, but we charged the client for it all and stocked the unused balance in a warehouse for our own future use.

Labour utilisation is a variable in the building trades, so when Michel took over the business, he closed the division that employed artisans and took some of them on as contractors who worked almost exclusively with us. We would try to occupy labour on other work between projects so the guys had some continuity of income, and Michel would pay them in cash so it didn't show in the books. That's how Michel built his two houses so cheaply, and then he sold the first one in 1985 or 1986 for two million francs. When you have a lot of cash, you have to move it on or stash it somewhere, so Michel is a major investor in Johnny Mendes's businesses, and he also distributes cash and presents to a lot of people to keep the peace and to ensure they owe him favours. That includes the police so he can drive around like a lunatic and not be prosecuted. That's another source of clients for Johnny's hotel too.'

'So what other businesses does Johnny have apart from the hotel?'

Philippe smiled again. 'You might think it's just a sleepy, one-star suburban hotel, with little to recommend it and not much in the way of business prospects, but in fact, it's a gold mine.'

'Johnny has invited us to stay overnight sometime,' admitted George innocently.

'Well, if you go there, apart from the lurid decor, you probably won't notice anything unusual. It's discreet, at least from the outside. It never lights up the town, but just make sure you are not in a room with one-way see-through mirrors,' he grinned.

George digested the possible implications of that but said nothing.

Philippe continued, 'On the surface it's a very modest business that peaks from around five in the evening. That's where Michel and his customers go. It has a two-way value. It oils the wheels of business for Michel and brings more clients and cash to Johnny. That's why Michel invested in it and in the new hotel Johnny is buying near the Champs Élysées. That's a complicated deal, but he's hoping for bigger budget clients there. Also, Michel wants to emulate some of the clubs he has been to where the guests provide their own entertainment, swingers, and the like, perfectly legal. But other things go on in the background, which may not be, but which are more remunerative.'

George wondered what part Ayida played in attracting Michel's financial loyalty and custom. He felt there could be more than one motive for the investment deals. Philippe added, 'The other area of expertise in the business is developing and maintaining a network of influence beyond the customers.'

'Who might that include?'

'Well, the police, as I said. That's an important source of information, and if they need someone to turn a blind eye, they can usually arrange that under some sort of deal. Then there are the planning authorities, getting things to move through quickly for customers and, of course, keeping the tax authorities on side.'

'Wow! Sounds like a tall order. How is that done?'

'Well, there is one particularly important contact, a tax inspector, who Michel meets in public places, art galleries, museums, and the like. They share a taste for modern art. Do you know anything about it, George?'

George dipped in and out of modern art. He had bought some contemporary pictures and owned mere copies of paintings by some well-known and now hugely expensive twentieth-century artists. He understood that an artist might seek to minimise traces of identity and any resemblance to anything, but some 'artists' seemed to be trying to reach a point where the work could hardly be described as art. Art consisting of simple geometric shapes could be decorative, but for him, it was without meaning or significance. George thought that the process of creating some of the larger metal assemblies from industrial materials must be like working in a third-rate factory. He had seen interesting assemblies of old car parts displayed in outdoor exhibitions and could imagine building them in cold messy workshops with the local radio playing in the background. He thought it would resemble the working conditions in a scrapyard.

George conceded that to be so successful, some contemporary artists must have found novel means to attract and satisfy buyers, which took very different forms to those with which he was familiar. He envied them. It was different. He didn't understand it and intuitively thought the undeniable popularity of bizarre works of art would quickly disappear, although some of those artefacts enveloping dead animals might end up in the Natural History Museum. He reflected on a sales-training course he had attended many years before. As a test, the class were each given a plastic paper clip and invited to prepare a convincing presentation for selling it at twice the price of a standard paper clip. That must be what selling modern art is about, he concluded. His mind wandered to something he had read about the most expensive cocktail on sale in New York—$590. Was that a work of art?

Philippe admitted that he felt the same scepticism but credited Michel for being selective in finding both new and old artefacts that were decorative and enjoyed increasing value. He continued, 'If things go well between Michel and the tax authorities, he may visit an art or antiques auction with his friend, and Michel buys him something to take home. That's the kind of relationship they have. The municipal planning relationships are useful for the building renovation work especially in old properties where the style police are involved, but they also help in obtaining planning consent for other building work, like if the customer needs a new home extension, for example.'

George was beginning to understand how Michel's passion for art and antiques was harnessed to money-making. He had naively believed that it was solely a hobby, a by-product of Michel's enthusiasm for decor and style in his business. Philippe studied George's face while he took all this in. He was feeling relieved that he had been able to unburden himself to someone he trusted and who understood the implications of what he was saying. He didn't mind what George did with the information; he just wanted someone to know that his own apparent facade of acceptance of events in fact covered a well of bitterness.

At that point, another guest from the Bodins' party sat down at the next table close to the pair and started chatting to them. She had the voice and delivery of a machine gun. It was extraordinary how fast she could speak, using a full range of high and low notes, at the same time, raising and lowering the volume and telling her life story in a single delivery. The two men sat for a while, wondering if and when she would draw breath but, like a songbird or bagpipe, she must have had an independent air reservoir which was not directly contingent upon breathing. It was extremely tiring to listen to and keep up with. Eventually, Philippe turned to her and laughed, 'That's very interesting. It's nice to hear how other people live. We are talking business, and we don't want to bore you. Please excuse us.' Then turning to George and lifting his elbow from the armrest, he said, 'Let's take a walk.'

They walked out into the burning heat across a lawn to a post and wire fence enclosing a meadow populated by one donkey and a large horse. They stopped in the shade of a walnut tree without speaking. George leaned against the trunk, still pondering on the fact that Michel's wealth did not come only from a legitimate business; it was built on black money from fraud, trafficking influence, and tax evasion. Any suspicions that he and the family may have had about a bit of tax cheating were washed away by the immensity of what he was hearing and amazement that it had been going on for so long without intervention by the authorities. A cousin of Thérèse, who was a tax inspector, once advised that anyone brave enough to think of setting up a business in France should at least have it registered in the Paris region.

'In the country, there are more tax inspectors with nothing to do, so they will be crawling all over you. In Paris, there are lots of government-directed tax inspections where the government is trying to intimidate some company that has declined to contribute enough to party funds. That leaves a shortfall of inspectors for regular business in the Paris region, so if you are small and insignificant, you are unlikely to ever see a tax inspector.'

George thought it was time to move to another subject, in case Philippe felt he had gone too far in his revelations.

'So why did you leave the company?'

'Oh it wasn't moral rectitude on account of money. Michel was fucking my wife, and that, together with the damage he did to her and our marriage, meant I couldn't stand the sight of him every day in the office, talking to me as if I didn't know he was feeding her drugs and throwing her to the lions at Johnny's place and elsewhere. It reached a point where she only came home occasionally, and she was sexualised to a point of frenzy, except she didn't want me. She didn't need me anymore.'

George let this sink in for a few moments. 'And yet despite that you came to the party yesterday.'

'Charlotte invited me, and I knew my son would be here. Michel doesn't want Sandrine any more, and she has found someone else. We divorced three years ago.'

'That's very sad, but I noticed that she was over by the pool with Michel. How do you explain that?'

'That's just the way it is. That's the facade that covers our underlying unhappiness. It's a pantomime.'

George recalled that he had heard that expression before from Michel.

'Do you think Charlotte knows all about this?' he enquired.

'She must know about the money, and she has seen what happened to Sandrine, though maybe she doesn't know about the part Michel played, but I think she can guess the rest. After all, she can see how he behaves in public, so what do you expect him to be like behind closed doors. She doesn't necessarily approve, but the guy is a first-class manipulator. He maintains a cash income so he can do what he wants with style, and his entourage want to believe in fairy tales. You might think I'm jealous, but I'm not. I just regret that we ever got mixed up with him. He thinks of himself as perfectly honest and caring in the same way as people think of themselves as honest and caring when engaged in the most deplorably antisocial or criminal acts. We have to accept . . . no, I have had to accept, that most of us live in a space that is defined by our political leaders, religion, social constraints, employers, the limits of our wealth, and the influence of friends, family, home town, bar, hotel, brothel, Club Med, and so on. It's there, you can't change it.' Philippe took a deep breath and smiled at the extent of his list.

George didn't know how to continue or end this conversation, so they just stood and watched the two animals amble slowly down to a parade of tall poplar trees lining the stream at the bottom of the field, and when they noticed mosquitos rising from the long grass, they headed silently back towards the hotel. George asked, 'What do you do now, Philippe?'

'I don't do anything. I'm suffering from generalised cancer and probably won't last till the end of the year.'

George was genuinely stunned. He had some difficulty responding to this blow. He stopped and turned to face his new friend. 'Oh, Philippe, I'm so sorry to hear that. I'm amazed at your equanimity. I have really enjoyed your company and our conversation. Could we stay in touch?'

They exchanged telephone numbers, but once George had accompanied Philippe as he loaded his case into the car on the gravel forecourt of the hotel and said goodbye, they never spoke again. George heard from Charlotte that autumn that Philippe Bouvet had died.

After the party at the Bodins' house on the Côte D'Azur, a crisis developed which was only explained in full much later. Michel told Thérèse that he was having trouble with his Moroccan caretaker, Mohammed, who lived on the estate in a large cottage with his wife and children. Mohammed was supposed to take care of the grounds, and his wife acted as housekeeper. At first, this arrangement seemed to work well, but, according to Michel, after the summer period, Mohammed was reluctant to work and did not inform Michel as to what was going on. This culminated in the whole central heating system freezing during the extraordinarily cold winter of 1997 and Michel having to take a team from Paris to cut out over thirty radiators and frozen pipework before they thawed. Mohammed had to go, but it was nearly another year before he was extracted from the cottage, and by then, Michel had had enough and so sold the property.

Towards the end of 1998, Charlotte and Thérèse were discussing their plans for Christmas and the New Year. Charlotte and Michel were going to Bali with Johnny and Ayida Mendes in January. Thérèse restrained herself from commenting, believing she had made her thoughts clear enough on that subject. Charlotte was concerned that her sister Sandrine, Philippe

Bouvet's ex-wife/widow, was currently steeped in more misfortune. After the loss of Philippe in the previous autumn, her new partner had been taken into hospital for intensive treatment of a serious kidney disease and was not expected to recover. His family didn't want Sandrine around, understandably detesting her because her partner had left his wife and two children to live with her, so she and her teenage son Christian were faced with a miserable year end at home. Charlotte left the idea dangling that someone might like to invite them for a short break. Thérèse and George were planning to spend Christmas at home in Ireland and had invited Charlotte's youngest daughter Lydia to join them in mid-December. After Christmas, they would travel to Branne, where they had invited an older aunt, Fleur Rocha, to join them for the New Year.

Knowing something of Sandrine's past depravities, Thérèse was not excited by the prospect of inviting her to spend the New Year at Branne or exposing George to the charms of a woman with such a reputation. But she relented, and after sharing the news with Fleur Rocha, who knew almost nothing about Sandrine's tumultuous past, invited Sandrine and Christian to spend a few days at Branne.

When Sandrine arrived in an elderly, battered lime-green Renault Twingo, George was surprised to observe that she had nothing of a sex bomb about her. She was poorly, probably cheaply, dressed in an ill-fitting cardigan and large skirt. She looked about six to ten kilos overweight. Her face was pale and pudgy, and her once elegant features were now less distinct. Her short unkempt dark hair, now with some grey flecks, hung in untidy strands around her plain features. To cap it all, she had a bad cold, giving her a red nose and streaming eyes. George found the transition from topless bathing belle to this hapless character in eighteen months hard to believe and reflected that Sandrine was unlikely to take her clothes off now.

Years earlier, this woman had been a middle-ranking executive with the Europe Number One radio station and subsequently moved to television to head up a department responsible for liaison between artists and programme directors. That was where she had introduced Johnny and Ayida Mendes's erotic dance routine to a television programme planner. But Sandrine was still only in her early thirties when her career began to unravel under the influence of alcohol and drugs and the pressure of life in the sleaze lane at work, and with Michel Bodin, Johnny and Ayida Mendes in her leisure time.

As the holiday progressed and passed through the period of condolences and sympathy with Sandrine's misfortunes, the Miltons discovered her to be a more interesting, cultured, and observant person than they anticipated. One afternoon, as the daylight began to fade early and while they sat by the wood-burning stove after a late and lingering lunch, the Miltons asked

Sandrine about her career and shared other thoughts about French life and culture that drove Fleur Rocha to take a siesta and Christian to take Fleur's dog for a walk, leaving the three others alone to talk.

Although Sandrine was never at a policy-making level, she had a lot to say about the relationships between the media and politicians. Thérèse commented that there were more women journalists and senior media executives nowadays. Sandrine explained, 'That's because most politicians are men, and it was a matter of policy to use attractive young women journalists to develop relationships with potential sources of information and opinion. France, especially Paris, is sexualised to a point of depravity so that's how the media gets closer to power. In France, you haven't got the same powerful media blocs that command attention, as in the UK, so we have to do things differently here.'

'Why do French journalists and media people accept that position then?' asked George.

'They are kept there by indecent levels of entertaining and presents.'

'And what does the French public think of that?' ventured George.

'You would think they are easily angered when you see street demonstrations against the government, but those are mainly set pieces orchestrated by interest groups such as trades unions, who look after their own interests above all else. No, the majority of the French public talk a lot but have only crushing apathy as their main reaction, even when something smells rotten. Let me give you an example you know about. Do you remember the sinking of the Greenpeace ship, Rainbow Warrior, in New Zealand by the French Foreign Intelligence Service?' The pair of listeners nodded.

Sandrine went on, 'In 1985, Greenpeace had been trying to disrupt French nuclear bomb testing in the Pacific, so the French government sent a team to blow up their ship while it was in port at Auckland, which they did, killing one man, a Dutch citizen who happened to be on board. As a result, two of the French team were caught and sentenced to ten years in prison in New Zealand but only served two. Why? Because the French government threatened a trade embargo on New Zealand. The rest of the team escaped to Australia, and because the Australian government invoked rules of limitation, they were released after a short period of detention. The French Defence Minister Charles Hernu and the Head of Security Admiral Pierre Lacoste were fired probably more for incompetence and being caught than for acting illegally, and Mitterrand ordered the Prime Minister Laurent Fabius to carry out an enquiry. Who knows what that revealed? It certainly didn't dig into the widely held view that the order for the attack came directly from the president. There were no other consequences. No pressure from the French public for Mitterrand's rotten government to resign. Journalists who tried to open up the debate were made to look like traitors,' Sandrine sighed deeply. 'There are lots more cases where journalists and others who reported abuses were simply not backed by public opinion or by the judiciary.'

'Is it worse here than anywhere else?' asked Thérèse.

'From what I have seen on business trips and read about the UK and the USA, sure, there are cases of abuse and dishonesty there too; Nixon and Clinton, for example. Nobody's perfect, but the difference is that they are more likely to be exposed, and when they are, there is a massive public debate, judicial proceedings, rolling of heads, and there is a rush to tighten the rules. Here there is no fuss, and although we have mostly the same rules as you do, the first requirement is that the hierarchy should follow them, but there is no will at the top to do so. When the judiciary could no longer ignore his abuses, Mitterrand got the members of parliament to vote an amnesty for themselves against prosecution. That vote was easy to secure because so many deputies had their snouts in the trough. Control of press by government is deemed normal here. There is strong centralised power and control of the media. When I was in television, the most important jobs went to trusted friends rather than more competent, but lesser-known, alternatives. By trusted, I mean they could be relied upon not to spill the beans on crooked dealings. If you consider that, most senior people in politics, political journalists, and judges all come from the same educational background. You can guess that they come with an existing network of people who have the same shared ethics and culture. That may simply sound like good personal marketing, and it is up to a point, but here, journalists and judges are influenced by the need to act within their cultural mould, and they are careful about what they say and don't say. It's a closed shop, so you don't comment adversely on those you rely on for your livelihood or do something that will surely stop your career in its tracks.

'There are a few critical newspapers. *Le Canard Enchaîné* is always entertaining and satirical, and there are a few brave independent journalists, like Jean Montaldo, but they have unusual courage and systems of protection that shelter them to some extent from threats, and they are tough enough to withstand the nasty personal attacks that come from little nobodies who have probably been paid by others who remain concealed, but it's not easy when family and friends' interests can be threatened. France is not a good place to be a victim, hence the expression, "Better to be a wolf than a sheep".'

'So are you saying that the French public will never be entitled to challenge government and ask the sort of questions you hear in the American and British media without that kind of treatment?' queried George.

'I'm not saying it's impossible, but at this time, and as things are today, the media with a few exceptions, will only attack a severely wounded animal.

Otherwise, no, never. These people are all mates. Leading journalists, who use "tu" in normal conversation with a minister as you do with your mates and family, revert to "vous" when they try to take some distance in a televised interview. It's all an act.'

(*Author's notes:* Wikipedia started in 2001, and Wikileaks was founded in 2006, and Twitter in 2007. They have made whistle blowing easier.

Dominic Strauss-Khan, a socialist presidential candidate, was seriously attacked by the French press when he became a 'wounded animal' as a result of his adventure in a New York hotel and subsequent arrest by the New York Police Department, leading to world publicity. Several previous cases brought against him within the confines of France had been dismissed or failed to go the distance.)

The subject of discussion moved to the role of women in the media, and the fact that several top women journalists were the wives or partners of politicians. Was there no conflict of interests there?

Sandrine smiled weakly, 'The words, "conflict of interests", have no currency here. When moral turpitude is an acceptable habit and improper relationships are part of doing business, there is no way out. The people in places of power believe that what they want to achieve takes precedence over the law. I know. I've been there and lived in that community. Although I was only an observer at first, it sucked me in and wrecked my life. My husband, Philippe, was a decent man, and I could still be living a decent life, with a decent family and a decent job, but I found rubbing shoulders with powerful people to be exciting and eventually got drawn into their lifestyle. God, I'm not going to tell you about that, but I immersed myself in the culture of immorality up to my neck and lost everything in the belief that I could do anything I pleased without consequences.'

Sandrine sniffed loudly, wiped her nose, and contemplated what she had said before continuing, 'Actually, it's not true that I would still be in a good job. The number of journalists and the number of media people supporting them has fallen considerably, so I probably wouldn't still have a job there. A lot of that work has been taken over by government media generators who cook up news and serve it, ready to eat, to journalists who gobble it up without question. Those people are absolutely barefaced about manipulating the news and using so-called "experts" to distort public opinion. For example, they will describe a commentator on the economy as an independent financial advisor, when he is actually a director of a bank. I've been present in conversations where they had to recreate the description of somebody as part of programme preparation to increase the credibility of what they wanted to say. Then you have weak interviewers failing to penetrate the defences of criminals who are protected by their status as ministers or senior government or party officials.'

'Doesn't that happen elsewhere though?' queried George.

'Obviously not to the same extent because I've seen a BBC television interviewer put a British prime minister on the spot and press him to answer sensitive personal questions about his honesty and good judgement. The viewers were left to decide for themselves how credible his answers were.'

As usual, it was Thérèse who asked the penetrating question. George thought she would have made a good investigative journalist. She leaned back and looked at Sandrine. 'What changed for you exactly, and why?'

Sandrine thought for a moment, uncertain as to how to summarise the complexities of how her life had decomposed and how much she could reveal. 'It started with alcohol, to be honest.' She breathed in deeply. 'I drank too much free alcohol at receptions and functions with people who drank buckets as a matter of habit. I thought I could handle it, but alcohol blurs common sense and morals and eventually alters your identity. Your inner conscience may be in conflict with the changes that occur to you, and you may even think you are coping, but the changes are relentless. You only find out where you are going and who you are becoming, when you arrive. Then you discover you have no identity, no substance, so you attach to something that gives you identity—whatever is available. You have no character, no principles, and no modesty.' She went on, 'You don't always live life the way you want to—destiny has a hand. I knew inside that I didn't want to participate in the mad life that my colleagues were leading, but I already had one foot in it. I had already cast off, and the boat was sailing. You have to decide whether to jump in it.

'You can always regret something afterward, but that has to be balanced with the desire at the time to feel real. You end up with no clear plans, but you can see your life as a changing image. Nothing you have learned helps you to find a way out or find a moral base that tells you when to stop. I couldn't. I just kept on till I fell over and was picked up and put back on my feet but not where I started. My old life had been destroyed forever, but at least, it gave me a chance to survive and start again.'

'So what did you do then?' pursued Thérèse.

'Hah,' laughed Sandrine bitterly, 'I started again, but this time with drugs.' She paused, raised her head with her eyes closed, and breathed in deeply. 'The first time you take drugs, you think, that's OK. I can handle that. At first, I thought I was really happy—nothing bothered me anymore. Then one day, you are found walking naked in the street or being used for sex by a group of men and sometimes women in a hotel room. Drugs are like death. They cut you off from every earthly constraint and give you the means to live life more freely than you would ever dare to do without them.' Emotion stopped her from talking for a while. Thérèse couldn't prevent herself from getting up from her chair and putting her arms around Sandrine.

'You survived. You're still here, and you have Christian to think about, so that's something worth fighting for, isn't it?'

Sandrine sniffed loudly and wiped her nose with a tissue. 'It's like being shut in a prison that you know you have to escape from, but you haven't got the strength to break out. Meanwhile, life goes on outside as if nothing had happened.' At that moment, Fleur Rocha came back into the room with a big smile. 'So you are having a nice siesta by the fire,' she beamed brightly. They all nodded. The conversation turned to the next meal and how it would be prepared.

George Milton and Johnny Mendes were drinking together at one of the Bodins' gatherings in a Paris hotel. The discussion turned to the reasons why Michel had sold the house on the Côte d'Azur. Was it all about Mohammed? They discussed the general difficulty of legitimately finding staff to take care of secondary homes in France because of heavy taxes on employment and the flourishing black labour market that is their by-product. George expressed some puzzlement about the affair and suggested that having a live-in caretaker must present another set of administrative and employment problems for the owners. Johnny leaned towards George. 'Can I share something with you in confidence?'

In George's experience, that question usually meant that the speaker had previously been lying or was telling only part of the story. He nodded to Johnny, put down his glass, and nudged it forward on the table like a chess piece.

According to Johnny, Michel's problems began when one day Mohammed went to get some gardening tools from the workshop—a spacious shed nearly fifty metres from the main house. As he approached the door, he saw that the padlock had been opened, and he thought he could hear a faint humming noise and gasping sounds. When he partially opened the door, he saw the resplendent back end of Catherine, Charlotte's sister. She was stripped naked and kneeling on a workbench, arching her back, while being enthusiastically serviced from behind by Michel Bodin using an electrical device. Mohammed closed the door gently and slipped away silently. He was shocked at the sacrilege he had just seen but not so shocked that he failed to identify an opportunity to ask Michel the next day for a pay increase to ensure his silence. Once Mohammed's powers of observation were made incontestably clear, Michel agreed.

Having thought it over, Mohammed was so shocked by what he had seen that he came to the realisation that he could not work for Michel anymore, so the next rung on the negotiation ladder was Mohammed's proposal that he should continue to live in the cottage with his family and be paid as usual but without doing any work. Michel would have to hire other contractors to maintain the estate. Michel found this imbroglio too difficult to accept and problematical to explain away to Charlotte, so there was a stand-off between the two men, resulting in the pipes being neglected that winter.

Michel tried to dismiss Mohammed, but the Moroccan knew all about employment tribunals in France and put the case to his boss that as he was a poor immigrant with a family, the tribunal would probably find in his favour whatever the circumstances, and in any event, French law prevented landlords from ejecting tenants between mid-October and March. Michel had no alternative but to ask how much Mohammed would accept to go, so that he could sell the place.

They did a deal. It was expensive. Charlotte never understood why her husband was so generous.

Mohammed took his family back to Morocco and bought a farm.

CHAPTER NINE

Paris Life, 1998-1999

How do you explain Paris?

(Sigmund Freud)

During another party in Paris, Johnny Mendes was advocating to George that he and Thérèse should come clubbing. George responded that they were a little old for clubbing.

'Oh no,' laughed Johnny, 'this is adult clubbing where husbands and wives are free to be daring and enjoy themselves.' The penny dropped.

'You mean a swingers' club?' George could just imagine Thérèse's reaction.

'Is that what you call it?'

'Well, it sounds like it. What goes on exactly?'

'The place has two parts,' elaborated Johnny. 'One is like a normal club where you can have a drink, listen to music, meet people, or dance—all quite normal. There's nothing sordid about it. Then, if you want to, you can go through into another private area and see what's going on through one-way mirrors or participate with anybody who takes your fancy, if they agree of course. That's what makes it exciting.'

'Do Michel and Charlotte go?'

'Yes. Charlotte was reluctant at first, but when she saw that Michel was enthusiastic, she softened up, and Ayida gave her some encouragement. Now she is quite a swinger. Last time we were there, someone offered ten thousand francs for her.'

'You mean you can sell your wife?'

'Shhh!' Johnny scanned the nearby guests. 'You don't sell your wife or girlfriend just like that, but if someone comes up to you and makes an offer, you can take it, subject to her agreement. It's the same for women too. They can select men.'

'And if it's a woman, does she know she has been sold?'

'Not in Charlotte's case, I suspect. She might not take kindly to that. You mustn't say anything, but there is this offer on the table for ten thousand, but it has not been, as you say, consummated.'

George was stunned but intrigued by this revelation. He had yet to work out how to differentiate between what was free and what you had to pay for in such clubs. He backed out of further conversation by explaining to Johnny that he was happily married and that he knew his wife would react badly to the suggestion that they should participate in the style of recreation Johnny had described. He resolved to say nothing about Charlotte either. Johnny ended on the cheerful note that maybe George would tire one day of always making love to the same woman, and if so, he should talk to Johnny about a variation on the theme.

At that moment, Michel approached with Thérèse. They had been dancing, and the conversation quickly turned to them. Thérèse mentioned that she hadn't seen Michel dance with Charlotte. Michel looked at her ruefully. 'Not today, not now, but maybe later.' He picked up a glass left by somebody else, drained it, and moved off to the bar. Johnny followed him, waving to George conspiratorially as he went.

'What was that about?' asked George.

'I don't know, but I suspect that something may be going wrong between Michel and Charlotte,' replied Thérèse. They moved on to the dance floor and said no more about it.

The club was in a side street off the Boulevard de Magenta, not far from the Gare Du Nord. An illuminated fragile-looking blue sign outside announced: 'Alive Bar and Hotel.' Michel Bodin and the Mendeses had agreed to bring Charlotte there and see how she reacted. At the entrance, they were confronted by a large man dressed in a tight-fitting dinner suit and bow tie, holding a stamp pad, and another man, equally large, who was collecting entrance fees in cash. Michel paid, and everybody had a red stamp put on the back of their hand. Once settled at a table, Charlotte looked around and saw nothing very different from any other gaudy nightclub, though some women were exposing more of their natural assets than normal, and there were several pairs of women and pairs of men. There was some interaction between the tables, and small groups sometimes moved away through double doors guarded by a steward. Johnny brought drinks, and they settled to observe the colourful display of people coming and going. Michel was busy talking seriously to one of the stewards near the bar.

After a second drink, Charlotte became aware of a nettle-like tingling between her thighs, so she decided to visit the ladies room, but as she rose, the world began to turn around. She couldn't reach her handbag on the floor and had to put a hand on the table to steady herself. Ayida got up and spoke, but Charlotte heard her as if through a tube. She was breathing deeply and could feel her heart pulsing in her chest. Ayida took Charlotte's arm and led her away.

When Charlotte partially regained consciousness, she was lying on a wide bed with Ayida. They were both naked. She rolled weakly away from Ayida and tried to get up, but her arms were too weak to support her, and she flopped back. She could not speak, and there was an echoing noise in her ears. Johnny and Michel were sitting in armchairs, watching. At that moment, a door opened and she saw another man enter the room. He approached Michel, smiled, leaned over him, and they chatted. The man nodded towards Charlotte, and there was further discussion. Michel looked up and laughed; the men shook hands and the newcomer walked towards Charlotte. Her strength was returning though her head remained confused, so when the man tried to pick her up, she struggled. He stepped back, said something to Michel, and left. Then Ayida came into view, fully dressed. Ayida helped Charlotte to dress, and by the time Charlotte's vision was able to focus more clearly and she could hear better, they were seated at the same table in the bar and in the same places they had occupied earlier. Ayida touched her arm.

'Are you OK now, dear? You flaked out for a bit.'

Charlotte asked what had happened.

'You had a bit too much to drink and nodded off,' Ayida reassured her.

'I'd like to go home,' said Charlotte determinedly.

'I'll take you if you like,' offered Johnny.

'No thanks. Michel, would you take me please?' insisted Charlotte.

'You will be all right with Johnny. I'll stay here a bit longer,' was Michel's response.

Charlotte was in no state to argue. She rose and moved slowly and unsteadily towards the exit with Johnny holding her arm.

Next morning, she challenged Michel on what had happened the night before. He maintained that she had dozed for a while, but nothing else happened. She asked if Johnny had undressed her and put her to bed. Michel had no idea how she got into bed as he wasn't there, and by the time he came home, Charlotte was asleep.

'Somebody spiked my drink, and you know who did it,' Charlotte confronted him.

'No, no. Nothing like that happened,' replied Michel.

'You are a rotten liar.' She removed one slipper and threw it at Michel, causing him to raise his arms in defence. Charlotte said nothing more to him for several days, and after that, there was even more reserve, one could say distrust, between them.

A few days later, Michel took a call on his mobile.

'Hello, it's Schmitt.'

'Yes, Schmitt, how are you?' He could sense what was coming.

'I am waiting for you to tell me when it's OK.'

'Yes. I'll get back to you soon. Actually, I think we may have been a bit ambitious. I think she may not be ready to play ball. I may have to give you the money back.'

There was a silence then. 'The money does not come back. The deal is a deal come what may, and if you can't fix it amicably, then we do it the hard way. Understand?'

The phone went dead.

Later that day, Michel took the ten thousand francs he had been given, put them in a large brown envelope, and had them delivered to Schmitt's office.

CHAPTER TEN

Break-In and Sequel, December 1998

The four cyclists rode rapidly up the short slope from the quiet side road in Maisons-Laffitte, a smart, low-density suburb in the Yvelines department to the north-west of Paris. The leafless tree-lined streets were sparsely lit, and there was nobody around to see the small peloton swoop into the cul-de-sac that served four large detached houses. There was a faint clicking of gears, and the riders stood on the pedals, taking the short climb easily. A bystander might have thought them to be athletes on a training ride, but this was just after one o'clock on a Sunday morning in December, when the night air was cold, clear, and clean. The shadowy figures were made darker still by their clothes—tight-fitting black tracksuit bottoms, black trainers, black zipper jackets with hoods over ski masks, and gloves to protect them from the cold. They leaned their bicycles carefully against the white-rendered outer wall of a garden and used them to assist their climb to the top. The last man handed up a backpack, and they silently lowered themselves to the ground on the other side, walked quickly across the lawn, and disappeared into the shadows at the back of the house, heading for the garden door.

Michel and Charlotte Bodin were in bed, both still reading, one of their favourite pastimes, especially when Michel came home late. It helped Michel to relax and prepare them both for sleep. Charlotte nudged Michel, 'Did you hear that noise?' Charlotte often heard noises at night, so Michel was not quick to respond. He looked straight ahead over his half-moon reading glasses, listened intently for a few seconds, pulling his lower lip with his fingers, and then heard a faint knock from downstairs. Sometimes the refrigerator made that noise when the motor stopped. It might have been that, but he decided to investigate, feeling irritated at having to put his book down and get out of a warm bed. As he opened the bedroom door, he felt a faint current of cooler air, but all was quiet.

He left the door open and moved slowly in the light cast from the reading lamps in the bedroom, across the landing towards the stairs, listening for any unusual sounds. As he passed the open bathroom door, he noticed the single, yellow, glowing eye of a deodorant dispenser watching him. It detected his movement and uttered a noise like a distant crow, causing him to jump in an involuntary reflex. He silently cursed the device and continued barefoot down the stairs without switching on the lights and checked the front door to ensure that it was bolted.

Nothing wrong here, he thought. Michel was familiar enough with the repertoire of natural sounds in his house to know there was nothing to worry about, but he was still curious about the sound he had heard. As he was about to turn towards the kitchen, he was struck by an almighty blow from behind. It had the effect of a bright flash. Michel sank to his knees in a daze but was immediately roughly pulled to his feet, and he took another hard blow to the left side of the face before he lost consciousness. He was vaguely aware that his arms were secured behind him and that he was being pushed up the stairs by several men. He stumbled several times, and before he reached the top, Charlotte came out on to the landing, saw what was happening, and screamed. She turned to re-enter the bedroom to reach a telephone, but one of the men bounded up the remaining stairs and thrust open the bedroom door before she could secure it. He threw her across the bed face down and held her there. When the others arrived, they opened a backpack and quickly taped her arms. They thrust Michel on to a small wooden chair, taped his legs to it, and put a double band around his waist. The buttons of his pyjama top had been ripped off in the struggle to drag him upstairs, so the tape was roughly stretched across his chest hairs. With one snatch, one of the intruders tore the bedroom telephone cable out of its plug.

Now they moved to Charlotte. They rolled her over to face up. One man ripped open her pyjama top while two others pulled off her trousers. They taped her ankles, now wide apart, to the lower bedposts. Michel was regaining consciousness. He could see very little out of his left eye, but he tried to focus on the raiders to detect any form of identification. There was none. There were not even the usual recognisable brand marks on any of the clothing or shoes the men wore. If any of them wore a watch, it was concealed by their cuffs. There was only a smell of sweat and warm clothing to identify the intruders.

One of the captors went to Michel's sports jacket which was hanging on the arms of a trouser press. He first felt the garment all over, then took out

Michel's wallet, removed a wad of high-value notes, and leaving the credit cards, put the wallet back in the pocket. Next, he reached into an inside pocket of the jacket and took out a large roll of banknotes and put those into the backpack. The same man came back to Michel and adjusted the chair so that he was facing his wife. He then placed a gloved hand on her pubis and shook it gently. Charlotte and Michel tensed as they guessed what might be about to happen. The attackers had taped the mouths of their victims and, by the time they left, not a word had been spoken and no sound uttered since Charlotte's scream.

A few days later, in a telephone conversation between Thérèse and Michel, when she commiserated with him about the break-in, she also probed his obviously defensive answers about the attack and suggested that the truth would set him free; Michel mis-understood the purpose of the question and responded, 'How do I say it? What is the right time?' He realised he had already said more than he wanted and cut the conversation short. He would always cut short an uncomfortable conversation and refuse to respond to any questions Thérèse put to delve behind Charlotte's intuitions about their relationship.

The loving relationship that had once flourished between Michel and Charlotte Bodin entered the final stages of its extinction from that time on. It had already suffered severely from Charlotte's increasing distrust and Michel's concealment of the truth. From Michel's viewpoint, his relationship with Charlotte was descending into bitterness. He had felt for some time that the atmosphere at home was becoming un-breathable, and he felt a tension in his chest from the minute he entered the house. Michel's problem was partly due to the fact that he could not accept that his life was changing and not only of his own volition. He was getting older, and things he had taken for granted no longer functioned on demand. He regarded the change as a poison that diminished him, but he could not accept that the cause lay within. The fault must lie elsewhere, and he must seek alternative forms of stimulation to overcome the shortfall.

Although external appearances remained plausible and they continued to share the same bed, there was no intimacy. Michel missed the warm contact of Charlotte's body, but when he attempted to touch her, there was no reciprocation. Though they lived in close proximity, the couple had become distant. There was no longer the same complicity and intimate connection. Michel's secrecy had destroyed that.

Michel rode a Kawasaki 650cc motorcycle for easier travel into and around Paris. It solved a practical problem and at the same time satisfied his love of fast motorcycles. One evening, a week after the break-in, he was riding along a narrow side street leading to the place where he usually parked on the pavement outside his office. There were cars parked all along one side, and he was probably moving faster than he should. A man briskly approached the kerb from the right at the next junction, looking towards the approaching motorcycle. Michel saw no immediate need to slow down but turned his attention to the man, expecting him to stop at the kerb, which he duly did, but Michel had been distracted a few seconds too long because when he saw another movement to the left, out of the corner of his eye, it was too late, and he collided with the front of a small van that had driven across his path. Michel flew across the bonnet of the van and lay dazed on the road. The van continued its journey, its engine revving fiercely, leaving passers-by to collect the victim. Nobody saw the driver or the number of the van. Michel was unhurt apart from a few bruises and a stiff shoulder, and his clothes were grazed, but the motorcycle was badly damaged, with bent forks and frame. He replaced it with a 4x4 car and stayed away from motorcycles for a while.

Within six months of the break-in, Michel sold the house at Maisons-Laffitte and the couple rented a spacious three-bedroom second-floor apartment near La Défence in Paris. It was prestigiously appointed, with a wide balcony looking out towards the centre of Paris, and it was just enough to accommodate the family, though two of the girls would have to share a bedroom if they all stayed at the same time.

Thérèse and George Milton never had a satisfactory explanation for the burglary at Maisons-Laffitte, but they understood why Charlotte would feel unsafe in that house with Michel often out at night, so they weren't surprised at the move, though they could not understand why the Bodins would give up serene verdure for concrete buildings, however prestigious.

The underlying reason for the move was that Michel was liquidating most of his capital assets and focusing on his new business. He had opened a small office in Paris, administered by his wife, while he continued prospecting his previous client network. This time, he acted only as an independent sales and design consultant, leaving the building and project management to others. Once again, Michel's charm and persistence worked, and the business, with lower overheads than before, performed brilliantly. Despite their differences, the couple worked together on a daily basis, and Charlotte continued to manage the accounts.

There was soon another discordant note when there was a break-in to the basement lock-up below the Bodin's apartment. Michel's substantial wine collection, temperature-controlled cabinet, golf clubs, and other sports gear were taken. It might have been a random initiative, but Charlotte was beginning to wonder if there might be more to it than that. She soon had confirmation that her hunch was correct.

A few weeks later, as Charlotte left her car in the underground car park of the apartment, two men in black leather jackets approached her, barring her way to the exit door leading to the apartments. She was just putting her car keys away and getting the apartment keys out of her bag when each man grabbed an elbow, and they started dragging her towards a large dark car where a third man waited behind the wheel. Charlotte's hand desperately groped in the bag and emerged with a pepper spray she kept there for just this eventuality. Both men received a paralysing dose full in the face, and Charlotte started coughing and crying too. She saw the third man getting out of the car, so she took off towards the hall entrance door, and once on the other side, she used the night-time security lock to bolt the door to the car park then ran into her apartment, again bolting the door behind her. She called the police, and they arrived within fifteen minutes. They looked around downstairs, found nothing, took her general descriptions of the men and their car, and left.

When Michel came home later that night, she told him what had happened. He frowned, said little, and they went to bed, both deeply concerned in different ways at what had occurred. Michel wasn't naive enough to believe that his run of bad luck was unrelated to the affair with Schmitt, which had to be settled. He had to find a solution, but as far as Schmitt was concerned, there could only be one outcome. The Bodins did not share their thoughts, and the next day went about their business as if nothing had happened.

Shortly after the incident in the underground car park, Michel Bodin made an appointment and went to meet Schmitt at his office. At first sight, it was not the sort of place you would associate with a successful businessman. The office was on the fourth floor of a derelict concrete office building which might have been at its best forty years earlier. The car-park area was partly occupied by loose rubbish, overflowing skips, and a few twenty-foot shipping containers pointing in different directions. At one side of this scene of desolation and neglect was a long, low, open-fronted hangar in which were parked a scattering of expensive cars, including a dark blue Mercedes 500, not unlike the one Charlotte had recently described to the police. Bodin walked through a fractured plywood ground floor door at the right-hand corner of the building and made his way up the concrete stairs, noting that his progress was watched at every landing by small idle groups of sullen African males. He had no idea what kind of business Schmitt was in and, so far, couldn't place it with certainty in any particular industry category. Once on the fourth floor, Michel walked carefully along a corridor strewn with broken glass, possibly from some of the office partitioning that had been clumsily removed.

He saw that the only possible working office was at a far corner, and as he reached it, he found the door was open to reveal a cared-for boardroom table, surrounded by comfortable chairs, with metal-framed windows on two sides, giving views across one of the more dismal areas of the Paris suburbs.

At the head of the table, facing him, sat Schmitt reading a newspaper and smoking a cigar. His suit jacket hung on a clothes hanger on a wooden, traditional type of hat-and-coat stand located just behind him. The man sported wide braces, a striped business shirt, and, incongruously, a bow-tie. With his feet up on the table, he resembled Humphrey Bogart in a Raymond Chandler movie. The soles of his light-tan leather boots, which were the closest point of contact to Michel, looked expensive, probably Italian-crafted, with a pattern round the outer edge that showed little sign of wear. Schmitt didn't rise to shake hands. Instead, he smiled and waved Bodin to a chair, offered a cigar, which Michel declined, and waited with hands locked high across his chest to hear Michel's news.

Michel, somewhat nervously and with a dry mouth, explained that their deal had been done when Charlotte was under the influence of a drug, but she was already regaining consciousness by the time Schmitt appeared, and the immediate opportunity for him to take control of her had been lost. Since then, the desired conclusion had always depended on Charlotte's consent. Clearly that wasn't going to happen now and further intimidation was only likely to lead to escalation of consequences and more trouble for all concerned. Michel omitted to say that Charlotte still knew nothing about the deal, and he had not attempted to broach the subject with her.

Schmitt appeared unmoved. After a period of silence, Michel suggested that they should do a deal which would release Michel from his bond and ensure that Schmitt was adequately compensated. Schmitt ruminated, leaning back in his chair and savouring his cigar, but said nothing. Michel was starting to sweat. He maintained eye contact and, as in a game of poker, tried to give no hint of what sort of hand he held or what he feared Schmitt might do to him and/or Charlotte, though he had already had a glimpse of the range of possibilities. After an interminable pause, which Michel found increasingly difficult to maintain, Schmitt was the first to speak.

'It must be nearly a year since we agreed to that deal. Maybe I took you by surprise at the time.' Michel nodded. He wasn't going to admit that he had no experience of such deals until this one, and he wasn't going to repeat the experience.

'Well, I guess that over that time, I have rather lost interest in your good lady. In fact, I can hardly remember what she looked like, though obviously she must have seemed attractive at the time.' There was another long pause. Schmitt looked up at his cigar smoke rising to the ceiling. He was thinking that he had only pursued the settlement as a matter of honour. 'I'll tell you what I'll do to make you happy. I'll accept one hundred thousand francs as a pay-off.'

Michel was about to reach for his cheque book and then suddenly realised he would look stupid. He nodded and swallowed. 'That's a tough deal.'

'You don't have to accept.' Schmitt produced an almost-avuncular smile.

'I'll have the cash delivered to you tomorrow.' This time Schmitt stood up and reached across the wide table to shake hands.

'Tomorrow then,' Schmitt turned to look out of the window, raised one hand to support his other elbow, drew on the cigar, and exhaled slowly. Then, after a few seconds had passed, he spoke to the window. 'Of course, if there should be any change of plan tomorrow, your wife will be the first to feel the effects.'

'There will be no change of plans,' Michel assured him.

When he reached the front door of the building and took his first breath of outside air, Michel realised that he was not only sweating profusely, but his hands were trembling. He reached for a cigarette and went for a long walk before getting back into his car.

Next day, Michel sent the cash with great relief. There were no more 'incidents.'

The next big event in his life was a new love for Michel. At first, it was a secret love, of which he spoke to nobody except Johnny, but it took over his mind to a point where he felt very exposed to discovery. Much of his life was transparent to those around him, so he had to maintain the really well-hidden secrets very diligently. He persuaded himself that this new relationship was an intellectual meeting of minds. She had the same passions as he did, and they thought about each other day and night.

He knew it would have to come out eventually. After three months, he could hardly contain himself, but his new love persuaded him to keep the secret. Sonja Alstrom was separated from her husband and desperate to find a man with the means to support her and her sons. At first, Michel declined to get involved in any kind of new relationship requiring finance. But as time went on, he softened, and by the time the deceit reached a crisis point, he was ready to accept Sonja's terms. She was the perfect lover, a friend par excellence; he could share all his thoughts with her, they could talk about anything, and she understood everything. It was perfect, but what about his family? More than ever, he wanted to be free to pursue his magnificent love story, but he still wanted to retain Charlotte for practical, financial, and emotional reasons.

CHAPTER ELEVEN

Discovery and Consequences, 2000

At the Bodins' home, the scenes and arguments multiplied, largely because Michel's ability to lie was no longer enough protection against Charlotte's intuition. She knew that he was in love with someone else. It wasn't the first time he had been unfaithful, but Charlotte's radar never failed, so much so that Michel could have believed she had supernatural powers. He didn't love her anymore, but Charlotte at least had one important element of power over her husband: they were equal partners in the business, and she had complete control of the joint accounts and investments and, as she felt the danger to their marriage increase, she held on tightly. She had only ever loved Michel, but she had reached a point where she could not trust him anymore and was aware of a heightened need to look after her own interests.

During celebrations for the millennium in their rented flat in Paris, the coolness between Charlotte and Michel was publicly obvious. Michel was absent for long periods, and when the rest of the family arrived, the atmosphere remained tense. Most of the family guessed the pair must have had a row, but the full truth was revealed only later.

The morning after the party, George Milton was having breakfast alone in the alcove next to the Bodins' kitchen at around ten thirty. There was a padded bench seat, a couple of wooden chairs; bread crumbs, shards of crust, and drops of jam on the table indicated that someone, probably Michel, had eaten breakfast earlier and left. George had managed to cut his section of French bread in half lengthways, buttered it, and applied a liberal dose of honey. When he tried to bite through the bread, he remembered why sharks have saw edges to their teeth; they are perfectly adapted to eating French bread. The more he bit and the more he pulled and twisted the bread with his hands, the more gobs of honey oozed over his fingers. He was just getting up to wash his hands at the kitchen sink when Charlotte appeared, looking unusually pale and stern, and came forward to kiss him. George explained what was happening to his breakfast and instead of the peal of laughter he anticipated, Charlotte just smiled weakly for a few seconds. Then she patted George lightly on the chest, bowed her head, and walked back into her bedroom with her hands over her face, shaking her head.

'There's something wrong with Charlotte,' announced George to Thérèse. 'I don't think it's because of anything I said, but she just started crying and went back to her room. I don't know if Michel is still there or not, but I thought you should find out what's the matter.'

There was indeed something wrong. The two women sat on Charlotte's bed, and she told Thérèse that she had found a letter in a pocket of one of Michel's jackets as she was preparing it to be dry-cleaned. It was from a woman thanking him for the generous Christmas present and explaining that she had taken herself to Bali for the holiday period, understanding that Michel had to spend time with his family. She would make it up to him later when they met—in the most lurid detail. It was signed, 'Your little cat, S'.

Thérèse was not altogether surprised, though saddened at this new element of confirmation of her worst fears. She tried to comfort Charlotte, but there was little to be done for now in the way of reassurance and pumping her up for the inevitable battles to follow. Thérèse had to leave her to take the next steps on her own. As Thérèse moved towards the bedroom door, Charlotte called to her, 'Am I a woman who dreamed of a love story?' Thérèse returned, and they hugged each other tightly. Both had tears in their eyes.

Thérèse and George left the apartment soon afterwards, taking Annick, on a shopping trip to buy her a belated Christmas present. They knew that Michel would be back sometime, so they intended to leave their hosts alone to face their new reality. As the morning progressed and the shopping was complete, George and Thérèse talked to Annick about her parents and what they had just heard, and she proved to be glad of the opportunity to discuss openly something that had bothered her for some time. Charlotte must have confided in her to a great extent because she stood in the busy street with tears running down her cheeks, articulating the hatred and disgust she felt towards her father.

'I can understand that he no longer loves her, but he was a coward and a liar to treat her that way. He has killed our relationship, and I will never be able to trust him as my father again.' George and Thérèse hugged her in silence, and after a few minutes, they continued walking through the crowded city, found a restaurant where they had lunch together, and learned more about recent events in the Bodin family from Annick's viewpoint.

Meanwhile, in the apartment, when Michel returned, Charlotte coolly put the letter on the table in front of him. She intended to ask him to explain, but at first, the words dried in her mouth. Michel realised he had passed the concealment phase and now had to make some directional choices. His wife accused him of deception and persistently lying to her. She told him that he had no talent for dissimulation, and she had seen all along that he was a dishonest coward. When they cooled, Charlotte asked why it was that she didn't need the kind of decadence that Michel sought in order to be happy. She asserted that the world they had shared still had a lot to offer, and they had had a good life to enjoy until he decided to hurt others in the pursuit of his pleasures. She added, 'I hope you realise now how much you have hurt me. My only regret is that I was too afraid to leave you earlier. I should have done it long ago.'

They sat in silence. Michel was not of a mind to reply and add fuel to the conflict, nor did he feel able to laugh off his predicament. Charlotte was meditating on the situation. Then she looked up at Michel. 'Do you know what all this signifies? All I have now is a terrible nostalgia of a life with you. I have had some very hard times and sometimes my nerves couldn't cope, but I think I have the strength now to go and make some new friends and a new life.'

To Michel, it was almost a relief. Now he would be honest and open with her. He wanted to maintain good family relations, but he still felt compelled to pursue his objectives to the absolute limit. There was no going back. He explained his plans to Charlotte. He would make financial provision for her if she would agree to him freely pursuing his 'leisure' interests. He suggested that she should become involved, and together they would live life in a happy, more open partnership. He explained that his temperament demanded a change which they both had to face.

Charlotte felt the drama overwhelming her, and she almost shouted at him, 'My tolerance has a limit, and you have reached it with your sordidness and despicable self-deception. As for your temperament,' she spat the words in his face, 'it's got nothing to do with temperament. Your problem is pride and your inability to accept that you are who you are now, and that is not the person you were.' To Michel's dismay, Charlotte would have none of his new proposition, and after a few days of fuming, he left the conjugal apartment and found alternative accommodation. They agreed to live separately, though they remained partners in the business and parents of three daughters.

How could she fight him? Some women among her friends were prepared to take their unfaithful husbands as they were, but though Charlotte still loved Michel, he had humiliated her repeatedly and intended to go on doing so with her permission. Well, she wasn't going to be such a pushover. For the time being, there wasn't much she could do about his new girlfriend Sonja, except hope they would rot together. She felt as though the instrument of torture, the uncertainty, had been removed, and she withdrew into a depressive solitude.

It was nearly two years later, in 2002, that Thérèse and George Milton next met Michel Bodin at a hotel in Evreux, to the west of Paris. They were heading for a channel port on their way home after staying at their second home at Branne. Michel rode out alone from Paris to meet them on his new motorcycle, and they had lunch together. His appearance had changed to replicate a magazine image of a middle-aged rocker with shaved head and three-day stubble, expensive leather trousers, a macho jacket with metal accoutrements, and, overall, a hardened attitude. Gone was any attempt to conceal or justify his behaviour. Instead, he challenged head-on anybody who dared to comment on his lifestyle. This time, he pre-empted questions by opening up with his views. He reiterated that for him the human race was made up of wolves and sheep. He was determined to be a wolf.

'I don't pretend to live by anybody else's moral code. Morality is an invention of those who don't dare to get what they want. Who else does it benefit?'

He maintained that he was acting responsibly towards his wife, who by this time looked as though she was in mourning. Her conversation was almost exclusively about her health and the treatment she was having for her various ailments.

Michel repeated his assertion that he was looking after Charlotte, and he was ensuring that she wanted for nothing. She was a beautiful woman, and she would soon find someone else. 'If you really love someone, you must be prepared to give her freedom.'

George nearly choked on his lunch on hearing this but decided not to inflame the situation by responding to Michel's moralising. By contrast, Thérèse was not someone to accept Michel's assertions without giving honest feedback. She described to Michel how his changing behaviour over several years before the separation had not escaped observation by the family, and she related how they had all suffered from loss and the stress of having to manage the new set up diplomatically and without showing disloyalty to Charlotte or Michel. She put it to him that his explanations were still only revealing part of the truth. She asked for no clarification, but advised him that he was playing a dangerous game on several fronts. 'I sometimes wonder, Michel, if your world is populated by other people or whether you feel like an isolated entity.'

'What do you expect, Thérèse?' Michel riposted. 'You and the family expect me to act what you call "normally". Normal is a poison. Nothing in life is certain, and you have to take initiatives to make things happen. I have decided to obey my own sentiments and follow my passions, so to that extent, I am alone and I accept that some pain is necessary to achieve that.' Thérèse was going to ask whether the pain was supposed to be exclusively endured by Michel or whether he expected the whole family, especially Charlotte, to share the burden. She decided to maintain silence.

On his way home, Michel reflected on this conversation. At first, he was tense and nervous, allowing his speed to build to over a hundred miles an hour on the A13 motorway before reasserting a measure of self-control. He was confused. He had thought that just as people get used to modern art, so they would get used to the fact that social norms were evolving and accept that he had joined that evolution. He had assumed that Charlotte needed to be looked after as she was still part of his plans, but things had started to go wrong, and they kept going wrong from the moment she found out the name of his mistress.

It was Charlotte's fault that things were not working out the way he had intended. He ought to wring her neck. He pondered upon two options: have her murdered or find her another partner so she would move into a different orbit. He laughed out loud at the realisation that the thought of having his wife killed had entered his mind. Then he thought about the possibility in more detail. He knew some people who could be hired for sensitive jobs like that. But what if was botched and could be traced back to him? There were several reported cases where husbands had hired killers to dispose of their wives and the killers had talked. If it led back to him, that would put the lid on all his visions of the future. He recalled the attempt to abduct Charlotte in the underground car park. That was almost certainly organised by Schmitt. *Huh!* He thought, *if a woman with a pepper spray could see off two hired kidnappers it would be potentially too dangerous to attempt to dispose of her cleanly*. He would keep that idea in abeyance. His thoughts moved on.

Curiously, it was only after his conversation with Thérèse that Michel understood the depth of disapproval in the family and the full effect of his actions on Charlotte. Until now, he had been able to believe the world was made up of people like his friends who could act as they pleased without hurting anybody or didn't care much if they did. Thérèse made it quite clear that she considered most of his friends to represent a nadir of selfishness and self-indulgence, and if he wished to continue deluding himself, that was his affair. She told him that she still found it curious that Michel should expect that he could be infinitely variable in his behaviour while those closest to him and who revolved around him should be absolutely stable and predictable.

Thérèse had asked, 'Is there a stable central kernel in you that you would call "yourself", Michel, or is everything about you reconfigurable according to your latest passion?'

Michel hesitated. 'No, I would have to invent a single description of myself. I am what people see, and that can be anything.'

'Does that mean you can do or think anything without consulting your conscience?'

'I don't know about conscience, but there are situations where I think "This isn't me", and I try to head in a different direction. I tell the truth but not all of it because I don't have the words to describe it. I am not a psychoanalyst. That's why I have difficulty expressing myself to you, Thérèse. I know what you are looking for, but I can't reply. I come out of conversations with you thinking more deeply about myself, and as a result, I am more able to cope with my life. I can more easily extract myself from the herd and do without the rails that convention wants to put us on.'

'Do you have *any* durable ideals or moral standards?' The tone of the discussion tensed.

'My family and protecting them.'

Michel looked up and smiled ruefully, lowering the corners of his mouth in a characteristic gesture of resignation. He raked his front teeth unconsciously across the top edge of his thumb and said nothing more. As he was thinking back on this conversation on his way home, Michel came to his senses with a jolt when a lorry buffeted past him. Unconsciously, he had let his speed drop to thirty miles an hour on the motorway. He cleared his head, accelerated again, and was home in less than an hour.

Thérèse and George had listened calmly to Michel's logic but summarised their feelings by saying that they felt a loyalty to him in spite of whatever he had done. However, they would always retain their affection for Charlotte and hoped to maintain contact with her, though for the past year, she had retreated into a shell and was quite uncommunicative. Charlotte later said she was too embarrassed to talk. She was psychologically crushed by the unavoidable fact of her husband's infidelity and the choices he had offered her—participate or be side-lined. Her handicap in reaching a firm and rational clean-break decision was that she was irremediably in love with Michel, and they still worked in the same office with everyday contact to keep the kettle boiling. But a limit had been reached. She was not prepared to make herself a public laughing stock such as happened when Michel tried to hire one of his girlfriends as a secretary. The woman gave herself all sorts of

choice of clothes and make-up, to which she replied, that was how Michel liked her to be.

Once Charlotte was installed at the Miltons' home and began to tell the story of her experience since the separation, the full devastation of her life became clearer. Charlotte's sisters had admitted that they felt more comfortable now that she had joined the ranks of badly treated women. They had envied her illusion of a faithful marriage that until recently she had enjoyed. They confided that they each had, at various times, succumbed to Michel's advances. Charlotte was sickened at this confirmation of something Thérèse had warned her about years earlier.

'Do you find it normal that they sit on his lap and kiss him?'

'Thérèse! You have a suspicious mind. They are my sisters.'

'Well, I wouldn't feel comfortable about it.' Then, laughing, she added, 'You'd better not do that to George.'

When Thérèse asked if she had found anybody else she fancied, Charlotte told her friend that so far, there was nobody and she wasn't looking. She had been shocked by the hypocrisy shown by several of her married male friends, including her lawyer, who had made her propositions of various kinds. She felt under observation, stalked by all the men who knew her. Johnny Mendes was among the first to advance, as might be expected.

'Actually, Johnny once said something to me which explains a lot. He said, "You don't have to like me to enjoy what I can do for you." The trouble is, Thérèse, I do have to like someone before I can enjoy physical sex with them, and I haven't liked Michel for years. When the trust goes, everything else goes.' Then, on reflection, Charlotte added, 'You can't help who you fall in love with. Thérèse, you know the thing that hurt me most was that all my "supposed" friends seemed to know what was going on before I did, so I think they are all rotten. Everybody knows and nobody talks,' she added. 'If I wanted sex that badly, I would have to find someone completely unknown, otherwise they'd all be discussing it. The men and the women are all just as bad. I don't think there is a single loving relationship among them. You are lucky, Thérèse, but it's rare.'

The two women discussed what Charlotte should do next, but there were still many unanswered questions. Charlotte was convinced that she had to do something, but what? She had to get above the situation, high enough to see it clearly and completely. She couldn't bring herself to tell Thérèse everything that had happened since her separation from Michel, but Thérèse knew from phone conversations with Annick in New York that at one point, her mother was phoning at any time of the day or night to pour out her feelings. She was asking whether it was worth living and seriously considered suicide. Annick and Thérèse took Charlotte's outpourings seriously and understood that she was entering a danger zone. It wasn't so much a case of what they could do to help, besides keeping in close telephone contact with Charlotte, but what could Michel do and not do to help Charlotte move forward? What lay behind his facade? Did he really care about Charlotte? Thérèse considered how the three daughters could intervene usefully. So far, they had avoided communicating their judgements to their father personally except that until now, Annick had used her residency in the United States to stay away from Michel and Sonja. She wanted to stand by her mother, and she responded to Charlotte's need to communicate almost daily without ever losing patience with her.

By contrast, Estelle accepted the situation without bitterness. She was living in Australia with a partner, so she too was able to keep a distance from the daily evolution of events. She wanted to maintain relations with both parents and was prepared to duck the issues in order to do that. Lydia was wrapped up in her own life. She saw what she wanted to see, but essentially, she wanted to be a wolf. She had become hard-nosed and selfish and seemed to blame her mother, not for the separation, but for not having the strength to cope with it.

In the end, it was Thérèse who contacted Michel after many attempts and ignored messages. Since he wasn't pretending anymore, Thérèse saw no reason to walk around the subject or mince her words. Thérèse first established her credentials to comment by emphasising that everybody in the family was affected, and they were torn in their affections. They didn't want to give up on him, although he had done the dirty on his wife, and Charlotte, instead of looking elsewhere for comfort as he had hoped, had decomposed and was contemplating suicide. She was unable to manage her life and was going to pieces, heading for a complete breakdown. Thérèse referred to the meeting in Evreux when Michel had assured the Miltons that he was looking after his wife, and she finally invited his comments.

At this point, Michel stunned Thérèse by announcing that he would make one more attempt at reconciliation if Charlotte was willing. Thérèse was truly lost for words. It had crossed her mind that Michel might want to return to a normal life with Charlotte at some point, perhaps when his relationship with Sonja had burned out, but she couldn't see how he could put the events of the last fifteen years in a plastic bag and dump them. To what extent did he truly expect to return to a life of suburban normality? A lot of what Michel had been doing involved enjoyment of risk whilst being in control. He liked to be the man of the moment, involved in real-life drama. Clandestine adventures were good for his adrenaline. When Thérèse ended the conversation, she could say no more than invite him to bring Charlotte to meet the Miltons when they were back together, believing that it would be a most unlikely eventuality.

A few weeks later, Charlotte phoned to say that Michel had taken her out to an expensive restaurant and offered a progressive reconciliation at a pace they could both cope with. They would continue to live separately for the time being, and apart from their daily dealings at the office, they would find time to share trips and continue meeting the family together. She didn't say what would happen to Sonja. She then asked Thérèse what she thought. Thérèse remained silent.

'I know what you are thinking, Thérèse, but I felt that it might be better than what I have now.'

'I'll pray for you that it will work out,' responded Thérèse. 'It's just that all common sense says that you are setting yourself up to be hurt again, and I find that very frustrating and very sad. I know it is hard for you to look back at what you achieved with Michel over the years, and what you built together, and think of it as finished. You survived all the business pressures and brought up three lovely girls. Yes, you had a good partnership for that period of your life, but it's over, and it's no good trying to turn the clock back. What exactly can Michel offer you now? You asked me what I think, and above all else, I want you to be happy, but I think there is nothing to be gained by you chasing someone who will never be there and has so little to offer you. He has changed forever, gone away, and we must all accept that, but for you, that is harder than for anybody else.' Charlotte was close to tears, so Thérèse moved into support mode and tried to reconcile her with making the best of the situation. They agreed that the Bodins would come and visit the Miltons as soon as it could be arranged.

When they did, it was for a long weekend, and although there were smiles all round, the Miltons had no belief in the integrity of what they saw.

'We must have faith,' said George quietly as the Bodins left. 'That's all there is.'

On the way home, Charlotte had time to think while gazing out of the window of the rushing aircraft. She reflected on conversations she had with Thérèse and tried to explain her decision to stay with Michel. She couldn't say it was because of the children. That excuse expired years ago. The unbearable oscillation between sentiments made her febrile and irritable. Above all, she needed stability, and reconciliation with Michel was not going to provide the stable platform she needed. She had no idea why Michel had suggested it or where it might lead. She hadn't dared to ask too many questions yet, in case he backed away. So at this point, Charlotte had no inkling of what was really happening or how it might evolve. She preferred not to take account of the obvious signs and attempts to extrapolate them into a picture of what would happen. She was with Michel again now, and they would find their way together as they always had.

Charlotte's dream was destined to be short-lived.

Nikko, the chief designer at the Bodins' business always started work early. He was an effeminate gay and was shy in the company of women, so he found that working in an office with several of them was unhelpful to his creativity. He liked to sit down alone in the morning, make himself a fresh coffee, light a cigarette, and ponder the current assignment without interruption. That was when he came up with his best innovative ideas. In this field, Nikko was extremely talented, and in his opinion, he was the main reason why the company did so well. The clients liked his quirky and original designs and appreciated his ability to extract the most commercial value from their workspace. That morning, Nikko made some changes to a plan on his computer and, when he was entirely happy with it, pressed the button to print on the large A3 size printer in the machine room. When he went to collect his print, he found the machine damaged and with Michel's note stuck to it. He saw a paper in the output tray and picked it up, but instead of his plan, he found a dark, life-size photocopy of coupled male and female sex organs. It was blurred, indicating that the photo had captured the participants in action. He smiled, folded the document in four, and placed it in one of the drawers of Michel's desk.

Near the end of the month, after Caroline had left the business, when she was looking for Michel's expense receipts in his desk drawers, Charlotte unfolded the document that Nikko had placed there and immediately closed her eyes to hold back her tears. It didn't work. She ran out of the office and didn't return that day.

The attempted reconciliation lasted only a few months before both parties had proved to themselves that it was unrealistic. Michel resumed his new life plan and eventually brought his mistress, Sonja, out of the background and presented her to the family in a forceful and arrogant way that brought more diplomatic problems for Thérèse.

'Sonja was not the cause of the break-up,' he insisted. He had met her after his separation from Charlotte. He obviously didn't know that the letter Charlotte found in his pocket had been discussed more widely.

Thérèse and George invited Michel and Charlotte to George's birthday party in 2005. In response, Charlotte phoned Thérèse to say that Michel had already told her he intended going with Sonja. Charlotte therefore declined the invitation.

Sure enough, without saying anything to his hosts, Michel turned up with Sonja and introduced her. It was the first time the family could observe Sonja in detail and compare her with Charlotte. There was a physical resemblance in that both women were slim, of similar height, and had dark hair. At first sight, Sonja looked older than Charlotte, though the gap was closing fast as the anguish of her situation gnawed at Charlotte's looks. Some of the guests, who knew about Michel's change of partners, thought it strange that Thérèse should have invited Sonja.

After this party, Charlotte was silent for several months. When Thérèse finally contacted her and asked what was wrong, she criticised Thérèse for inviting Sonja and making her welcome, while she had been left out. It was some time before Charlotte was able to accept that Michel had managed the whole thing and had treated Thérèse with the same disregard as he had Charlotte.

Michel bought one Paris apartment in their joint names for Charlotte and rented another where he lived with Sonja and her two sons. The two properties were within ten minutes of each other, near the Eiffel Tower. Having recently sold his second business, Michel felt relieved of one part of his burden of responsibility and was satisfied that he had converted most of his assets into cash and deposited it in offshore accounts. Once again, he was working as a consultant to the new owners, and getting around Paris, visiting clients as before on a motorcycle. He invited Thérèse and George to stay with him and Sonja, which they did on two occasions, getting to know Sonja a little better. In their private discussions, they speculated on where the relationship might be heading.

Although publicly, intimate conversations between Michel and Sonja were lovey-dovey, Sonja appeared to be entirely dominated by Michel. His behaviour towards her was more oriental than European. Observers got the point that this was exactly the life Michel wanted, the life he couldn't have with Charlotte, who although compliant up to a point, insisted on having a voice of her own. Maybe Sonja had developed more subtle ways of managing the situation.

In discussion with Sonja, Thérèse found an opportunity to ask her how she felt now that she had met Charlotte at a recent family gathering, at which the Miltons were not present. Sonja replied confidently that she had no regrets on that score. 'Charlotte seems to have understood that it's a law of nature for couples to become bored. The girls are grown up now, and once she comes to terms with reality, she will realise that their marriage was over.' Her tone irritated the Miltons, but they accepted that there was some foundation for what she said, and they had no immediate intention to argue.

Thérèse and George speculated on Michel's rationale. He clearly took pride in trying to be avant-garde in some aspects of his lifestyle but that did not include his domestic life where he was very conservative, not to say reactionary against current perceptions of women's roles. They wondered why he had married Charlotte, who wanted to be an equal partner in everything, when in fact he only wanted someone who would look after the house, washing, food, children, accounts, and warm his bed, leaving him as undisputed head of the household and free to follow his fancies. If that was his philosophy, he had made no progress since his ancestors. When he had allowed Charlotte to participate in the business and use her talents, he appeared to do so without shame, but there must have been some insurmountable inner tension. He was happy to accept the benefits of her participation when it suited him, and looking back, it didn't seem to bother his conscience that since their separation and until the sale of the business, Charlotte had been meeting him daily at work and running the company administration and their private bank accounts. In his own mind, Michel must have felt that before the truth spilled out, resulting in their break-up; he had found the right balance with Charlotte, a balance that enabled him to live in his own way at home, making it easier for him to freely pursue his 'real' life outside. He had not considered Charlotte's sentiments, only the practicalities of home life and the freedom he needed. Only when Charlotte declined to follow him into his new existence was it necessary for him to find a new running mate and somewhere else to live.

Until their separation, Michel had felt that, unlike others who abandoned their wives or who hid their mistresses, he could bring the two together into a harmonious sublimation of wives, mothers, housekeepers, and lovers. He would be their benefactor. He was acting responsibly and was financially generous towards his wife and the girls. He was resolved that if the rest of the family had difficulty accepting this, then relations may have to become more distant, especially with his aunt Thérèse, who on the one hand he admired greatly, but who on the other hand, he thought, was too drawn towards questioning his attitudes and his behaviour.

Though she could know little of the details of his secret life, Thérèse, like Charlotte, had enough intuition to guess the rest and that was enough for her to feel that Michel could not be trusted or believed. This conclusion opened an irreparable crack in their relationship. Michel preferred debate to be channelled towards theoretical ideas and concepts where he would never lose his sense of humour, whereas Thérèse explored more personal questions that irritated him and made him suffer from an acute persecution complex when in discussion with her, making it difficult at times for him to stay cool in the way that Thérèse was always able to do.

His initial tactic of making a joke out of serious questions didn't work with Thérèse because she would always return to her point repeatedly until he felt obliged to close up. Also, Michel was fully aware that Thérèse and Charlotte were close, and he unfairly assumed that they concocted plots to exclude him and Sonja from their circle.

Only Johnny Mendes was a really reliable friend. He admired Johnny and judged him to be more talented and brilliant than himself. He had recently become more intimate with Johnny and his family and was confident enough to quote him in discussions as if he were a hero and an authority on matrimonial matters and lifestyle decisions. He clearly shared a passion with Johnny and maybe with Ayida and Beatrice, but did Johnny have reciprocal feelings towards Michel? Thérèse thought Johnny incapable of such elevated sentiments. She had no detailed knowledge of Michel's partnership with Johnny and the investments he made, nor did she know for sure that Johnny was willing to trade his wife and daughter to achieve a level of dependency by Michel and others. Thérèse had previously noted during visits to the Bodins that Johnny would call Michel at almost any time of day or night, and Michel responded without delay, never explaining what was going on. Sometimes Michel would put on his motorcycle jacket and leave the house for an hour or more, without explanation.

Having thought over his plans for Charlotte yet again, after the short-lived reconciliation, Michel was reviewing his options and changing his mind. He now saw himself as wanting to escape from a marriage that imposed more responsibilities than he could accept if he were to realise his dreams. He wanted more freedom to be a student of everything, following his insatiable desire to taste, learn, meet, exchange, and share his ideas. He didn't mind with whom he made contact, and he showed the same interest and respect for scholars as for dropouts but mainly his friends were streetwise, self-made and, usually, like Michel, running a business of some kind. The job he had retained with the new owners of his business still earned him all the day-to-day money he needed, and it left him time for research and testing opportunities to reach out and express himself in whatever way he wanted.

Nobody in the family could see or know what Michel was getting in return for his generosity and submissiveness bordering on obsequiousness towards Johnny, but Michel felt that Johnny had taught him a lot and given him confidence to realise his own ambitions. It was Johnny who showed him how to target a new mistress and make her current married lover feel inadequate thus opening the way for his own proposition. That was how he had won Sonja. For, although her husband was effectively out of the way, she was already involved with one of Michel's friends. Michel followed Johnny's advice, talked to the friend, and aroused his scruples by making him see that he could not support Sonja and her sons financially, and it would be better to let her go. Events swung in Michel's favour without him needing to refer to what might be the implications of the man's wife finding out what was going on. Michel then made his move with Sonja, and she allowed herself to be flattered by his extravagant advances. To him, it was now a tested method, taking him to a new level of capability to achieve the desired result. It had worked in the heat of battle, so Michel was tremendously excited by his success, and grateful to Johnny, though he could not share his joy with the rest of his family.

Sonja had every reason to mould herself to Michel's requirements to gain a level of security for herself and her sons, which she could never have achieved alone after the small cafe that she had been running with her husband had to close and they had gone their separate ways. Her husband's way was to lose himself in alcohol, while Sonja was left to fend for herself and her sons.

Another lesson that Michel had learned from Johnny was that a few instructive hours with a beautiful and willing prostitute are nowhere near as exciting as gaining control of an unwilling participant and bending her to your will. In pursuit of this new passion, Michel had found he was leaning towards periods of madness, destroying reason and requiring a supply of enslaved victims to achieve satisfaction. He had started developing a taste for exploring this perversion with increasingly younger girls at the Alive Club, where one evening Michel was visiting with a client. As they moved along the corridor, viewing action in the rooms through the windows, Michel came across a room with a double bed occupied only by a girl, who looked no more than fifteen (at that time, the age of his youngest daughter). The girl was sitting on the bed with her knees pulled up to her chin and the sheet tightly covering her up to the neck. She had a look of sheer terror on her face as she gazed at the locked door. Michel went to a steward and asked about the girl. She was new and available to the highest bidder. She was indeed around fifteen and had been brought in from one of the Balkan countries by an older sister. The steward asked if Michel would like to make an offer. He did and returned later that evening after parting from his client to claim his prize.

The Miltons concluded that as Michel had found in Sonja a partner to do his every bidding, while she was happy to fit into that mould, all would be well between them. The set-up resembled the Roger Timmonier model that Michel so much admired. Was Michel planning to maintain a ménage à trois, or more, of compliant women? Charlotte had declined to submit in this way, though the Miltons still felt that, in some important respects, Charlotte's behaviour was ambivalent.

'How can you walk around nearly naked and overtly titillate men and tolerate other women doing the same to your husband without expecting a reaction?' Thérèse asked George one day. 'Are those men all eunuchs?' She went on, 'Although the women maintain that they are happy to behave like that, it all goes wrong when someone gets hurt as badly as Charlotte.'

Their discussion returned to the display of outstanding femininity at the Bodins' garden party on the Côte D'Azur. They came to the conclusion that it was part of a feminine power game to say to men, 'If it provokes you—tough—that's your business. I am free to dress or undress how I like'.

'I am not opposed to nudity or shocked by it,' admitted George. 'It's one of life's luxuries to swim naked in the sea or a pool and to see attractive women without their clothes, but as far as I am concerned, it's a personal matter. I just find it embarrassing when family or friends thrust their nudity upon me. It changes the relationship from platonic to potentially sexual or, at the other extreme, just plain nauseating. The rules of engagement might all be tacitly agreed, like "look but don't touch", but what happens when they experience mission creep and someone decides to push the boundaries?' George went on, 'There are plenty of men about who believe that what's on show is available and what about men from cultures which don't respect the imaginary glass wall? And what about lesbian women? Aren't they getting a privileged front-row seat?'

George's mind went back to an incident involving an English friend Alf, a self-made man who enjoyed a jet-set lifestyle with a large sailing yacht and house on Menorca. Alf was happy to share his wealth with friends, and the Miltons were happy to be among those who sailed with him. They once spent a pleasant week at his house overlooking the harbour at Mahon, looking down from the sunny terrace on to the moored yacht in the glittering estuary below and spending several days sailing it around the island.

Later, when a different party of visitors were there, Alf's twenty-two-year-old daughter, Amanda joined the party. She was an experienced yachtswoman and could skipper Alf's boat from the Solent in England to Menorca with a crew of three, but her appearance was not the least macho. She was tall, fair-haired, and her T-shirt displayed a chest like a full spinnaker.

When the Miltons were staying in Menorca, they had noticed some of the female guests stripping off to sunbathe on the terrace, and on this later occasion, Amanda had joined them, revealing golden orbs and a flat belly to tempt male hands. One night, a married guest found his way to Amanda's bedroom and slid an exploratory hand under the sheet, feeling his way towards a plump breast. The tension must have been palpable. Just then, Amanda partially awoke and rolled slowly towards the man, giving him an exquisite handful of smooth, firm roundness. He must have thought he was about to win the prize, but Amanda opened her eyes, focused them in the semi-darkness, and suddenly began screaming. Amanda screamed and continued screaming until the whole household came running. After what must have been huge embarrassment, the poor man and his wife left early in the morning.

When George first heard the story, one evening as he and Thérèse were preparing for bed, his only question was 'Why did she scream?'

'You are missing the point, darling,' warned Thérèse, as she removed her jewellery, placing it carefully in a decorated wooden box in the bedside cabinet.

'I reckon she was expecting someone else,' suggested George. Then after a pause, laughing, 'I wasn't there though.' He went on, 'I know it's about feminine power and men are not supposed to act naturally, but I can't understand why her father allows it.'

'You know why,' teased Thérèse, sliding into bed.

'No. I am really missing the point here.'

'Because he likes to see them. It's his titillation.'

'It may be just titillation for an old man like him, but you can see what happens when you do that to a red-blooded male. You get a predictable result. What do the women expect? Why don't they go to some of those hedonistic resorts that specialise in "anything goes" holidays?'

George thought about it some more and then added, 'I can't believe some of those women in France would scream. They may be misandrists, but I bet they would be more receptive if the same thing happened to them.'

'We don't know that though, do we? I think you are indulging in wishful thinking, and anyway, where did that word come from?' Thérèse enquired.

'I found it in the scrabble dictionary, though I adapted it with artistic license. It is the female equivalent of a misogynist, a person who hates women, so a misandrist is a woman who hates men, and there seem to be quite a few of those about.'

'Yes, sometimes with good reason,' sighed Thérèse. 'Now come close to me.'

George remained silent, remembering that Thérèse was not aware of Gigi's stunt and Ayida's reaction at the Bodins' party back in 1997.

Soon after her parents' separation, when Lydia Bodin was in her fourth year of the five-year master's course at Sciences Po, she had to be brought home sick to her mother's apartment. For the first day or so, Michel stayed away and showed little concern, but a few days later, he paid a visit to check on Lydia's progress. When, in the toilet, he noticed residual blood stains that had resisted flushing. He raised his concern with Charlotte.

'Has she got piles or something, or is it some feminine disorder?'

Charlotte explained that she had called the doctor to examine Lydia and would know more when he reported. That evening, after the doctor had left, Michel returned and asked again what was wrong with his daughter. Charlotte made him sit down and prepared him for what must be a shock. She then summarised what the doctor had told her.

Lydia had suffered an anal fissure, probably as a result of insertion of a large object that had exceeded the limit of flexibility of her anus.

'Lydia told me that it happened at a university party, and it seems there is a culture of abuse of female undergraduates in this way.'

'Are you saying she was raped?' burst out Michel, jumping to his feet.

'There is some doubt about that. She was probably coerced but was at least partially cooperative. She was probably drunk at the time though.'

'How can it be treated?' Michel started biting his fingernails.

'The doctor advised that it may heal over a couple of months, but if that doesn't work, she will need to have surgery to repair it.'

Michel sat down again, looking at the floor and breathing heavily. He couldn't focus on what he felt. Anger that such a thing should have happened to his precious daughter, anger at the authorities for allowing it to happen, and anger at the perpetrators. Michel was also pondering on how violence was taking the place of sex in his own life. However, in his mind, there were rules, and there was a big difference between what he did with other consenting adults and this.

Next morning, before Michel and Charlotte had decided what to do, there was a phone call to Michel's home from the university. He listened and made some notes. He had a very concerned look when he ended the conversation. 'Yes, we'll be there. Thank you.'

He picked up his piece of paper and immediately telephoned Charlotte.

'I just had a call from someone called Ségolène Ravel. She is a member of a joint committee at the institute responsible for life on the campus. She wanted to know how Lydia was, and she told me that another girl has complained about the abuse that goes on and described what had happened to Lydia as one example. We are invited to discuss it with her this afternoon.'

Ségolène Ravel was a very large lady who only just fitted in her chair. The degree of compression necessary for this feat was measurable in the columns of bulges that protruded on both sides between the bars supporting the armrests. Her ingratiating and sympathetic smile on greeting the Bodins faded suddenly to a look of deep concern as she addressed the parents. She first apologised for what had happened to their daughter. Then she went to some length to explain the event and repeated several times over that the assault occurred off campus, but the university authorities believed that there was a wider problem of drinking among the students that must be addressed.

'If undergraduates drink themselves silly, they take the consequences. But the university is a caring organisation and wants to encourage dialogue between the parents, the students, and the authorities to reduce the problem.' Ms Ravel continued, 'We know what goes on, and we feel in particular that the ritual humiliation of women undergraduates is an extraordinary erosion of personal liberty, coupled with massive disrespect.'

Michel had a simpler way of describing it, but kept his temper and asked what action the university could take, other than report matters to the police, thus facilitating prosecution. Ms Ravel frowned and admitted that the university had only planned to go as far as expelling known offenders. She referred again to her argument that if students drank excessively and lost control of themselves, they could easily become victims. It was unlikely that a prosecution would succeed in those circumstances. A defence lawyer would make a laughing stock of anyone claiming they were a victim. Michel agreed to talk to Lydia when she was well and discuss what to do next. In the meantime, he was considering a private investigation to be followed by making examples of the perpetrators.

It was several weeks later, when Lydia appeared to be making an almost complete recovery, that parents and daughter discussed the situation. At first, Charlotte tried to keep Michel away, thinking that it would inhibit Lydia, but he insisted, and as usual, he had his way. He arrived early and expected to be waited upon, but Charlotte put a coffee pot and cups on the table and left him to serve himself. It was a new experience for him to get up to fetch the sugar and a spoon, rather than ask for them to be brought to him.

Lydia described the event as she recalled it. A group of about ten students had gone to one of their watering holes to celebrate a birthday. They assembled in a back room, normally reserved for private functions, because that night the landlady wanted the rowdy students out of the bar, and she let them have their privacy. At some point, when all had drunk enough to kill a horse, the birthday girl started to dance and strip to the encouragement of the mainly male audience. That particular cabaret turn ended with the girl having sex on the floor with beer being poured over the participants to cool them down. Then, as the only other female present, Lydia was invited to entertain with her own turn. At first she resisted, but help was provided in the form of many hands to remove her clothing and place her on a table to perform. All she could do was wobble uneasily with her arms across her chest, while the group whistled and booed. Then she was pushed forward into a crouching position, and something was rammed into her. She screamed; the barmen came running, and the place was cleared. The landlady arranged some form of first-aid dressing, and Lydia was taken back to her apartment to recover. Next day, she phoned for help, and Charlotte came to collect her.

Charlotte repeated the essence of the conversation she and Michel had had with Ségolène Ravel. Lydia shook her head,

'I don't want to go back there, Maman. There's no point in following it up. I couldn't face them, and I wouldn't feel safe whether I report it or not.' Both parents reluctantly agreed that their daughter should not resume her studies but should find a job and rebuild her young life from this tragic setback. Michel relented from taking vigilante action only because Lydia was firmly against it. She was such a genuinely sweet girl that nobody was to be blamed for anything. Lydia found a job with one of the large grocery retailers and, on the surface, seemed happy in her new position as a marketing graduate trainee.

After a few years of separation from Michel, Thérèse detected that Charlotte sounded a little brighter during one of their phone calls. She said that having seen the world with Michel, she was now seeing it in new and unexpected ways, and she was seeing someone new. She explained cautiously and coyly that they were just friends for the moment, but they shared recent turbulent histories and had developed a mutual empathy. Tomasso Nencini, Charlotte's new friend, was from an Italian background, though born and educated in France. He was a successful communications engineer working for one of the largest European telecoms companies. His work had brought him into contact with Annick Bodin, and they had become friends as well as business collaborators. At a party to celebrate a birthday in Paris, Annick introduced Tomasso to her mother with the objective of finding someone decent to at least give her a chance to develop a new friendship and maybe encourage her to make a new life away from Michel. At this time, Charlotte and Michel were still meeting regularly for 'business and family matters'.

Tomasso was younger than Charlotte, tall, well-built, cheerful, with all the charm of an Italian, and was also absolutely genuine and sober. He fell for Charlotte immediately, and they started visiting each other's apartments, becoming firm and trusting friends despite their past unhappy experience. Tomasso was divorced and had a teenage daughter. The divorce had been acrimonious, and although he still had a responsibility for his daughter, it was difficult for him to develop a relationship with her because his ex-wife's vindictiveness was poisoning his daughter's attitude towards her father.

Several years after Lydia Bodin's sudden departure from the Sciences Po, the Miltons had an opportunity to meet her again when Annick Bodin came to stay with them at Branne as she often did during her visits to Europe from the USA, and this time Annick announced that she had persuaded her sister Lydia to join them, so it was set up to be a combined business and social break. Normally, during Annick's visits, they enjoyed discussions about the family, and Annick helped the Miltons get the most out of their business information systems, an art in which she excelled.

The Miltons had not seen Lydia since she left Sciences Po. They knew she had no regular boyfriend and was still working with the grocery retailer in Paris, where she had received several promotions. When they first saw her at Branne, they could hardly hide their dismay at the metamorphosis from golden girl to the caricature before them. Lydia was painfully thin, her face narrow and grey, with deep creases between her eyes. Now still in her mid-twenties, she had already lost the poise and the glow of youth, was a restless chain-smoker, and her routine language was foul even by French standards. She wore tight, torn jeans with frayed bottoms covering skeletal thighs, scruffy trainers with trailing laces, and a shapeless off-shoulder top that only partially covered her underwear, showing there was little to reveal underneath. Her hair was cut very short and ragged, and she sported a tattoo on her neck. Her facial expression was one of repressed anger and vindictiveness. Lydia paced up and down as she spoke with her arms folded tightly across her chest or gesturing sharply with a cigarette between her fingers. She had become the kind of person who would make anyone share her nervousness.

George and Thérèse learned that Lydia had advanced to become a buyer with the grocery retailer and was responsible for the flow of goods into the retail supply chain. She demonstrated, in George's opinion, a new low standard of appearance and manners for retail management. Her conversation was vituperative in the extreme, and it was hard to fathom how she held down such a demanding job, judging by the attitude she expressed towards her employers and their suppliers. George concluded that she must be one of the Rottweilers used by retailers to beat down supplier prices. In other circumstances, she might be fired for transgressing company limits of decency and mutual respect in business dealings. George recognised the same characteristics in several senior media executives and 'celebrities' currently on trial in the UK for misdemeanours to which top management had turned a blind eye. Lydia looked and sounded like a Patsy in waiting, but of course, he remembered, things were different in France.

The visit passed without sparks, and after Lydia had left for Paris, the Miltons had a couple of hours with Annick to compare their impressions before she flew back to the US. They packed up and loaded Annick's affairs into the car and continued their conversation all the way to Bordeaux-Mérignac Airport. They started by commenting on how Lydia had changed and asked Annick about the causes of transformation in such a promising girl.

Annick explained that immediately after the attack at the university, her sister had maintained her positive attitude, but it took long and painful months before she completed her medical treatment, during which further tests discovered that she was also suffering from infections in her reproductive tract, from damage due to abuse which threatened her ability to conceive children. George and Thérèse were mortified to hear this. They knew there had been problems but were still deeply shocked to hear Annick's synopsis of what had transpired.

While still at Sciences Po, Lydia had found a boyfriend, supposedly a builder, who stunned the family by his lack of any perceptible compatibility with Lydia, yet she said she was going to marry him. Michel was, at first, close to combustion but later softened, hoping that Lydia would soon tire of whatever she saw in the young man. They didn't marry, but Lydia had become pregnant while still a student. There followed a miscarriage that was carefully concealed from Michel and Charlotte. When, after starting her job, Lydia did announce that she was pregnant (again), there was a predictable howl of dismay from her parents and strong pressure from Michel to have an abortion.

Charlotte took Lydia to a counsellor, hoping that she would persuade her daughter to have an abortion, but when Lydia came out of the consultation room, she announced that she could not have a termination. It was only after probing that her parents found out about the previous miscarriage and her overall medical condition. In the event, Lydia had a second miscarriage and was advised that she must avoid any more pregnancies.

At that time, Lydia and her mate were still living in the student studio flat that Michel had bought for his daughter when she first went to the university. Soon after the miscarriage, Lydia told her parents that her salary and the fact that she and her partner were living rent-free were not enough to prevent her getting into serious debt to the tune of about €25,000, which she was prepared to admit. Michel and Charlotte were dismayed and baffled by this revelation, and although they wanted to know how they could help, they insisted on full disclosure as to how Lydia had got into this mess.

Lydia's boyfriend Eric had not worked for over a year. Nevertheless, he had expensive tastes which he financed by dipping into their joint account to feed his Range Rover and gambling habit. Lydia knew that he had lived with other women in the past and had children by some of them. She thought it was possible that he was still seeing other women and possibly had children by them too. She loved him and was prepared to do anything for him but now felt she had come to the end of her stamina for punishment.

Whereas in the past, Michel might have leapt in with threats and bombast, he now asked Lydia coolly what she wanted to do. Lydia explained that she wanted to clear Eric out of her life once and for all. She would be happy to settle her debts and continue living in her apartment alone within her own space and really focus on her job as the outlet for her talents and energy. She wanted to be challenged and thought that once the distractions of her present lifestyle were out of the way, she would seek more recognition at work and take on more responsibility. On hearing this, Michel agreed to settle her debts and wipe the slate, relieved that she had not succeeded in bringing more children into the world.

About six months later, Michel was cruising across Paris on his motorbike when he realised he was approaching Lydia's apartment. It was around dinner time, so he stopped to buy some food, intending to have a quiet tête-à-tête with his daughter, and walked to the entrance of the building with a carrier bag of goodies. It occurred to him suddenly that he should have announced his visit, so he called Lydia on his mobile.

A slightly dazed voice answered, 'Where are you?'

'At the main door.'

'Christ, you don't give me much notice!' The phone went dead. At that moment, another resident came to the coded security door, dialled the code and Michel smiled, picked up his bag of food, and walked in with her. He rang the doorbell at Lydia's apartment and waited patiently. A long time passed without any movement, so he rang again. This time the door opened to reveal a ghost-like figure, wearing pyjamas, and with nothing on her feet. The place reeked of smoke that Michel recognised was not tobacco.

'What's going on? Are you OK?' Lydia turned her back on him without greeting, and he followed her into the small bedsit. Stretched out on the sofa-bed was Eric, in a daze. He was wearing a T-shirt and nothing else. Michel carefully put down his package of food on the galley worktop and turned to face Eric. Eric waved a hand limply. Michel took a deep breath and seized him by the shirt, lifted him up, thumped his head against the wall, and was about to continue pounding this drone to pulp when Lydia intervened.

'Papa, stop! Let him go. Please.' Michel was breathing heavily. His head was spinning, and he felt murderous. He grabbed Eric again and dragged him unresisting towards the door. He continued dragging him across the granite floored lobby, opened the front door, and threw him out into the street where his body slapped limply against the wet paving. He sat in his nakedness, leaning against the outer wall of the building with his legs outstretched. It had started raining again, and passers-by paid him no attention from under their umbrellas. Michel returned to Lydia, and they sat for some time in silence before he regained his breath and composure. When he spoke, it was quietly and deliberately, 'Is this really what it was all about in the first place? Drugs?'

Lydia said nothing; her vacant expression and rolling eyes said it all. Michel was faced with a serious problem. His daughter needed help and, above all, supervision. In a normal family unit, he would take her home where Mum would take care of her. What could he do now? He decided he would take her to Charlotte's apartment, so after phoning his wife, he went out and stopped a taxi, planning to return later to collect his motorcycle. As he loaded Lydia, now wearing a dressing gown and trainers, into the car, Michel noted that Eric had somehow crawled or been carried away.

When they arrived at Charlotte's, the distraught mother put Lydia to bed, so the parents were able to discuss the situation privately for several hours. They would contact her employer and try to maintain her job. It was clear that Lydia would have to attend a detox clinic, and finally Michel must track down Eric and put the fear of God into him so that he never came near Lydia again. Michel felt he could call on some reliable contacts for that mission.

The next day, Michel called at Charlotte's apartment again in the late afternoon. As Lydia regained her wits, Michel insisted on knowing how her drug habit started and who her supplier was. If it was Eric, he was determined that Eric would meet with a serious accident.

'Oh Papa,' Lydia began wearily, 'don't you know? Remember when I was a kid I used to do my school homework in your study at Maisons-Laffitte? One day, I needed a stapler, so I opened a desk drawer and found a black drawstring bag. Sounds familiar?' Michel felt as though the blood was slowly draining from his body.

'I used to take a handful and smoke it outside. Then, when I left home, I used the same contacts as you.'

'Who were they?' Michel thought he knew the answer.

'Estelle's friends. Zu and Ahmed. Ahmed has done well since those days when you used to finance him. He drives around Paris in a Porsche Cayenne now.' Charlotte lowered her head slowly and put her hands up to her face. Michel felt a terrible pressure across his chest, and his mouth was dry. He said no more, but left Lydia with Charlotte. He needed air, so he went for a long walk, winding his way through small groups of people ebbing and flowing on the wet pavements and crossing side roads as they were going out for the evening or taking their dog for a walk. He was unconscious of anything around him. He didn't even notice that the rain had started again because he was so deep in his own gloomy thoughts, but eventually, he arrived back at his point of departure, Charlotte's apartment building, where he had left his motorcycle several hours earlier. First, he wanted to go back inside and be with Charlotte, but then he automatically wiped the glistening raindrops off the seat and windscreen with a gloved hand, put on his helmet, and, without looking around, drove away on the shimmering wet street into the busy evening traffic, leaving a faint whiff of oil smoke in the still, damp air. A car alarm went off nearby, its doleful tone adding to Michel's sorrowful mood.

By the time Lydia visited the Miltons in Branne a couple of years later, Annick informed them that she had survived and conquered most of the obstacles she had faced, but the experience had taken a toll on her. She no longer trusted people, especially men. She had become aggressive, and built a hard carapace, and she was making her way in the tough career she had chosen, though she had become resentful because it was certainly not the intellectually demanding path she would have chosen if she had completed the course at Sciences Po.

Annick concluded, 'Lydia doesn't have a particularly romantic temperament. It's not her style. She has no illusions about her poor chances of attracting a mate, but I think she has come to terms with who she is.'

'She is lucky to have you to talk to,' said Thérèse, without further comment on Lydia's situation. Then, having taken another sip of coffee from her paper airport cup, she asked, 'Is it my imagination or is life particularly difficult for women in France?'

'Do you see a difference between Paris and New York, Annick?' Annick gazed into her cup before replying,

'Yes, there are differences, but first remember that Paris is not typical of France, and New York is not typical of the rest of the USA. They are both coping at different speeds with transition from a strict moral base established throughout history by religious groups and a set of traditional social norms, to a much more liberal society, and there are tensions. In theory, freedom is better than repression, but the sudden sexual freedoms have caused explosions in families, and I think that women and children have suffered as a consequence. In the 1960s, Simone de Beauvoir was able to say that France had the legislative framework for equality of the sexes, but even now, you can see it's not being applied. It's not the case in real life, and I believe that is because you can't change male attitudes by legislation. For hundreds of years, men expected to receive the sexual services of women and retain them as housekeepers and mothers. In return, men were supposed to provide protection for the weaker women and that *chevaleresque* attitude and sense of ownership have not altogether evolved to match the potential of modern life for women in France, and in some cases, those repressive traditions are still applied in a covert but organised way to the detriment of women. What I see as ironic today is that whereas in the past a man was looked down on if he was unfaithful or abandoned a woman, nowadays they consider it normal behaviour, and the woman who is left behind by her partner is often made to feel guilty. She can actually become a victim of so-called "friends and neighbours". It shows a misplaced, hypocritical, prurient, and punitive attitude that's completely wrong in my view, and it makes France look backward compared to the USA and the UK. We are not all perfect, and we all mess up, but different countries have different speeds in applying the same three options. You can see them being played out with greater or lesser flexibility in, for example, Paris and New York.

'The first option is that you can choose to live alone all your life and have no children if you wish, depending on friends rather than family as in the TV series *Sex and the City*. There is no longer any stigma attached to that.

'Second, you can remain a traditional lifetime couple, though that seems to be on the way out.

'Or third, you can be a liberated couple that confronts choice—that is problematic because it brings in the concept of polyamory, multiple partners, and the hard part is accepting that someone you really care for and want to spend the rest of your life with only considers you as part of his harem.

'Leibnitz said, "To *love is to be delighted by the* happiness of someone, or to experience pleasure upon the *happiness of another*." So if he was right, the polyamoury concept is not a route to happiness.'

'So where do you place yourself in those options, Annick?' asked Thérèse, always ready to put the more personal question. 'Or am I being indiscreet?'

'No, your question is not indiscreet, Thérèse, but the answer may be. Love is a great privilege. Real love is very rare, but I know it enriches the lives of the men and women who experience it. I would like very much to be part of a traditional couple like you and George, and I could accept the constraints that it imposes, but there are so many pressures today which can drive couples apart and put temptations in their way. I just don't know how things will turn out for us.'

'Will you get married?'

'There is no hurry. We are both making our way in our jobs, and I guess if a baby comes along, we will have to think about it seriously.'

'Doesn't that mean the exit door is left open?'

'Yes, we just have to confront the choices as they come, and there is an abundance of choice. The life we want and are encouraged to adopt nowadays is often at odds with happiness in married life. I can see that, and we just have to move at a pace we can cope with. I do know that. Neither I nor my partner fit the new criteria of gaining sexual experience according to the Internet, where you have to put what you feel into words and hope that a word match will put you in contact with the right person. Neither do we believe that you have to have serial sexual experience and build sexual capital to attract lots of people.' Annick paused and smiled broadly. 'Do I sound old-fashioned?'

Thérèse's answer was to put her cup down and give Annick a hug. At this point, the three looked at their watches, rose unhurriedly, and strolled towards the boarding area.

CHAPTER TWELVE

New Life in Haiti, 2009

During one of their phone calls, Michel announced to the Miltons that he and Sonja had been to Haiti on the Caribbean island of Hispaniola, with his friends Johnny and Ayida Mendes, and they had both bought some adjoining land in the north of the island near a large town called Port-de-Paix. One of their French friends had bought some land near there some years earlier and was developing a resort. Michel intended to build an idyllic home and possibly develop a holiday business when he retired fully. The Miltons' first reaction was that it was a mad scheme set in a dangerous country, but they wished him luck with it.

What Michel did not disclose was how they were able to buy a substantial tract of prime land by the shore of a large bay, when sale to foreigners was supposed to be restricted. Michel had done his research carefully, using his extensive library of travel books and by putting Sonja to work on the Internet. He found out that Port-de-Paix is probably one of the most beautiful, most peaceful areas of Haiti. It's a place that Christopher Columbus named Valparaiso (Paradise Valley). Now a sprawling city of over two hundred and fifty thousand people (about the size of Orleans in France or Trenton, New Jersey, in the US), it forms one of the principle centres of the remote northern region which is sufficiently cut off from the violent politics of the south to have created its own economy and commerce based on access to the outside world via the sea. Visually, it resembles many cities on the African continent with contrasting colonial-style public buildings and larger, opulent, nineteenth-century, three-storey residences similar to those found in smarter Paris suburbs. However, unlike Paris, the leafy gardens and colourful churches are surrounded by high cantilevered security fences, topped by razor wire. The spread of building is immense; not-yet-painted, grey concrete buildings with ornate pillars and arches extend down to and into the sea. Others display an amazing optimism in spreading out into bays and estuaries, using concrete piles to gain more space. The city centre is characterised by its immaculate white and varied colour-washed buildings and ornately paved public spaces, contrasting with crowded main streets with narrow pavements forcing all traffic including pedestrians into roads shared with all types of vehicles and animals. Towards the periphery of the city, there is a shambles of incomplete buildings, muddy access roads, piles of building materials, and rubbish. Look up, and electric wires and telephone cables slice up your view of the sky. The music you hear and the people you see are unmistakably African.

As you move away from the city with its overwhelming smell of drains, the landscape opens up to reveal a coastal tropical paradise, where a few modern luxury hotels occupy prime sites along the margin between the vegetation and the beach. This was the area that Michel and Johnny hoped to exploit by investing in cheap land and building a tourist complex along the same lines as their friend who was already established and attracting holidaymakers from North America.

When the Mendeses, together with Michel and Sonja, flew into Port-de-Paix Airport, they were among the few tourists and aid workers on the plane. In the next seats across the narrow aisle from Michel were two Haitians from Toronto, Canada. The man was dressed in immaculate white trousers, a bright red T-shirt and huge multi-coloured trainers. The woman had her hair carefully combed and braided and wore clothes that suggested, no, demanded closer observation of what was underneath. Michel started chatting to the man, speaking loudly to overcome the noise of the turbo-prop aircraft engines, and his neighbour's partner occasionally leaned across to add her comments. The Haitians, who were about thirty years old, explained that they were flying into Port-de-Paix (*Podepe* in Creole), rather than to Port-au-Prince because some of their friends had been robbed in the capital within a few minutes of leaving the airport. The armed robbers were not satisfied with cameras and contents of the tourists' cases, but wanted their clothes too, and they left the victims standing naked behind a derelict cinema after hijacking their taxi.

In another story told by the Haitians, a white woman had been kidnapped from her hotel, and the kidnappers had issued a video of her being carried out of the hotel naked. She disappeared and was never seen again. It was said that she may have been used as a voodoo sacrifice, though there was no evidence that humans were still used in this way.

When Michel asked a question about voodoo belief in modern times, the woman explained that our modern view is dominated by physical, touchable reality, but in Haiti the spirits are as real as your wife or your dog. Michel asked if they had any plans to settle in Haiti or buy a property there. Both the Haitians laughed, the woman's ample breasts bouncing up and down as she did. The answer was no. Anybody with any education and ambition would choose to leave at the earliest opportunity as they had done, and whilst some expatriates felt it would be nice to go back and help the country of their birth to progress towards modernity, and everybody hoped that one day the economy might be able to develop, most felt that the security situation still made any such ideals too risky. No, they were just here for a holiday and to look up some family contacts. Michel pressed again to find out if they knew how to buy land for investment.

The Haitian woman by the window leaned across her partner's lap and shouted across the aisle. Michel leaned towards her and found the close proximity satisfying, though the information he gained was not. The woman began to explain,

'In Haiti, you can legally own the land on which you live and have a primary residence. If you are a non-black, non-Haitian, you cannot own rental properties or business properties. But people do all the time, subject to deals. Just be aware that as you are white, your testimony is inadmissible in a court case, just as the testimony of blacks was inadmissible in some parts of the USA during slavery times. Haiti is not signed up to many international conventions on law or human rights and reconciliation.

'If you are going to buy land anyhow, be aware that if someone can squat on it for more than six months, you have to go to the higher court to evict them. You might not succeed, especially if they are Haitian and you are not. Also, make sure that you get a decent lawyer to do an *Extrait des Archives*, basically a title search, because due to the incredible corruption of the Haitian courts, there may be four or five people with 'deeds' to any given piece of land. You buy the land, the other 'owners' run to court, and you will never, ever be able to live on that property, but you won't get your money back either.

'If a man sells you his land and dies years later, his inheritors can come to your house with machetes and try to run you off. I saw that happen to a Frenchwoman whose Haitian husband died. I personally would never, ever, buy land in Haiti, and if you do, you'll probably be sorry!'

As this was entirely consistent with what Michel had already heard from Ayida and others, he had little more to say but decided to shelve his dream for the time being.

As the passengers descended from the plane, the small group of American Haitians seeking to rediscover their roots were immediately distinguishable by their designer-branded clothes, 'cool' sunglasses, digital cameras, and loud English language. There being no radio contact with the ground, before landing, the aircraft had overflown the airfield to give the ground attendants time to remove as many bystanders, children, and goats as they could from the narrow runway which ran alongside encroaching dwellings, but the aircraft was surrounded by a band of sightseers as soon as it stopped. What the ground team could not do was remove the gravel, including stones the size of eggs covering the landing and taxiing surfaces. It was no surprise to the visitors on descending from the Saab twin turboprop aircraft to see that the plane's tyres had bare patches and the underside paint was badly scarred. Michel estimated that by the time it reached Port-au-Prince after another take-off and landing, there would be nothing but canvas showing on the tyres. He later learned that the Port-de-Paix airfield is one of the most dangerous in the world, but what would normally be defined as emergencies are an everyday affair and so go unreported. At that point, he made a mental note that in future he would fly in and out of Cap-Haïtien, the other northern airport, even though it meant a longer car journey.

A few days later, the French visitors were sunning themselves at their superb, modern, low-built hotel near Port-de-Paix, when a young Haitian man approached them. He looked about sixteen, was painfully thin, with a hollow chest, large sunglasses that seemed to cover most of his face, and a worn but clean shirt and long shorts. He carried a clipboard as if it were a symbol of authority, though the cracked ballpoint pen attached to it looked exhausted. His name was Stephane. He asked if they were having a good time and whether they might like to stay longer in a property of their own. The two couples explained that they had planned to buy a property that they could develop as a combined residence and business but had so far shelved investment plans on advice from all quarters, including the woman on the aircraft, which had left them with a picture of insurmountably obstructive legislation, bureaucracy, and risk. The young man sat down with them, removed his sunglasses, and revealed a habit of rolling his eyes disconcertingly, so that at times while he was speaking, his listeners could see only the whites.

'I work for the local government in Cap-Haïtien, and they are keen to open up this area to tourists. They have tried by building lovely hotels like this one, but still the people don't come in sufficient numbers to boost our economy, so we think it would be better to sell some land for residential development to prime the pump so to speak.' He paused and then asked, 'Would you be interested?' They said they might. Ayida spoke to him in Creole, and there was much nodding and head shaking, eventually leading to a suggestion that they should look at a piece of land now. They packed their things, put on their shoes, and followed the man towards the beach; they walked for about twenty minutes along the waterline until they could no longer see the hotel or any other building. When they saw the land Stephane described as for sale, they were overwhelmed. It was vast, beautiful, and cheap for the surface area and location. It was the perfect spot to start their enterprise. The blue water of the sea showed no signs of the pollution that poisoned most of the estuaries and ports along the coast; the sand was immaculately clean, and the whole bay area was surrounded by mixed jungle growth leading up to a steep green mountain with exposed rocky crags near the summit. They stood and looked in each direction, admiring the curve of the bay and the flights of tropical seabirds and appreciating the absence of any signs of other human beings.

'I must warn you,' said their guide, 'that the administration is not totally straightforward because a small number of people are opposed to this kind of sale. We must be very discreet and resolve to win allies in the right places. You first need to obtain an *Extrait des Archives* to confirm that a land purchase is possible and will not be disputed by other certificate holders, and that requires some work to be done on your behalf by a person in authority.' Michel and Johnny had a fair idea as to what this might mean and anticipated the level of personal inducements required, but they agreed to the proposition so far.

'If you are really interested, you will need to come to Cap-Haïtien for a few days, and my boss will describe to you in minute detail what needs to be done. In less than a week, you could be the owners of this land and go ahead with your building plans.'

They agreed to discuss the proposition over dinner, and Stephane, the 'realtor', as his grubby business card described him, said he would return next day.

That evening, the discussions and speculation went on till late. There would have to be bribes. How sure could they be that the sellers were the only owners and that they were entitled to sell the undisputed freehold of the land? If they bought it, would they be free to build or was there another set of obstacles ahead? Who would look after the property when they were away? Once the word got around, would their asset be in danger of locals taking revenge? These were just a few of the questions debated by Michel and his friends before they agreed to explore the idea further and arrange the trip to Cap-Haïtien during the next week.

Cap-Haïtien, where Ayida Mendes was born, is a smaller city than Port-de-Paix but still with 190,000 inhabitants and suffering from the same urban sprawl degenerating into favelas around the edges. It lies about forty kilometres along the coast to the east of Port-de-Paix and is a colourful historic centre with a wealth of French colonial architecture in the same style as New Orleans in the USA. The buildings are surprisingly well preserved, proving that it shares the same advantages as the other northern region towns of its remoteness from the south. Its local government and merchants have benefited from the comparative stability assured by the dire transport links to the capital Port-au-Prince, which insulate it from the violence and political instability that plague the south of the island.

Haiti has a long history of brutal authoritarian dictators, who lived like kings but impoverished the once wealthy country. A coup d'état in 2004 had done little to restore order and provide any semblance of modernisation. One reason for the continuing poverty, given by a Haitian national staying at the same hotel as the Bodins and Mendeses, was that African tribalism prevails, and leaders, whether in power by armed domination of their competitors or elected by whatever means, act as though they had won the lottery rather than become servants of the people. Possibly because of the background of slavery, the mere suggestion of providing any kind of paid or unpaid service is often seen as a personal insult. The population is comforted in its poverty by superstitions, voodooism, and alcohol. Those who are not thus comforted and who show any kind of dissent often become victims of naked violence.

It was as a result of one of the pogroms launched by former President 'Baby Doc' Duvalier, to bring the northern region local governments into line and no doubt skim off some of their wealth, that Ayida decided to remain in France at the end of her studies and later met and married Johnny Mendes, thus ensuring her joint Haitian-French citizenship. Her family had been largely eliminated in the violence because they were mixed race, tending towards white appearance as a result of interbreeding with white landowners before independence.

Far from any immediate threats, the four visitors installed themselves in the Mont Joli hotel, which Ayida considered to be one of the best choices for a stay in Cap-Haïtien. The rooms were large, clean, and comfortable. The air-conditioning was old but functional. Wi-Fi access was problematic in the rooms and only worked well in the reception and bar area. The breakfast buffet was a real treat, taken by the pool while they waited for Stephane, their realtor guide, to look them up again. When he did, he announced that his boss Mr Fedji Wilsen, a name which they quickly shortened to Freddy, would see them in his office that morning.

The walk to Mr Wilsen's office depended on some agility because it required them to climb and descend numerous steps where no taxis could go. It was a short journey, but the heat rose in waves from the road surface and reflected from the buildings, so by the time they arrived, the four needed a drink. They were shown into semi-darkness, and when their eyes adapted, they saw that they were being served still, iced, slightly clouded water in pewter mugs by a girl who looked about twelve years old and had an urgent need of corrective dentistry. They were contemplating what might be the bacterial population of the ice when Mr Wilsen entered, filling most of the available space with his huge frame. He shook hands and demonstrated that, like over ninety per cent of Haitians, he spoke reasonable French. Nevertheless, he greeted Ayida in Creole and spent some time in conversation and looking her over.

When they got down to business, it was much as the two French men had anticipated. Sale of land to foreigners by Haitians for anything other than a main residence was forbidden by law. Only the government could sell land for specific purposes and issue licences. The proposed acquisition would require research and various permissions which must be paid for. In the case of Johnny and Ayida, it would be better if the property could be in her name as she retained joint Haitian and French nationality. For Michel and Sonja, Mr Wilsen suggested that Stephane's name should be on the register of ownership alongside Sonja's. When asked about his authority to conclude a legal deal. Mr Wilsen said he was close to the president and showed them minutes of a government meeting at which approvals were given for this kind of sell-off, presumably because they needed the money.

A sum of money must be lodged immediately to start the process, thus mandating Mr Wilsen to ensure that everything ran smoothly and on time for the buyers to return to their base as owners. They discussed building permission and what kind of interest the locals might show. Mr Wilsen leaned across the large dark-wood desk, tapped with his forefinger for emphasis, and in a deep, sincere, and conspiratorial voice explained that if they placed enough money with the government now, they would receive a licence to build any kind of property for residential or commercial use, provided it was completed within five years. As to the locals, he was more guarded. 'You could expect some silliness, but you have to take them into your confidence. My advice would be to involve them in some way that they value as a personal benefit.' He eyed the two women lasciviously and suggested that perhaps this was something they could discuss between men on the way out. It was agreed that they would sign documents, then the men would draw the necessary funds in US dollars immediately, before the bank closed for lunch, and Ayida would take the payment to Mr Wilsen that afternoon.

When Ayida returned to the hotel later in the evening, she looked shaken and angry. She said nothing but handed over a large brown envelope containing official-looking documents that had been drawn up in the names agreed, stamped, and signed. Once in their hotel room, she explained to Johnny what had happened.

'I knew that bastard wanted me as part of the deal, and I was prepared to take the hit, but when he got me cornered, I found there were four of them waiting for me.' They forced her to strip and took their pleasure variously and repeatedly in a dirty bedroom above the offices, while the documents were being prepared downstairs. The necessary administration took most of the afternoon before she could be released. Then the men cheerfully offered her a drink and a cigarette before sending her on her way.

Johnny and Ayida knew that Haiti has one of the highest HIV/AIDS rates in the entire Caribbean.

Neither of them slept well that night.

While Michel and Charlotte were in business together, as an equal partner and centre-pin of administration and accounting, Charlotte controlled business and private transactions. So from an early stage, she had worked out how Michel was milking the cow and knew that he must be receiving large payments in cash to avoid VAT and reduce corporate tax. She was happy enough while she thought she was a beneficiary of that process, but how much cash Michel collected now and how he spent it was not visible, and that had become a very contentious issue between them since their separation. Charlotte was burning with resentment in the knowledge that he was in all probability spending their joint money on his adventures and on his mistress. Had the land in Haiti been bought in Sonja's name? Michel denied it. When Charlotte tackled him on this and on the fact that he was continuing to spend from his/their cash reserves, which remained hidden from her, he explained that now as he was no longer the owner, there was no inflow of personal cash. Charlotte disbelieved this story like so many others. When she heard about the land deal in Haiti, she immediately referred to the bank statements she held, but there was no sign of the source of funds or a payment for the land transaction.

Michel would not tell Charlotte where the money for the land had come from, so she concluded that she was increasingly being excluded from Michel's financial arrangements, and it strengthened her suspicion that he had large sums of money in accounts that were invisible to her. In a conversation with Thérèse, when asked why Michel was going to Haiti of all places, Charlotte quoted Michel as saying, 'If there's a possibility you may have to answer criminal charges, it's best to do it from a long way away.' Thérèse wondered what threat Michel feared and what form of protection he was planning.

After three years of separation and having consulted the family and her lawyer, Charlotte accepted the conclusion that her initially hoped-for reconciliation with Michel was unrealistic. She had hoped he would tire of Sonja after a while and come back to her. But on the contrary, after Michel's short-lived attempt at reconciliation with Charlotte, the relationship with Sonja seemed closer than ever, and the longer the present financial arrangements remained in place, the more their joint wealth was likely to leak into assets or accounts which could benefit Sonja or some other mistress.

Charlotte decided to follow Thérèse's advice and persuaded Michel to come and see their lawyer with a view to initially separating their assets, opening the way for a later divorce. According to a later conversation between Charlotte and Thérèse, the lawyer had explained to the couple that their position was one where tax would remove a large part of any settlement and Michel had therefore decided not to cooperate in any disclosure. Charlotte's now felt that she had no choice but to live with the current situation.

They sat around a huge oak-panelled, leather-topped desk in an office filled with books and spectacular sailing ship models. Colin, the lawyer, creaked back in his captain's chair, steepled his hands and began, 'I've known you two for some time, and I believe you to be down to earth, practical, and pragmatic in business matters. Am I right?' They nodded. 'Let me get straight to the point. The position is this—if you decide to formally separate, you will be required to present a sworn statement of all your assets wherever they are held, and they will be valued independently and officially at your expense. When a decision is made to divide the ownership as a first step towards a divorce, the French state will impose a tax on the totality of your wealth.' He paused for effect, then explained the full financial implications and set out the details of tax that would be levied.

'Do you wish to leave now, or will you have another cup of coffee?' They stayed. Charlotte asked what other options there were.

'Living in sin maybe untidy and emotionally irksome for both of you, but fiscally, you will not do better.' He sat back in a self-satisfied way, with a rigid smile on his face.

Charlotte banged the desk with her fist. 'I am not living in sin! He is!' She pointed to Michel and bowed her head hopelessly.

'I'm sorry, Charlotte,' Colin added hastily, his smile quickly removed. 'It was an inappropriate expression. I mean that if one of you is living in concubinage, that characterises the relationship. I didn't mean it to be any reflection on you.'

After leaving the lawyer, Michel and Charlotte sat down at a street cafe and ordered drinks. Michel leaned towards his wife. 'Whatever he says about money, I will not agree to a divorce.'

'Why not?'

'I have my reasons.' He pursed his lips. Charlotte understood this was a sure sign that no further comment would emerge.

Charlotte went home and shared her thoughts with Thérèse, who had been advocating a clean break. When she heard the outcome of the meeting, Thérèse realised that Charlotte was economically and emotionally trapped. The tax imposition was extortionate, and there was no way that Michel would reveal all his assets to his wife or the tax authorities, and second, the status quo appeared to be a way for him to control Charlotte, who, whatever she said, was handicapped by her residual love for Michel.

Thérèse and George agreed it was a mess and one that Michel could exploit to keep Charlotte on a string. He already found and delighted in every opportunity to meet her to discuss family or joint financial business and Charlotte always agreed to meet him, usually over a meal. Thérèse thought she must be a willing collaborator, signalling that she maintained possession of Michel to spite Sonja. Her real motives remained unclear, but it seemed odd. Although she said Michel's lies and cheating had reached a point where she couldn't love him anymore, this might not be a true expression of her deeper feelings, despite everything that had happened and all the pain she had suffered.

George Milton expressed his exasperation when he heard the latest.

'Why should we worry about all that? They worked together in the same office every day until he sold the business. They have cosy lunches to discuss "family business", so I don't see why we have been pussyfooting around their sensitivities when Charlotte can't bring herself to make a clean break because of the cost.'

'But she can't, can she?' asked Thérèse. 'There has been the complication of the fact that she still loved him until she abandoned all hope, and then it's not just a question of the financial cost, she has to get his cooperation to make the separation.'

George puzzled over this.

'I am not a lawyer, but I know that lots of people seem to get divorced without the cooperation of the other party. She has every justification, so surely she could if she wanted to? It's a complete mess just rolling on like this.'

'But look at it pragmatically, George. At least, she controls the bank accounts,' added Thérèse.

'Yes, but that's no big deal for Michel. He still has various sources of income, and he can just set up bank accounts elsewhere.'

There was no conclusion from the conversation, but the Miltons agreed it looked a mess and that Charlotte remained as economically and emotionally dependent on Michel as before their separation.

News Item from Haiti

On 12 January 2010, there was an earthquake measuring 7.0 in magnitude, which killed 220,000 people and destroyed millions of homes and public buildings.

With the passage of time, Milton family attitudes had settled into a form of resignation about the Bodins, and it was now possible, when there was an anniversary, for the Miltons to invite Michel and Sonja to Branne at the same time as Charlotte and her partner, Tomasso. During one such visit, Michel found it necessary to have a private meeting with Charlotte in her bedroom.

'What the hell is going on? What impression does she think she is giving?' George fumed to Thérèse. Their sympathy with Charlotte as a victim was giving way to impatience at her behaviour. Was she trying to irritate Sonja, or was her undying love for Michel making her soft in the head? What impression did it make on Tomasso?

When George and Thérèse opened the presents that guests had brought, they were surprised to find in an envelope from Michel and Sonja, a brochure from a Paris hotel with a card saying that it was a voucher for a one-night stay with a free glass of champagne in the Dark Star Hotel just off the Champs Elysées. It was signed by Michel, Sonja, Johnny, and Ayida. The photos of the hotel showed that it was modern, brash, and brilliant. The walls and furniture were in large slabs of primary colours that assaulted the eyes. It was ostentatious and exorbitantly excessive, and although, at first, they concluded that it looked like a high-class brothel, on reflection, realising that they had no experience of such establishments, they laughingly concluded that maybe even a high-class brothel should be decorated in more subdued tones so as not to overexcite the customers.

Thérèse asked Michel cautiously about the design and colour, testing to establish whether it was an example of his creativity before causing any offence by faint praise. Michel explained that the concept and colour scheme represented a 'commitment to pleasure, enhanced by inspired design'. As Thérèse was slow to react enthusiastically to this, he took her hesitation to be disapproval. Thérèse thanked Michel for the present and added that as they didn't go near Paris very often nowadays it was unlikely that they would use the voucher in the near future. This response had the effect of another pinprick to Michel's sensitivities and their relationship.

Another low spot was reached when George asked Michel how the earthquake in Haiti was affecting his investment there. George had read a US embassy warning to the effect that travel within Haiti was hazardous and incidents of violence and mass demonstrations in the capital were significantly limiting the embassy's ability to provide emergency services to the US citizens outside Port-au-Prince.

Michel shook his head in irritation. 'I guess we won't be going there for a while. You know I built a house there?' George nodded.

'Well, it's just abandoned for the time being, and by the time we get back, the locals will probably have occupied it.'

George got the impression that what piqued Michel most was not the potential loss of his investment but knowing that the family felt they had been right about it all along. He could see that Michel was reluctant to go into more detail, so he asked no further questions on the subject. Facts that later emerged confirmed that Michel was highly irritated by the delay to his plans and did not welcome enquiries on the subject.

During the several days of this same family celebration, George had thought to prompt a neighbour, who was joining them for dinner one evening, to brief his wife on the domestic background of the split couple and new partners to avoid embarrassing questions. After dinner, outside on the terrace, in the warm summer evening air, cheerful conversation continued late into the night. A large parasol kept the warmth in, and although it felt as if one of the severe summer thunderstorms, frequently experienced in southern France, was approaching, no rain had yet fallen. Michel and Sonja said relatively little and remained at one end of the table, smoking. Most of the conversation was at Charlotte's end, where Tomasso Nencini, one of his friends, and the neighbours surrounded George and Thérèse. At one point of calm in the discussions, the neighbour's wife Clare looked around the table and asked Charlotte in halting French, which of these men was her husband. There was a silence.

Seeing Charlotte's hesitation, Thérèse stepped in. 'That is Charlotte's husband over there with his partner Sonja. This gentleman here is Charlotte's partner,' indicating Tomasso.

Sensing some tension in the air, Clare quickly apologised, 'Oh, I'm sorry if I trod on any toes.'

Michel tried to put everyone at ease with a broad smile. 'Not at all, no embarrassment whatsoever. That's the way it is, and we are all happy.' He put his cigarette back in his mouth and sat back, relaxed.

George could not restrain himself; turning to Michel, he let out, 'Michel, if you believe that, you'll believe anything.'

There was no response from Michel other than turning down the corners of his mouth in one of his characteristic expressions, and it was some minutes before the discussion resumed.

Afterwards, as the party broke up and they were alone, George walked towards his neighbour pretending to strangle him.

'I am so sorry, George. I forgot to tell Clare what you told me.'

There were no recriminations between them. George was not someone to bear a grudge, but he had underestimated how badly Michel had taken the exchange and couldn't know that he now blamed Thérèse and George for being undiplomatic about him in public. Their relationship was permanently damaged from that moment.

For the next year, Thérèse and George Milton had no communication from Michel Bodin, though they talked regularly with Charlotte. When asked why Michel was brooding, Charlotte said she did not know, so the mystery remained.

CHAPTER THIRTEEN

Disappearance, 2012

Although Thérèse and George sent Michel regular news of their movements and invitations for Michel and Sonja to join them, they were met by silence, until one day they received an emailed circular from Michel in New York, where he was visiting his daughter Annick, and a new grandson. Broadcast to around a dozen addressees, it was an effusive and poetic outpouring about the stunning atmosphere, the overwhelming happiness he felt at being in New York and seeing the buildings and sites with which the world thinks it is familiar. There was no personal information.

Thérèse contacted Annick to see how the visit had gone. 'He came with his woman again. He keeps pushing her forward. I've told him that I don't want her here, but he just says that if I want to see him, she comes too.'

Thérèse responded to Michel's message from New York with a more personal message, but there was no reply. After another month, George sent a text message and email saying that he had understood that the silence was deliberate and invited Michel to explain why he had cut himself off from them.

After a few weeks, there came a muddled and hurriedly typed SMS from Haiti, apologising for the delay in responding because of poor network connectivity. Michel had to go up a mountain to obtain a signal. He said he would reopen communications with his aunt in September on his return to France. He expressed his love and emphasised that this message carried greetings from him and his *partner* Sonja.

Michel Bodin did not call in September 2012, and when George and Thérèse Milton contacted other members of the family in October, including his daughters and parents, nobody had heard from him since his last text message to George Milton. Annick Bodin called some friends in Paris, and they talked to the police.

The French police contacted counterparts in Haiti and asked them to check. It took a month before a report came back saying the local police had been to Michel's address and interviewed madame Sonja Alstrom. She had maintained that Michel Bodin left for Paris early in September. The police had found his white Mitsubishi Pajero in the Cap-Haïtien International Airport car park. However, there was no record of a Michel Bodin buying a plane ticket or using his credit card. Having acquired this information and passed it on to the family, the French police filed a missing person report and showed no enthusiasm for further investigation.

Sonja Alstrom had been feeling for some time that things were turning sour between her and Michel, but the relationship had so far met most of her objectives. They had been together for over ten years now, and since meeting Michel, her life had been transformed from one of constant worry about money and survival to one of financial comfort and sensual excitement. She had accepted early on in the relationship that, in truth, she was a sex slave, housekeeper, personal assistant, and dogsbody, but in return, she lived well, travelled extensively to glamorous destinations around the world, and she had no more financial worries for herself and her sons, who were now launching into a good careers after completing private study to compensate for lost years in education.

Now she had only herself to think about, and she was concerned at how the emotional price she was paying was increasing, and as she felt that she was now past her best physically, it was becoming harder for her to play the role of mature swinger that Michel had originally defined for her in the subculture he frequented. At first, when Michel introduced her to Johnny and Ayida Mendes, she took to the lifestyle willingly and with a frisson of excitement as her sexual comfort zone was extended by new experiences, some of which frightened her at first, but she had to admit, it brought enhanced pleasures too. Once she overcame her inhibitions and was considered to be a member of the community of daring adventurers, she could look down on 'straight' people, who were constrained by their puritanical morals based on superstition or were simply too unattractive to market themselves for recreational sex in the way she could.

With Michel, Sonja had been able to free herself from constraints and enjoy the experience to the full by keeping herself in good shape physically and by using her increased funds to take good care of her presentation. She was happy to be admired and openly approached by men in the way that Michel encouraged. The key to the right balance was consent. Michel and Johnny had coerced her to extend her boundaries of experience, and she had become willing to allow that to happen, feeling confident that they would protect her. However, once the novelty wore off, she was increasingly concerned that her protectors were also capable of becoming her exploiters and was worried that, although in the past when she indicated that a limit of her sexual fantasies had been reached, they relented; they had also shown that they wanted to push her further. Sonja's boundaries did not extend to filmed gang rape and the more or less public humiliation scenarios that she had witnessed at the club. So although she was becoming concerned that there was a risk of things getting out of control, until they arrived in Haiti, she had felt that the uncertainty added to the excitement, and she could still protect herself by using her influence with Michel and, therefore, continued to believe that she could still trust Michel and Johnny to look after her. However, events in Haiti proved that her confidence was misplaced.

The single issue that created a rupture was Michel's rejection of the need for her consent. No single explosive argument had done more to destroy Sonja's faith in Michel, and it forced her to the inevitable conclusion that more than ten years of love for Michel lay in ruins. Maybe that is as much as she could have expected. After all, the relationship had served her original purpose. She must now decide what to do next and, knowing Michel, anticipate and counter any harmful plans he might simultaneously be making for her.

A shabby, much-dented pickup truck arrived in a dust cloud outside the smart, brightly painted wooden bungalow near Port-de-Paix, on the northern coast of Haiti. It gasped to a halt, and the passenger-side door cracked open loudly, causing the chickens and other animals to scatter. It looked as though the driver's door of the pickup must have been jammed shut by the obvious accident damage because two uniformed men emerged from the one working passenger-side door, wearing grey short-sleeved shirts and red-and-blue shoulder flashes with PNH (National Police Force) badges, white socks, trainers, and sunglasses. The men put on blue caps and approached the table under an awning, where Sonja was drinking coffee and eating a papaya.

'Madame Bodin?' asked one of the policemen.

'No, I am madame Alstrom,' replied Sonja without elaboration. She was thinking that as she was alone, she should exhibit some authority by not offering further information.

'We are policemen, madame, and we are making enquiries. May we see your passport?'

'May I know why?'

'We have been asked to check on monsieur Michel Bodin. Some relations in Paris have reported him missing, and the French police have asked us to investigate.'

'I am monsieur Bodin's partner, and he has gone to Paris.'

'When was that, madame?'

'A few weeks ago, early in September.'

'Have you heard from him since?'

'No, but that's not unusual because the telephone reception is so bad here.'

'OK, madame, let us see your documents please.'

Sonja got up and went in search of her handbag. Her pulse was thudding so much it sounded as though someone was walking behind her. She looked around and saw that the two policemen were still by the table. She fought to keep control of herself. As she came back to the table, the policemen were standing facing her, eying every detail of her skimpy clothing and the way her body moved underneath. She smiled and presented her passport.

'Do you rent this place?' enquired the policeman, as he took her passport.

'No. monsieur Bodin bought it in my name.'

'That would surprise me very much, madame.' He made no further comment, but flicked through the passport and read every page including the blanks, leading Sonja to think smugly that for her, at least, there had been a way to acquire the property and doubting if this man could read the passport.

'Now, please tell us exactly what were monsieur Bodin's plans and intended movements when he went to Paris?' The policeman recorded the passport number and added some notes in a large, lined, hard-backed book with yellowing pages and battered cover, proving that he was more literate than Sonja had at first imagined.

Before leaving, the police officers removed a sun-bleached plastic jerry can from the back of the pickup and asked Sonja to fill it with water so they could top-up their leaky radiator. The men watched Sonja's hips swing as she carried the container to an outside tap which served a large water trough, and they continued watching as she bent over it while it filled. The jerry can once had a tap at the bottom, but this had broken off and had been replaced by an ill-fitting cork which leaked once the can was filled. There was still some water left by the time Sonja returned to the car.

The vehicle started with a noise like a cockerel and bumped away down the track from the house, leading to the main track to town, leaving a cloud of dust drifting away with the light wind.

The policemen chatted in Creole. 'She not worried. Not surprised he gone.'

'No, the *béké* (white man) has done a runner. I could take over though. Give her a taste of the tropics.' They both laughed and lit cigarettes as they bounced along slowly with a wisp of steam already rising from the radiator. They didn't have far to go to town.

Late in 2012, Patrick Mastrolli, the ex-policeman friend of Michel Bodin, phoned Thérèse out of the blue. He had retired and was now living in Dakar, in Senegal, where he had previously worked on secondment for several years. He had been on a liaison assignment there, liked the place, and decided to stay there when he retired. He asked if Thérèse could get him some business information in England. Thérèse took a note of what he wanted and then asked if he had had any recent contact with Michel Bodin.

'Not since I have been here. I have rather lost contact with my Paris friends.'

After a long update, Thérèse asked Mastrolli if he could do anything to elucidate the circumstances of Michel's disappearance, as his parents and the family as a whole were increasingly worried.

'It would take time and money,' he explained. 'The French police have no jurisdiction in Haiti, and there is another problem in that there has been no settled government there since the earthquake. It is quite a dangerous place to be.'

After further discussion, the two agreed that they would communicate via Skype and emails. Mastrolli would get some facts together and present Thérèse and George with a proposal, either for further investigation, which he could set up or alternatively advise them to drop it.

A week later, Mastrolli called Thérèse on Skype.

'I've looked into this, and there are strange and unexplained elements to the story, but the French police are conscious of the cost and difficulty of pursuing this as a case. It really should come under Haitian police jurisdiction, and they are unlikely to do any more than they have already. The earthquake in 2010 has left the whole country in disarray, and although the UN is pouring in resources, the poor state of infrastructure and political instability before the earthquake means that it is still a mess. The French police had to put money on the table to fund the Haitians for the initial investigation. As you know, the relevant family witnesses are scattered from Australia to New York, Ireland, and Paris, and the current breakdown of whatever administrative functions existed in Haiti before the earthquake makes it difficult to obtain facts at that end.

'As to what might have happened, it is quite possible that Michel has done a disappearing trick. I heard that he was being threatened by some people in Paris, which is one reason why he went to Haiti. He was also concerned that the French tax authorities were closing in on his past business dealings and historical tax returns. They want to interview him. In addition, I believe he was tiring of his relationship with Sonja. People disappear with fewer reasons than those.'

Thérèse was not surprised to learn why Michel had left Paris but still believed that, one way or another, some harm must have come to her wayward nephew. Did he really buy the land in Haiti in Sonja's name as Charlotte feared? Could it have been a leaving present?

'Patrick, how much would it cost for you to carry out a more thorough investigation and visit Haiti for long enough to draw your own conclusions based on evidence, even if there is no complete explanation?'

'Could you get the key witnesses together in, say, Paris or London, so I don't have to travel all over?' asked Patrick.

Thérèse considered this. 'It might be possible.'

'OK, but I won't go to Haiti myself. I know someone there who is much better placed to get to the truth than me. He knows the area, and I know his methods.'

Thérèse agreed to the proposition, subject to Mastrolli taking overall responsibility. They agreed a sum to cover the enquiry up to the point of a report.

Members of the family, including Annick, Estelle, and Lydia, and Michel's parents met Charlotte Bodin and the Miltons in the bar of a three-star hotel near the Opera in Paris, and then, over a meal in an excellent nearby restaurant, they briefed Patrick Mastrolli on what they knew.

It was apparent to Patrick that although the family shared mixed emotions about Michel, the strongest of those emotions was anger. Each of these people felt a strong sense of the loss of someone, who had been a landmark in their lives, and anger, not because of his recent disappearance, but because of the way he had conducted his life and made his earlier choices. He had, to a greater or lesser extent, ended the life they shared before and then sought to impose himself with his mistress, forcing them to accept a new relationship. The one who took the new situation with most equanimity was Estelle, who seemed quite fatalistic about it and was trying to maintain a balance of relations with both her parents without judging them. The others were making their own way in life without Michel; he was still a husband, father, or son, and until recently, he wouldn't go away, and more irritatingly, Sonja wouldn't go away. The two were constant companions, and until his disappearance, Michel would not meet other members of the family without Sonja in tow. Was that a case of Michel imposing his will, or was it Sonja, clinging close to fill any space left by Charlotte? They were still a family, and there were still parties, anniversaries, weddings, and grandchildren to bring them together, so it was hard to keep him out.

By the end of his briefing, Patrick concluded that although everybody had their views on what had been taking place, they were light on relevant facts and detail. They did not have much idea as to how Michel operated in recent years. Even his wife could only see what happened in the bank accounts she managed, though by now, Patrick felt sure most of Michel's money had been shifted to new, probably overseas, accounts. Beyond that, Charlotte was in denial about Michel's private life and intrigues. Armed with this thin information, he prepared notes, added some thoughts of his own, and transmitted them to Eugène Kotor, his associate in Haiti, requesting a detailed investigation with extraction of the truth.

CHAPTER FOURTEEN

Investigation and Explanation, 2012-2013

Besides the paved streets in the capital, Port-au-Prince, there are only two paved highways in Haiti, which link the northern and the southern regions of the country. National Highway One (Duarte Highway) extends north from Port-au-Prince to Cap-Haïtien via the coast. Despite international funding and some government improvement efforts by the National Road Maintenance Service, the roads are in very poor state. A journey of just a few kilometres on such roads, even in a well-adapted vehicle, can leave passengers and drivers feeling numb and needing to lie down on a stable base.

When Eugène Kotor arrived at Michel Bodin's house near the beach, a few kilometres outside Port-de-Paix, he had travelled nearly 200 kilometres in a Toyota Land Cruiser with two colleagues, stopping first to rest in the back room of a bar, which was infested with mosquitos, and later to make some enquiries at the local bus station in Port-de-Paix. He was in no mood to sit patiently and listen to Sonja's lies. He knew that the version she had given to the police was untrue. Before setting out, one of the questions in his mind was how to confirm his theory that she had returned to Port-de-Paix *after* parking Michel's car at Cap-Haïtien Airport nearly forty kilometres to the east.

Assuming Sonja Alstrom was acting alone and in no hurry, the most likely methods of travel would be by Tap Tap bus or taxi. If she had taken one of those options, it was likely that someone else from Port-de-Paix had travelled at the same time or seen her getting off. Kotor had followed that hunch at the bus and taxi station. There were so few whites living in the area that it was easy to get some useful input before turning to Sonja.

The bus station was no more than a Y junction in the road with a concrete bund wall in the centre to contain spillages and protect the fuel pumps from carelessly driven vehicles. In the narrow streets, on either side of the fuel bunkers, buses and taxis were parked where they could between heaps of tyres and vehicles under repair. A butcher's shop doorway was piled with half-open cartons of meat, and huge, high-sided tipper lorries, which are also used for passenger transport, blocked the streets outside. Between the larger vehicles and other obstacles zoomed flocks of cheap Chinese motorcycles. Once a bus was fully loaded, it was some time before it could lumber away to find its route out of town, but the slow progress of heavily laden, mostly overloaded, vehicles along the streets served a useful purpose of crushing rubbish that was deposited there, to be thus reduced to mulch. A bus journey towards the edge of the city would be at no more than walking pace in order to avoid wheelbarrows and flat trailers loaded with sacks and powered by humans. Other obstacles to be negotiated included errant animals, files of immaculately uniformed schoolgirls in tartan kilts and boys in perfectly pressed long khaki trousers. A bus driver spent several minutes following an attractive young woman in a short skirt, beeping his horn so she would look round. Most of the women to be seen on the street were either pregnant or had recently given birth and were accompanied by tiny, brightly dressed infants.

A Tap Tap bus may get its name from the fact that you tap on the metalwork to stop it, or according to other opinions, because "tap-tap" means quick in Creole. One could argue that the low speed of the buses in town should discount the latter source, though excessive speed and overloading is a major cause of frequent bus accidents on country roads. Whatever the source of the name, a Tap Tap is a work of art, an engineering miracle, and an essential part of public life in Haiti. They are mostly privately owned Mercedes, or of Japanese origin, and whatever the dubious state of mechanical units that propel, control, and stop the buses, the bodywork is kept in supreme condition by one hundred per cent paint coverage in colourful graffiti. The themes are often religious or related to voodoo but with a heteroclite blend of subjects and styles, for example, sex; crime, especially shooting; or a scene in which Brazilian football heroes peer over the shoulder of the Virgin Mary. Open ventilation windows on some buses are positioned so low that passers-by can see only the legs and lower bodies of passengers, a form of public entertainment for passing motorists. Some buses carry a steel tube bumper extension supporting a full-width platform on the front of the vehicle, which serves the dual purpose of nudging people and animals out of the way while, at the same time, carrying a further five standing passengers between the outer fender and the engine compartment, thus partially blocking the driver's view of the road ahead.

Kotor made himself comfortable in a bar out of the heat of the sun and sent his two colleagues to talk to drivers who plied the route between Port-de-Paix and Cap-Haïtien International Airport and told them to hand out a few packets of cigarettes in the event of a truly useful disclosure. After an hour or so, they came back with credible information that only a bus driver could deliver.

About a month or so ago, a slim, dark-haired white woman wearing a white dress revealing her bosom had travelled from Cap-Haïtien Airport to Port-de-Paix. She was remarkable because she carried only an expensive handbag and did not look like a tourist. She smoked cigarettes and used bright-red lipstick. As always, the bus was crowded on departure, but as the passengers thinned out, she moved to sit closer to the driver to be sure she would get off at the right place. The driver remembered talking to her, and he showed Kotor's associate how he had to adjust his internal rear-view mirror so he could keep an eye on the woman as he drove the bus.

The driver couldn't help laughing as he recalled the details. 'Every time we go over bump, she bounce.' He demonstrated the action with his huge hands. The two men laughed. 'So I find more bumps.' The driver was now laughing uncontrollably, revealing his few remaining teeth and with tears running down his cheeks. So infectious was his laughter that all conversation stopped until the two were able to recover.

'One last question—where did she get off?'

That place was about five kilometres short of the outskirts of Port-de-Paix.

Now she was coming towards Kotor from a low, painted-timber house where a garden table and chairs were arranged under an awning. She was barely dressed, like so many shameless European women he had seen at holiday hotels, and she was smiling nervously as she approached the strangers. She shaded her eyes with her hand against the white glare of the sun.

Bantam-sized chickens and guinea fowl mingled with small dark pigs and a goat wandered the bare earth, while crickets provided continuous music interspersed with squawks from unidentified creatures in the jungle close by. Sonja took in the fact that there were three men, one of whom, dressed in black shirt and jeans, was leaning against the car scratching his groin. The other two wore expensive civilian clothes and stood side by side in front of her.

Sonja was puzzled by the appearance of these men. Not many people here drove the latest model land cruisers and certainly not the police.

'Are you from the police?' Sonja enquired, her throat tightening.

Kotor ignored the question, wasted no time on introductions, and got straight to the point. 'What happened to monsieur Bodin, and where is he now?'

Sonja blanched and reached for a cigarette in the purse she carried. Her hands were trembling, and her mouth was more rigid than when she greeted him. 'I don't know anything. He left here and said he would not be back for a while. The police came here and told me he was reported missing.'

Kotor knew all about the car parked at the airport and her journey back by bus, so he decided to confront Sonja with that, knock her off guard, and save a lot of time. 'Why did you fake the trip to the airport and lie to the local police about what you already knew?'

She looked down at her cigarette and didn't answer, though she was breathing faster.

Kotor motioned to his two colleagues who quickly moved behind Sonja and attached her elbows behind her back with a frayed red Terylene rope. The lighted cigarette fell to the ground as they bundled her into the land cruiser, so she was sitting between the two men on the back seat while Kotor got into the driving seat. The engine was off and the heat inside the car without air-conditioning was like an oven.

Kotor reached down and turned with a Colt M1911 ex-army pistol in his hand and pointed it at Sonja's head. Beads of sweat rolled down from his forehead. The whole car smelt of sweat.

'You have one minute to tell me where he is or where his remains are.'

Sonja slumped and mumbled incoherently. One of the men pulled her hair to raise her head.

'Speak!'

'What's going to happen to me if I talk to you?'

'Probably nothing, but we can't guarantee what the authorities might do. You'll have to take your chances with them. But you do have to tell us, now.'

'I can't. I can't. I don't know,' pleaded Sonja.

Kotor holstered his pistol and got out of the car. His colleagues pulled Sonja out roughly and threw her to the ground. They dragged her to a water trough used for the animals, picked her up, and threw her into the dirty water, face up, and pushed her under. Her hands were still tied behind her back, and the men handled her breasts with some satisfaction as they pushed her down. She thrashed her legs, but they caught and held them.

They were excited by what they saw, but for the time being, Kotor remained focused. 'Lift,' he commanded. They pulled Sonja out. She was gasping for breath, her eyes were closed, and her head was thrown back. For a moment, Kotor was not sure she would survive.

As soon as her fit of coughing subsided and she appeared to breathe normally again, Kotor repeated his questions. This time Sonja's face remained puckered for some minutes. She wasn't crying, but she couldn't or wouldn't speak. She wore sandals, a red bikini, and a partially transparent robe to shield her from the sun, now soaked and clinging. One of the men ripped off her clothes. Then they picked her up and dumped her in the trough again, holding her down while she thrashed about. This time, Kotor counted up to thirty, and when they lifted her out and held her upright there was no sign of breathing. Kotor punched her in the solar plexus, and she doubled over, making a terrible retching, vomiting sound and then emitted a loud gasp as she inhaled and remained bent double.

Shortly after, the men carried her to a rough wooden bench by the house and stretched her out full length on her back, arms still attached, and legs spread either side. Kotor pointed his pistol at her genitals.

'This may not kill you immediately, but it will not give you much time to think. Speak now, or I will pull the trigger.'

This time, Sonja started sobbing and coughing. Kotor gestured, and they let her sit up. She could only speak quietly and, that too, with interruptions for more coughing. No one offered any help.

It wasn't her fault. She and Michel were walking up to the top of the mountain, which they usually did once a week, to make some phone calls. On the way up, Michel, who was overweight and unfit, started wheezing. He had been suffering from a dry cough for a few days and was complaining of breathlessness. Suddenly, he fell over. Sonja thought, at first, that he had tripped on a boulder, but when she bent over him, she could find no pulse. He appeared to be dead.

The mobile phone still did not work, and she didn't know where to turn for help. She sat with him for several hours and, then descended, leaving the body where it was. She did not contact anybody else but instead came up with the idea of making it look as though Michel had left the island as they had planned to return to Paris that month anyway. She had indeed concocted the idea of parking Michel's car at the international airport and returning by bus.

'Why did you do that? What did you have to gain? You could have had him declared dead. Instead you made it look like something suspicious.'

'Before leaving Paris, we took out life insurance policies on each other. It wasn't much, but it would have allowed me to live here, but that is impossible now.'

'Why? Surely, if you had a life insurance policy, you had no interest in concealing his death. You were going to benefit financially if his death was natural. Was he also going to leave something to you in a will?'

'No, he wasn't. We had several arguments because he was unwilling to hand over any lump sum to me or discuss what he would do for me in the future. He was naturally secretive. It was his way of controlling me. I had to do what he wanted, and some of that was pretty disgusting. He dribbled money in my direction to keep me dependent on him.'

'You chose to go with him and stay with him. You knew what he was like. It must have been worthwhile,' pursued Kotor.

Sonja now straddled the bench with her hands tied behind her back, trying hard to breathe and keep herself under control. It was a very emotional woman who finally answered Kotor's questions. 'The way it turned out it was not worthwhile, but most of the time, I had no choice. At first, he was kind to me, and I thought I understood that the basis of our relationship was that he would look after me financially and I would help him deal with his devils, but as time went on and my dependency on him increased, he would abuse me more and more. He was impotent. He got his kicks from seeing me having sex with his friends, male and female. Then when we moved here, he used me to entertain and pacify neighbours from the village who showed an interest in what we were doing here, and he started inviting them to do whatever they liked with me while he watched.'

'Is that why you killed him?'

'No, I didn't kill him. He just died, and to be honest, at first, I felt a great burden had been lifted from me. I wanted a bit of freedom and enough money to enjoy it. But then, I guess I just panicked. I realised that I couldn't stay here, not after what happened. It won't be long before those men from the village come back for more of their entertainment, and I will be alone to deal with them. The locals resent us being here and buying "their land". They don't like foreigners, and they think that an offer to abuse a white woman is an opportunity for vengeance. Michel stood by and watched while those men raped me. Sometimes, it went on all night,' she cried again, deep bitter sobs. She took a deep breath and recovered enough to speak between sobs. 'And do you know the cruellest irony in all this?' Kotor waited. 'I found out after he died that we don't own this land at all. We are only entitled to rent it. The certificates of ownership turned out to be a kind of tenancy agreement.'

Kotor was unmoved.

'So what happened to the body?'

'I don't know. I didn't go back. It was months ago now.'

'Let's take a look anyway.'

They picked up the limp and unresisting Sonja and threw her robe over her shoulders. She was still completely naked underneath.

They got back into the land cruiser, and Sonja gave them directions. She sat with her arms still attached behind her back, shivering with fear despite the heat.

After more than half an hour bumping along at walking speed, the track was intersected by a narrow, barely visible footpath leading to higher ground. The vehicle could not turn on to it because the path was too narrow and strewn with boulders. They got out of the car, and one of the men picked up a coil of rope from the back and slung it over his shoulder. Sonja was still wearing her sandals if little else. The hard earth, warmed by the sun, was hot enough to burn naked feet. The four made their way with difficulty up the steep path with Sonja leading, conscious that the men were watching every movement.

Sonja's mind went back to the day when she had last come here with Michel. They had had a severe argument, which had continued most of the way up. Michel did not like arguments. He preferred silent brooding. It was more effective in unnerving his opponent and keeping up the pressure on them. He did not know what to do about Sonja. She was disrupting his state of mind and getting in the way of his personal plans. She had run her course, and although he would miss her as she had been in the earlier stages of their relationship, sexually he had run out of things to do with her, and he was trying to work out his next move.

As the pair crested a ridge and the fantastic perspective opened up before them, Michel paused and moved towards the cliff edge to survey the ribbon of jungle below, stretching almost to the shore. Over the horizon, somewhere out there to the north, was Tortuga Island, the Bahamas, and eventually Miami. He edged closer to the brink, daring himself to place one foot in front of the other and sensing the feeling of vertigo creeping upwards from his intestines. His arms began to tremble, and he breathed deeply, folded his hands behind his back, and gripped tightly to regain control. He continued to relish the sensation until he became aware that Sonja had sidled up to him without a sign of nervousness. Suddenly, he knew exactly what to do. No word was spoken. He breathed in as if savouring the pure air and then he suddenly thumped Sonja in the back with his right hand, pushing her towards the rocky edge and the one-hundred-metre drop below.

Instead of punching her square in the centre of the back where he intended, Michel's hand hit Sonja's shoulder; so although she lost her balance and fell, she failed to reach the edge as he expected. Instead, she spun and fell to her knees, rolling on to her side with her feet towards him. She turned to look up at him with a pained expression on her face, and then, first folding her legs as if to rise, Sonja kicked him hard behind the knees. Michel's legs buckled, and with nothing to hang on to, he first flailed his arms in a wide arc and then leaned back as his feet briefly scrabbled the edge, and he was gone, followed by a scurry of small stones. It all happened in slow motion, Sonja recalled. Then suddenly, she returned to consciousness.

'So where did you leave him?' asked Kotor.

'Somewhere around here, I think.'

Kotor moved behind Sonja, grabbing her hair in one hand and her neck in the other.

'Now you listen to me. You used to come here regularly. You were up here for several hours with the body, you say. So you had plenty of time to look around and remember where it happened. So take your time, and when you think it's the right place, we are going to throw this rope over the edge to mark the spot. Then we are going to search down there because either you threw him down or maybe someone else did. If we don't find remains up here, that's where we are going to look. If you suffer a lapse of memory or if we don't believe you, it's likely you will be on the end of the rope.' He released Sonja from his grip.

Sonja's arms were still tied behind her back and had become numb. She turned her neck with some difficulty and looked at Kotor's black, sweaty face and bulging eyes. He probably meant what he said. She bowed her head submissively and moved slowly away. She covered about twenty metres, then raised her head, and turned as if she were looking around for a landmark. The man with the long length of rope had lifted it off his shoulder and was organising it on the ground. Kotor and the other man were talking a metre or two further away. The man with the rope stood up and made a lewd gesture, pointing in Sonja's direction. Whoever they were and whoever had sent them, she had no doubt that they considered her as part of their rewards package, to be claimed before disposing of her. She first walked slowly towards the band of scrubby trees running almost parallel to the cliff edge, thus opening the space between her and the men. She looked studiously each way along the band of short dry grass, turned to face them, as if to announce some finding, and then ran straight to the edge and jumped into the void.

Mastrolli called Thérèse a few days later. 'I thought I should give you this verbally, and then you can tell me if you want anything else done.'

'OK, go ahead, Patrick.'

'My contacts in Haiti think it's possible that Sonja killed Michel by pushing him off a cliff, although her story is that he died of a heart attack.

Whatever it was, she admitted placing the car at the airport as a diversion, so it's likely she was trying to cover up something.'

'Have they found a body?'

'No, and it's most unlikely we'll find anything now. We are not certain where it happened, and the terrain at the foot of the cliff where he might have fallen is rocky with impenetrable jungle. Bodies and bones disappear quickly there.'

'What will happen to Sonja?'

'She decided to end all speculation by killing herself. She jumped off the same cliff, so I don't think we will ever know the exact details of Michel's disappearance now.'

There was a long silence as Thérèse registered the fact that her nephew was dead and Sonja too. Her initial sentiment was anger, but that was soon replaced by deep sadness as she absorbed the fact that a central character had disappeared from her life. She explained to Patrick that for more than ten years the relationship with her nephew had delivered pain and frustration. Before that, for nearly twenty years, they had bathed in the glow of a genuine loving relationship.

She realised that she must be grateful for the good parts and rely on selective memory to obliterate the rest. Another thought came into her mind. 'Are you sure he is dead, or was this just part of a disappearance plan?'

'I can't answer for sure as without body identification we can't prove he's dead, but the way the events have been reported, I think that is the more likely conclusion.' Thérèse still hung on to the idea that this was the kind of scenario that Michel could have organised. But if that were the case, why had Sonja killed herself? The reality for her was that the insurance company was unlikely to pay Sonja without a death certificate. The property in Haiti was a liability, not an asset. Michel had left Sonja nothing in his will, and he appeared to have abandoned her. It added up to enough reasons why she would feel desperate and choose to end her life.

'Thank you, Patrick. What, if anything, can we do now?'

'I don't think we can do much more, and I doubt if there will be any further official investigation. I will complete my report and send it to you. It might be useful for informing the family and of course for reference if there are any police enquiries. Sonja had a son, didn't she?'

'Yes, two sons, and there are quite a few other people who will want to know what happened, and now we can tell them. Thanks again, Patrick, for your good work and support.'

'I'm grateful for the opportunity to clarify what happened, at least to some extent, but I can't help thinking that from what you say, Michel's bank account of goodwill needs to be redressed somewhat.'

'I really don't know what you mean, Patrick. His bank account of goodwill, as you call it, had been in deficit as far as the family was concerned. We saw him in recent years as a selfish and insensitive pleasure-seeker. Maybe he wasn't always that way, but that is what he became. I have two boxes of memories of Michel. One contains the happy and good memories, and the other contains bad or unhappy memories. I sometimes allow the good memories to influence what's in the bad box, but I never allow the bad box to invade the good memories. In Michel's case though, the contents of the bad box still exceed those of the good box.'

'That's fair enough, based on the facts as you saw them. Everybody makes their own life choices, but there was another side to Michel. Good people can do bad things, you know? Even great men do bad things.'

'I don't know what you know about Michel that I don't,' Thérèse replied, 'but one day I would like to find out more.'

'Listen, next time, I am in your part of the world, I'll call on you, if I may, and I'll tell you what I can. Maybe I can reduce the stuff in your bad box or at least add to what's in the good box.' They both laughed wryly. Thérèse switched off, crossed her hands in her lap, and cried.

CHAPTER FIFTEEN

Clarity and Conclusions, 2013

Thérèse and George Milton pondered on the report, the accusations it made, and the light it shone on events that had been taking place far from their sight. They concluded that as Michel Bodin had led his life as though the law and any moral constraints did not exist; he had been lucky that the day of reckoning had not come sooner, by the hand of one of his detestable 'business contacts' or some other person whom he had debauched or betrayed.

In February 2013, a tax inspector arrived unannounced at the offices of what had been the Bodins' Paris company, which was now under new ownership. He asked to see M. Bodin. The new owner, Marcel Picard, explained that he had bought the company in 2009, and he had heard that M. Bodin had died recently in Haiti. The tax inspector withdrew and reported that further enquiries should be addressed to madame Charlotte Bodin, monsieur Bodin's wife and co-director.

When looking over files in Michel and Sonja's computer, Annick Bodin found an incomplete email message from Michel to his daughter Estelle, drafted but never sent. Michel Bodin expressed himself thus:

'All my life, I have been forced to do things that didn't suit me and to turn my back on those which appealed to my taste, my talents, and where I had a good chance of success. I think I am a reasonable moralist because that is an art requiring honesty, a lot of deep thinking and great sincerity with oneself as well as with other people. You have to be self-critical and ignore the art of self-forgiveness . . .'

The message stopped.

It was another six months before Patrick Mastrolli called, and George Milton answered the phone. There was a big murder enquiry involving the French police travelling to England, and Patrick had been called out of retirement to assist in the coordination of the combined UK-French police operations. Would it be possible to meet sometime? He was prepared to stay on for a while after his assignment was finished, but for the time being, his availability would be limited and uncertain, so some flexibility might be required.

George and Thérèse were planning a trip to London on business, so they agreed to have dinner with Patrick at a hotel near Hyde Park, and to their relief, he arrived on time. He now looked quite elderly compared to the last time George had seen him in the garden at Maisons-Laffitte nearly thirty years earlier, but he was tanned and slim and just as quietly self-assured as before. His thinning grey hair reminded them that they were all getting older.

As dinner progressed, Patrick began to ask questions about Michel and how his behaviour was understood in the family. George referred to the relationship with Johnny Mendes and suggested that it was a contributory factor in Michel's midlife obsession with pleasure in whatever form. He mentioned Johnny's hotels and the swingers' clubs the Bodins and Mendeses had attended. It seemed to the Miltons to be a classic case of a man who had everything destroying himself by always wanting more and dragging others down with him.

Patrick listened as if noting every word and nuance and then, when the Miltons felt they had put the case in sufficient detail, he asked if they knew about the relationship he had with Michel. George said he thought it was about cancelling speeding tickets and probably offering the police special deals at Johnny's hotel to get them to turn a blind eye to what went on there. As he said this, George watched Patrick for a reaction, feeling that he was being maybe too provocative in his condemnation of the French police.

To his surprise, Patrick laughed. 'I didn't have anything to do with speeding tickets, but Johnny's hotel was an important centre of information-gathering for the vice squad at the time when I controlled undercover operations linking several departments.' Patrick's audience was silenced and holding their breath in anticipation of more,

'Enough time has elapsed for me to give you more information, but none of what I am going to say changes anything with regard to Michel's behaviour towards his family. He did what he did for reasons that he explained to you, or at least tried to explain, though sometimes even he didn't know why he did things. He was driven by impulses and passions which were sometimes incompatible with happiness for him and others around him. I think he understood that, but he decided to follow his passions. He preferred excitement over contentment, not like me. When I was younger, I got all the excitement I needed in the police, and now I'm living a contented and quieter life. But despite everything I have said about his faults, Michel was always a good and generous friend and very useful to me in some of the sensitive cases we handled.'

'You mean he worked with you officially?' asked George.

'Not officially in the sense that he was on the payroll. Let me give you an idea of the kind of cases we worked on.

'At one time, I was concerned with a case that developed from a long-standing awareness of the systematic import into France of large numbers, and I mean thousands, of young girls from the Balkans and former eastern bloc countries, for prostitution. The girls were often lured into a trap with promises of jobs by young men who were paid by gangs to recruit girls by befriending them and becoming romantically involved with them but only for as long as it took to gain their confidence and take them on a trip abroad, supposedly to find jobs, or alternatively, they would simply be rounded up, loaded into a truck, and shipped across the border like farm animals.

'Once the girls were in Italy or France, the gangs took control, removed the girls' passports, if they had any, and forced them to work as prostitutes to earn their keep. Girls were routinely drugged, and as they became dependent, they were easier to manage. In the context of our territory, they were often initially being confined on large construction sites, mainly around Paris, like the huge Bercy redevelopment and La Défence, where the size of the project justified a resident international workforce housed on-site in temporary personnel accommodation.

'In 1984, when the building was at its peak, we estimated that there were over a thousand girls at any time held in on-site brothels. The girls never saw the light of day. Eventually, they might be released into the secondary trade, either as street prostitutes or into clubs where they would continue to serve until they were past their prime or got sick. Then they would disappear or at best be shipped back to where they came from. We had a good idea of what was going on, but my department's role was not to make raids and make life uncomfortable for a few perpetrators. If you do that, you are just pruning the weeds but never eliminating them. The local police act in that area if they can, to satisfy public opinion, but our job was to cut the heads off the organisations, and that is hard to do when you have several jurisdictions, some of which see no reason why they should step in, and others are actually making money out of it. We needed a lot of information leading to names and locations and an absolutely clear understanding of the business structures that held it all together. We had to map the processes and the cash flows. These guys operate very professionally and often have legal businesses to provide legitimate transport and warehousing facilities. You can understand that witnesses are reluctant to expose themselves to an uncertain judicial system and risk the revenge of the gangs, especially if the case gets bogged down by government red tape or interference and the perpetrators are left free.

'Now, at the swingers' clubs, we had opportunities to covertly interview some girls by hiring them for private sessions. That's what Johnny and Michel did. It didn't work very well because the girls didn't speak much French, and we didn't speak their language. You can't invite an interpreter to your session with a prostitute without arousing suspicion. We were moving very slowly, and the government was not of a mind to increase resource funding, partly because they were themselves being paid huge sums by the large building contractors in the Paris region, and they didn't want anything to rock that boat. Those building companies said afterwards that they had not offered bribes to the government. It was the government who demanded their cut. Whatever the truth, those building companies are now respectable global businesses with fingers in many other pies. Only a few journalists were on the case, and they were mainly digging into the issues of fraudulent conversion of public money, bribery, manipulation of contract tendering, and other forms of corruption, which were rife in the administration during the Mitterrand and Chirac eras and still haven't been stamped out completely.

'Then we had a massively publicised case which had to be cleared up fast. It literally put a rocket under our investigations. Suddenly, more resources became available, and the politicians and judiciary were prepared to listen where they had turned a deaf ear before.'

There was complete silence around the table. Muffled voices and a clatter of plates came from the kitchen, but the other tables were now empty. Patrick continued, 'A French journalist named Clara Rémy was working for a national newspaper that had linked-up with a radio programme to run a series on street prostitutes. She managed to get some of the girls to talk about their history and where they came from, and from that, she mapped out the connections between recruitment in Eastern Europe, the forced induction centres around Paris, and the eventual conversion into street prostitutes. She got some names, documents, and photos and pieced together what looked like a good case to report on apparent police apathy and government and judicial corruption too. Clara brought a draft of the article to the police and told them that she intended to publish but was prepared to hold back if they would commit to a full investigation, in which case she would turn over copies of her files in exchange for an exclusive on whatever action was taken. Our head of department went straight to the editor in chief of the newspaper to have her shut up fast.'

'Why?' interrupted George.

'What she was going to say would stir up the wasp's nest and would not only be dangerous for the journalist, it could also disrupt our on-going investigations. Anyway, the newspaper people declined to cooperate on various grounds, and we could not get an agreement with them. Our position was that although the article stated correct facts, it delivered no proof that we could use to secure convictions at the right level. Telling the world that it was going on would achieve nothing useful where we were concerned. On the contrary, it would only serve to tighten security among the gangs.

'The press ignored us and published the first part of the story a few weeks later, promising to name names and print photos in further issues. It turned out to be more useful than we anticipated because we immediately detected unusual communications and movement of individuals who were previously in the background. After a few days, that all stopped and nothing more happened until the husband of the journalist reported that she hadn't returned home. After a week of enquiry, there was absolutely no progress. The papers were associating her disappearance with the article, and we saw headlines like: "Investigative Journalist Disappears in Paris. Police Have No Clues as to Her Whereabouts" and "Paris Just Like Moscow. Who Kidnapped Our Clara?"

'The press closed ranks to make sure that the authorities could not forget that this victim was one of their colleagues. My department had a pretty good idea where she was, though we couldn't prove it yet, so we needed a daring and trusted informant to help confirm our assumptions and prepare the ground for us to act decisively. Johnny Mendes was top of the list for that job. After all, he was one of their outlets for sale items. Just like a retail store manager, he put in his requests to one of the middlemen, based on his customers' fantasies, and the human goods would be delivered to the hotel within a week or so. It was trafficking to order.

'By working with us, Johnny was risking his life. Anyway, he fed in the idea to the suppliers that he could be interested in a more mature woman. This journalist was a very attractive lady, for those who appreciate more-rounded female forms. He didn't expect to get what he wanted, and he was afraid that they would guess he might be fishing. If there had been any suspicion of that, he would have been in big trouble, and we would have had to bail him out quickly. However, a few days later, Clara Rémy was part of a new consignment to the hotel.

'The only reason I could think of for the captors to fulfil Johnny's order was there was so much heat that they decided to put her somewhere where she might later be found without a trace back to them. Even at this stage, it was difficult for us to intervene by grabbing Clara without blowing Johnny's cover, though people at the top in the police were getting jumpy and pressing us to act decisively.

'Then Johnny received a message from his suppliers, suggesting he should call the police to say he was suspicious about the activities of one of the guests in his hotel and not to mention his contacts if he wished to remain healthy. This break came at a good time for us because we were still trying to think of a scenario whereby we could release Clara Rémy without implicating Johnny. It was just what we needed, and within hours Clara was freed.'

'What state was she in by then?' asked Thérèse.

'Let me explain here, the gang has what it calls a "doctor", who keeps the girls sedated for most of the time. This man was important to us because he had contact with the operational leaders, and thanks to Johnny, we knew who he was and were thus able to monitor his supply and distribution routes. So this journalist was first conditioned with drugs, then initiated into the working stables at a building site, and was being visited by between ten and twenty men a day. Before she was transferred to Johnny's place, we managed to get someone in there who was able to talk to her and confirm who she was. For protection of our sources, we couldn't use that information widely. We tried to find out more, but it wasn't much because she had no view of what was going on, and she was kept in solitary confinement and under sedation all the time. But the fact that we had confirmed she was there, added to what we already had, gave the public prosecuting attorney enough confidence to authorise an operation once she reached Johnny's. You might notice that even at that stage the authorities were not prepared to authorise a raid on the building sites. Well, anyway, as a result, we managed to clear the whole chain going right back to Bulgaria where we sent in a snatch squad, and in collaboration with the local police, came back with two of the top men in the syndicate and several other financiers and beneficiaries. All were sent to prison for long periods, and that perhaps explains why Johnny and Michel wanted to lie low in Haiti.'

There was a long silence after this.

'What part did Michel play in all that?' asked Thérèse.

'He was the single-link man. We couldn't make any direct contact with Johnny, but Michel was perfect for feeding back information to us and sending down instructions or advice to Johnny. They just acted normally.'

'Did he really do that alone?'

'I believe he had a team of young hopefuls who did some of the running for him—messages, money couriers, and the like. He made it look as though he was running a dope ring, but that was just a front.'

'Zu and Ahmed?' volunteered George.

'They were involved, but since then they have all converted into decent businessmen,' Patrick chuckled.

'I thought Ahmed was now a drug baron,' said George.

'Where did you get that from?'

'I thought that's what Michel or Lydia told me.'

'No, they wouldn't know because they are out of touch now.' Patrick explained. 'You may remember that one of Charlotte's sisters had a son who was in computer technology?'

'Wasn't that Christian? The one who spent Christmas with us once and later got a degree in international business studies?'

'That's right. Well, in his student days, he started making videos at Johnny's club. Some were commissioned by the clients themselves and others by us. He was the house photographer. Later, that developed into a business, and they received government grants to acquire more professional cinema equipment till they had a fully operational, high-quality pornographic movie operation. Zu and Ahmed were involved too. That's how they made their money. Christian designed and operated websites as outlets for their movies, and Michel continued to invest, though I don't think he knew exactly where the money was going. Johnny recruited actors from the throughput of young men and women at the hotel. His daughter, Beatrice, became quite a star.'

'How did Johnny start up in that business?' asked Thérèse, with a frown of disapproval.

'I understand that when they were younger, he and his wife were very fond of dancing, and they worked up an exotic dance routine that they took around various clubs. It was considered very suggestive for its time, and it evolved into a combination of a strip show and live sex on stage. Very arty and stylish, I am told. Then Charlotte's sister, the one who was working in the media at the time got them a slot on a television show, and they never looked back. By the time they were in their thirties, they could afford to pay others to do the arty work.'

George remembered seeing something like that years before on French television during a chat show with guest performers. A couple performed a strip-dance routine surrounded closely by a rousing audience. The sequence ended with both participants naked and having sex, which looked vigorous enough to be real rather than simulated. George had been shocked at the time but, in retrospect, thought it was more artistic than the regular mush on UK television. What he saw might have been Johnny and Ayida. It must have been Sandrine who got them the break. He continued to debate in his mind what constituted erotic art and where pornography begins and concluded that it was just a matter of personal taste. He emerged from his reverie to hear

Thérèse ask a question. 'Christian designed our web operation. Does that mean we have been inadvertently financing porn movies?'

Patrick laughed loudly. 'I think it's the other way round. You have benefitted from the porn movies because that is where they make the money and develop the techniques that they apply to other respectable businesses. You probably paid a lower price because of the more obscure work.'

The conversation moved on, and eventually Thérèse asked, 'Why was Michel's house broken into, and then he was robbed and hit by a car? Was that because he was involved with drugs and pornography?'

'No. It wasn't directly related to that business. Apparently, he promised something to someone that he couldn't deliver and that was just a shot across his bows, so to speak. Small stuff really!'

'Wasn't Michel at risk with his investments in what were illegal operations? After all, he was financing some pretty marginal activities,' queried George.

'Anyone seeing massive returns on investment must suspect that either it is a Ponzi scheme where eventually a lot of people will lose their money or the money is funding racketeers who want to dilute their dirty money with a fresh supply of clean investment. So yes, there was a risk, but no doubt, he got a lot of satisfaction from that too. He got big kicks from taking risks.'

Thérèse was quietly relieved to be able to add some weight to Michel's 'good box'; even if it could not justify the harm he had done to his family and others. She could, however, still not reconcile herself to what had happened in Haiti. There was still a niggling doubt that the story had ended, even though the investigation was closed.

'Where do the big flows of dirty money come from now, apart from the French government?' asked George provocatively.

'Yes, we were watching that too,' responded Patrick, raising the palms of both hands. 'It varies over time, but these days; there are massive investments in criminal activities from corrupt regimes around the world who want to divert public money into private accounts and from there, through legitimate banks to "investments".'

'But surely you can trace those movements back to source with the systems available now,' commented George.

'Yes, technically it can be done, but all sorts of procedural and political obstacles stand in the way, not least because the French government has made its own illegal money movements to and from European and other tax havens. Do you remember the speech Sarkozy gave at the beginning of his period in office? He was condemning the tax havens around Europe and virtually declaring war on all of them. Then one of the journalists in the audience pointed out that he had missed Monaco off the list. *Sarko* replied that Monaco complied with French banking regulation. So we all know what that means.

'Some of the big corruption money has been channelled through "legitimate" companies like Urba, who were set up by the socialists, before Mitterrand was elected President, to skim a percentage of local government contracts and channel the money to party funds from where it settled into all sorts of accounts. There are several cases in the courts now which have dragged for thirty years, frustrated because the tradition of party funding in France is based on corrupt appropriation of public funds for private use. I've seen quite a few watertight cases of corruption filed for no further action because of intervention from high up in the government. Remember the president is the head of the judiciary. All judges report to him. Threats are levelled not only at the person considering or making a revelation, but also at their family, and it could mean they suffer penalties while the perpetrators go free.'

Thérèse asked, 'Do you not think sometimes that you are fighting a losing battle, not knowing who is honest, who you can count on, and especially when you know how high the corruption goes?'

'I still don't understand why such a large proportion of politicians and heads of industry can get away with such antisocial behaviour when France is supposed to be a socialist republic,' added George.

Patrick grinned widely before replying, 'It's in our history, stemming from a sociology of political centralisation. Look at how Napoleon behaved. Emperors, monarchs, and, more recently, presidents succeeded each other in excess, and every Frenchman dreams of emulating them. It's a dream everybody shares.'

'So it's a re-enactment of George Orwell's *Animal Farm*,' George mused.

'Yes,' agreed Patrick. 'The behaviour of the pigs in that story is part of human nature. Power corrupts, and France is a nation which, with a few exceptions, has been corrupted by a succession of leaders and their acolytes of every political stripe. They all want to travel in executive jets and helicopters, rather than by train. They still treat public money and resources as if they were their own.'

'So is there a solution? Is the new socialist government likely to follow Mitterrand in robbing the country?' asked George.

Patrick thought for a while before responding, 'I suppose it's about what we deem to be legal and acceptable, not just in France, but there are global precedents too. The last American presidential election cost the Democrats over a billion dollars. Obama's presidency has so far cost $1.4 billion in personal expenses, but I don't hear the American taxpayers shouting that they are being robbed.'

'Our problem today is not just the economic one that most countries share. France needs fundamental changes in the way the country is governed and where the power lies. Some commentators say François Hollande has made a bad start, but others say he has made no start at all. Maybe he is going nowhere because he doesn't understand the first thing about what business needs to grow, or if he does, he fears to confront the changes needed. Whatever he does to move money from non-productive areas to help to generate new business, he will be opposed by traditional socialist supporters, and so he may be waiting for the economy to get bad enough for there to be a stronger consensus on what to do.

'The public sector cost in France is fifty-three per cent of our gross national product and rising. We are champions in public expenditure, so there isn't much left to develop new commercial and wealth-creation initiatives. Where we have had good ideas, they have been badly and expensively managed by the state who appoint people to important positions, not for their competence, but because they have worked for somebody in the power clique. Why can't we move forward? It's a good question. I think one reason is what I just said, that making the right moves would mean the socialists would have to admit that their election promises and political principles are not only failing to help, they are actually damaging the country, but the Left fears any loss of centralised power because it works for them.

Patrick took another sip of coffee and meditated briefly. 'It's not reasonable to expect governments to be completely transparent, any more than parents expect to be completely honest with their children. I'll give you an example of where the press and others can take a variety of opinions and pass them on to the public without really knowing what has happened and why.

'When Sarkozy was in power, the government passed a law offering a deal to illegal Roms, travellers, or gypsies, whatever you like to call them. They are the ones who populate camps around Paris, bus child pick-pockets into the tourist areas, and roam the provinces in marauding groups. The deal was €300 each to travel back to Romania. Now, anybody with any sense knew that they were likely to abuse the offer and be back in France within weeks of taking the money, and that's exactly what happened. François Hollande has just repealed that legislation on the grounds that it was costing too much, and as far as anybody can tell, the Rom population in France has actually increased. Now, did Sarkozy make that law as a political gesture, an act of compassion, or was it to prove to sympathetic liberals that we were dealing with untrustworthy exploiters of the French social system? The politicians and most of the press simply won't call a spade a spade.'

Patrick poured more coffee. 'Coming back to your point, George; French politics these days is driven by selfish pride and a privileged class who have proved themselves unfit to govern, which makes us observers sceptical of anything the government may do, however well-intentioned it might appear. Nevertheless, we can't be high-minded about it. The reason corruption is so well entrenched is that so few people have a clean pair of hands that there can be no acceptable immediate solution. It's more of a utopian journey. It can take generations to eliminate corruption and to realign the people behind their elected leaders.

'In our profession, you soon realise there is no simple measure of honesty because it's a variable, just like democracy. You can never be sure what level of honesty people have at any particular time and how much pressure they may be under to do something dishonest. Everybody has their limits. Everybody has their price. There is a saying in the police force: "The incorruptible man is more expensive than the others".

'I must stop making speeches though.' He took another sip of coffee.

'No, do go on,' urged Thérèse. 'It's interesting because what you are saying explains a lot of what we suspected all along, but sticking with France, what do you think can be done?'

Patrick took a deep breath. 'Well, as I said just now, the solutions tend to be slow and uncertain, and anything that can only be solved in the longer term irritates politicians and others who are judged in the short term, but if you make comparison with the eighteenth century, some things have improved,' replied Mastrolli emphatically with a big smile. 'Denis Diderot, the great French philosopher, who was a victim of state abuse, quoted from Greek mythology when he was asked how it might be possible to bring morals to a corrupt people.

'He replied, "Just as Medea the witch[2] restored youth to Pelias, you cut it up and boil it," and, adding a purely French touch, 'with a little garlic for extra flavour.'

'Yes, that's what we need,' concluded Patrick thoughtfully, reverting to a straight face.

(*Author's note:* Arcadia was possibly the ancient Greek equivalent of Buenos Aires. See Backdrop Notes referring to Jean-Michel Boucheron.)

---

[2] Medea went to the palace of Pelias and persuaded his daughters to make mincemeat of their father and boil him, promising to make him young again with her magic potions. The naive daughters of Pelias did as the witch instructed, but since then, no one has heard anything more about Pelias, whose daughters, some say, immigrated to Arcadia.

EPILOGUE, 2014

The Miltons were sitting at their dining table at Branne drinking coffee and eating a *Quatre Quarts* cake late one November afternoon as the autumn wind screamed around the house and rattled the shutters. They were discussing Annick Bodin's forthcoming wedding in New York and the absence of her father, Michel.

'Do you really think he gave up his family completely to disappear into some obscure hiding place, never to emerge?' wondered Thérèse.

George thought about the range of possibilities while his mouth was full. 'We can't say. I suppose practically and financially he could have cut himself off, and probably there were few emotional ties. He no longer had any feelings for Charlotte. The girls are grown up and running their own lives in different places. He was fed up with Sonja, and anyway she is out of the picture. What else? He went to New York to see his new grandchild in 2012, so I guess that indicated he still had some sentiment for them. I just don't know how big the threats were to offset that. Who knows?'

'I know who might know,' suggested Thérèse, popping the last piece of cake into her mouth.

George was mystified. 'Patrick Mastrolli has done all he could for the time being, so who did you have in mind?'

'Think about the person in whom Michel confided most, his partner in crime.'

They both said together—'Johnny Mendes.'

'Do you still have those vouchers for a free night at their hotel?' George grinned.

The Dark Star Hotel had changed its name to The Crescent Moon. Johnny Mendes met the visitors with a big smile and supervised the unloading, then George drove the car to a nearby underground car park and walked back, finding Thérèse and Johnny in the bar chatting amicably over a drink. It was clear that having heard Patrick Mastrolli's story about Johnny's secret life, Thérèse now felt better-disposed towards him. The 'bad box' was still heavy, but the 'good box' had gained weight.

Thérèse turned and brought George up to date. 'We haven't been up to the room yet, but Johnny was suggesting that he takes us on a quick tour of the hotel now while he is available, then he has invited us out to dinner later.' George was happy to accept, and they picked up their drinks and followed Johnny in a short and admiring view of the ground floor where the original colours had been toned down and the elegance turned up compared to the images in the early brochures.

Johnny was dressed in a smart, beautifully tailored, dark suit, expensive shoes, and an immaculate white shirt partly concealing a thin gold neck chain, an ensemble which made him look every inch the successful businessman dressing down only by omitting to wear a tie. He explained that the main hotel building was run as conventional tourist accommodation, mainly for wealthy Arab and Asian clients. 'We have no kitchen or restaurant as such, but we serve breakfast in the bar area and use a nearby top-class food service supplier for room-service orders anytime of the day or night or the same food can be served in the bar.' The two guests looked around admiringly. It was like a smart nightclub with a stage and sound system for musicians, a small dance floor, and probably thirty tables. The bar was around ten metres long and decorated with a pattern of changing soft lights inside the bar itself. The overall effect was palatial in the style of Las Vegas, though on a smaller scale.

Johnny continued, 'There are twenty-six standard suites on two floors, and the top floor is a single penthouse apartment, which I can't show you today because it is let long-term. Did you see the long building next door with the arched carriage entrance?' George said he had noticed it on the way back from the car park but could not see beyond the front wall.

'We bought that for very little about three years ago. It was built in the time of Louis XV as an arms depot and base for his militia. Later, it was used as a warehouse, and then it was abandoned to become one of twenty thousand empty properties in Paris. We originally intended to convert it as an extension to the hotel, but it was a listed building and the cost and complication would have been prohibitive, so we worked out a scheme with the local authority, whereby we would buy it from them at a reasonable price, and they would guarantee us an income from its use as a dormitory for homeless people.

'We did the deal, and now, Beatrice runs it as a commercial operation. There are three sleeping areas, each with forty beds and washing facilities and a dining area in the middle. We get paid per head per night, and we take anybody except illegal immigrants, *les sans papiers*.'

'So if one of those girls imported by force to become prostitutes managed to escape, you wouldn't take her in?' George queried.

Johnny thought about that, swirling his glass under his nose. 'There are refuges where they can go, but if one came to us, I would probably find her a room in the hotel.' He grinned broadly and drained the glass.

'What happened to your other hotel on the east side of Paris?' asked George.

'We sold that because we were having increasing difficulties with some seedy characters that were using the place, and it was getting a bad reputation with the police, which made it uncomfortable for us. In any case, we couldn't run both, and once this was up and running, we sold the other one.'

When Thérèse and George reached their second-floor accommodation, George checked the mirrors by shining a lamp close to them. He didn't know how effective this method would be, but he felt it necessary to check. The Miltons sat on their bed in their spacious and comfortable suite and pondered on the questions that had arisen as a result of what they had just seen and heard. They decided to save the questions for later over dinner.

When they came downstairs an hour later, Johnny insisted that they should have their free glass of champagne in the bar with him before walking round to the restaurant, and it wasn't long before the conversation returned to the hotel and how it had evolved.

'We originally conceived this as a club for swingers,' admitted Johnny cheerfully. 'We always had the middle-eastern and Asian markets in mind. That worked well for a while, but then some shady characters tried to muscle in, and we decided we could earn almost as much for doing a lot less, so we reverted to *hôtellerie*. Nowadays, I have to keep my hands clean. I'm a pillar of the local establishment.'

'How did the dormitory building come about?' asked Thérèse.

'First, it was just sitting there, festering on our doorstep, so it was a neighbourhood liability. Second, Michel needed a tax shelter because he had sold some property in France and had to roll over his capital gain to avoid paying tax. At first, he was getting a share of the revenue from the municipality which proved to be quite generous. Now that goes to Charlotte and their daughters, of course. I am a local councillor, so I was able to follow the acquisition through the system and negotiate good terms.' He winked.

'So you are a municipal councillor. I somehow don't see you as a citizen, Johnny,' goaded Thérèse. Johnny chuckled, then took another swig of wine, and rolled it around his mouth appreciatively, enjoying the luxury.

It wasn't long before the Miltons asked where Ayida was and how Johnny's investment in Haiti was progressing.

Johnny explained that Ayida was in Haiti now, doing some tidying up of their affairs there.

He leaned across the table. 'If I confide in you two, it's because you know the background, and I trust you to understand that there would be a very high price to be paid if it got out.'

'If what got out?' Thérèse bounced on her chair and leaned forward.

Johnny looked down and examined his fork seriously. 'What we set up in Haiti was never intended to be our end game. Let's just say that things here were getting uncomfortable, and it was necessary for Michel and me to have a bolthole where it would be more difficult for unwelcome people to approach us. If that move became compromised in any way, we could move to plan B which was all set up and funded in advance.'

'So what was plan B? Is that in operation now?' asked George.

'I can't give you any more details. It wouldn't be fair to you or the other people involved.'

'But . . .' insisted George.

Johnny raised a hand. 'It's no good pressing me, George. What happened to Michel was very unfortunate, and he is no longer part of our concern. But I and my family could still need the protection we have set up. That's why I can't tell anybody about it.'

The Miltons realised they would get no more from Johnny, so the evening continued amicably, and it wasn't long before the conversation turned to comparisons between the UK and France during which Johnny made a remark about the class structure in the UK. 'So do you see the French as classless?' countered George.

'Not at all. There are just more layers of them now compared with the classic three estates, and they are perhaps more widely separated.'

'So what do you see to be the important classes in France at the moment?' nudged George.

'Well, you've got the political classes, mostly with the same political-administrative education and the same ambition to gain or retain power. You have big business, very similar in many ways and equally corrupt. There are the politico-intellectuals who don't take office, but form opinion and generally favour the left, even when its policies verge on the insane.

'There's the massive civil-servant lobby, a very privileged class who don't want to give up positions they have fought for and won over a hundred years. Alongside them, you could include industrial workers, though they have shrunk as a group and are mainly trying to retain jobs where they are now, a futile battle really. These two groups represent the core attitudes of

French workers. They have made a set of choices which are different from the Anglo-Saxons. They asked the question, "Why work?" And their answer was, "To do as little as possible to maintain the best possible lifestyle". I guess that despite sharing the same problems as the US and UK and constantly complaining about the economy, we are still here and probably no worse off than most Americans and Brits. Our big companies are profitable and still buying utilities and other businesses in the UK and US.

'We have an expression that a fish rots from the head down, and these groups are for me where the rot has set in at the top and the others take on the same odour.

'Then there are the middle classes, made up of people who are trying to gain a standard of living and a safe environment, just like the others but with a more limited scope.

'The *agriculteurs*, people who work on the land. They fall into two subgroups: one subgroup is made up of those who are business-like and are generally hard working, but heavily burdened by taxes that would cause a revolution elsewhere. They worry about rising cost and inflexibility of labour, and fuel costs, which make them less competitive.

'The other subgroup is made up of subsistence farmers who have the reputation of being narrow-minded and obstinate. They are locked into a culture which they describe as "traditional", which to them means "good", as opposed to towns, especially Paris, which are modern, meaning "bad". They keep going by subsidies as part of the government's social policies because if they migrated to towns they would become an even bigger social burden.

'Next, you have the *commerçants*, small businesses, hard-working people with traditional values but also buried under wasteful administration and costs imposed by government. Napoleon described the English as a nation of shopkeepers, but they couldn't have been so successful here because of the bureaucracy.

'And of course you have the immigrants, large numbers of outsiders, both official and illegals, some of whom are well integrated into French life and contribute, while the rest are either a social-benefit millstone around our necks or, in some cases, which have been fully reported in the press, are truly malignant and are actually here do harm.'

'You didn't mention the French aristocracy, who manage to live like royalty and retain their wealth despite all government efforts,' George pointed out.

'You did say important classes,' Johnny tilted his head with a fixed grin. They all laughed.

'Where do you fit into that list, Johnny?' asked Thérèse, tapping the table as if to bring the meeting to order.

'Ha! Not in any of those categories. That's what Michel and I had in common. We wanted the best for ourselves and our families, but none of the structured avenues on offer suited us, so we kind of made our own different paths to success and happiness.'

'And did you achieve it?' asked George. There was a pause.

'Achieve what?'

'Happiness.'

'I am happy,' replied Johnny emphatically. 'I'm not sure that Michel was ever happy. He was never really satisfied with anything he achieved. He liked approbation, but his mind was restless, and he was always looking to the next project.'

'And didn't that quest leave a trail of unhappy people behind?' asked Thérèse.

'Possibly, but it depends on what they expected and whether their expectations were realistic.'

The conversation petered out so they sat with their own thoughts for a while. There was no tension between them, and it felt as though they had cleared the air without a storm.

The waiters were laying tables nearby for the next day, and the other diners had left, so the three rose, Johnny paid, and they walked slowly back to the hotel.

George and Thérèse continued their drive next day to Bordeaux. On the long car journey, they were able to compare notes from their conversations with Johnny and consider whether they should leave things alone or probe deeper into 'plan B'. Within a day of arriving, Thérèse contacted Patrick Mastrolli. She put it to him again that the Haiti scenario could have been only the first step in a possible disappearance plan.

Patrick accepted that as a possibility. 'But supposing Michel had arranged his disappearance, for what were to him very good reasons, what would you have to gain by tracking him down? Don't you think it might do more harm than good to him and the family?'

'You're right, Patrick, but could you try to find out what might have happened without going into detail, without necessarily obtaining confirming evidence, and keeping it as discreet as possible?'

'If we did that, what value would it have for anybody, including you, Thérèse?'

'It's not a question of value. It's more about sentiment and what memories we carry. Some people are happy to believe any fairy story, but I need to know more, even if there are some gaps. You can edit what you tell me if you think it's too sensitive.'

'Whoa! Who said I can or will do anything?'

'Patrick,' Thérèse turned on the charm, 'you are the only person who can help, and I would be very disappointed if you said, "no".'

Patrick decided to start by putting some hypothetical questions to Eugène Kotor and see what he thought. He made it clear in a message that no investigation should be entered into which might stir up the wrong kind of interest.

Report

Date: 2014

To: Patrick Mastrolli

From: Eugène Kotor

In answer to your hypothetical questions, here are my thoughts:

Identity Change: It would be relatively easy for a European with enough cash to obtain a new identity here. At least a new passport and driving licence could be provided for a credible third-country nationality (i.e. not Haitian), and that should be enough for international travel and to open bank accounts.

Ideal Location: Next to Haiti, sharing the same island is the Dominican Republic (DR). It's a different world to Haiti and has become a major Caribbean tourist resort. I know from personal experience that it is easy to open bank accounts there. The DR is a preferred money-laundering centre for Columbian drug cartels and about eight per cent of cocaine entering the USA comes from there. The southern part is heavily populated, but if you were looking for a quiet place to hide, the northern coastal area is quieter, and there is some nice land for development at Puerto Plata, for example.

Feasibility: It would be easy for a European to fly out of Haiti to say Miami, on one identity, and fly back to the Dominican Republic on another. Alternatively, from the northern coast of Haiti, you could just sail east along the coast and land in DR. There is no sophisticated immigration control, at least for whites, and a small amount of money goes a long way.

Miscellaneous Information: I thought this was all I would have to say on the subject, but then I found out that madame Ayida Mendes was in Haiti, at Port-de-Paix recently. She is an almost white Haitian Creole, still very pretty, though she must be in her fifties. The Mendeses were friends of the Bodins and had also tried to buy land here almost next to the tract the Bodins rented. While she was here, madame Mendes tried to visit a madame Cassandra Mantou, a forty-year-old Haitian widow and a very attractive one, I was told. Her husband was shot and killed in some sort of turf war down in the south. However, the important bit is that when Ayida Mendes was enquiring after Cassandra Mantou, she described her as a friend of monsieur Bodin.

I don't know what importance that might have, but consider this: madame Mantou has disappeared; she is said to be visiting relatives in the mountainous Côtes-de-Fer area, which is completely inaccessible even for aid workers, so I think that story is unlikely. Could madame Mantou have gone off with monsieur Bodin? Not to DR, because blacks are not welcome there and have been persistently persecuted or sent back to Haiti by successive governments.

My reading of the situation is that madame Mantou may have been helpful to monsieur Bodin in some way, but for what and when? If, as you say, he could still be alive, is there a connection? And if there is a connection, he may have rewarded her with enough money to enable her to set up somewhere else, possibly in Haiti, but more likely in the USA or Canada. I doubt they are together, though I may be wrong. There is no evidence either way at the moment. This is pure speculation on my part. The fact that they may have been friends before he died is not of itself a lead, but her disappearance raises questions, though it does not yet shed any light on Michel Bodin's fate.

One more point is that the nice wooden house monsieur Bodin had built on his rented land is now occupied by a Haitian family, and no Europeans have been there since madame Alstrom died. I am not washing my hands of this subject, but there is no more I can do for now. I will let you know if anything interesting is brought to my attention about these people.

Important Note: I had to go to the US embassy in Port-au-Prince to send this, so you may appear on WikiLeaks before long.

(PS. Thanks for the package.)

Signed
EK

Backdrop Notes
to the Story

Kleptocracies

Kleptocracy describes corrupt forms of autocratic and nepotistic government in which no outside oversight is possible. Kleptocratic rulers typically treat their country's treasury as though it were their own personal bank account, spending the funds on luxury goods as they see fit. Many kleptocratic rulers also transfer public funds into secret personal bank accounts in foreign countries in order to provide them with continued luxury if or when they are eventually removed from power and forced to leave the country. (*Source:* Wikipedia)

It was Ambrose Bierce, in his *Devil's Dictionary*, who called an election, *an advance auction of stolen goods.*

In 1981, François Mitterrand was elected president of France. He and his socialist entourage proved to be one of the most corrupt regimes in several generations. A foreigner might marvel at the powerlessness of the judiciary faced with systematic abuse of power on a massive scale at municipal and central government level—the fraudulent use of public money and its diversion into the accounts of individuals and phoney companies created uniquely for the redistribution of wealth towards party funds, the president's personal purse, and those he wanted to keep in his service. (*Source:* Jean Montaldo, *Mitterrand and the Forty Thieves.* Published by Albin Michel, 1994.)

Paris, 1986: François Mitterrand was keeping his mistress, her family and their illegitimate child, at taxpayers' expense, in government apartments. (*Source:* Jean Montaldo)

In 1988, one week before the French general election, a German newspaper exposed yet another embarrassing high-level French government fraud. French financial intermediaries were invited to arrange a loan from Saudi Arabia of more than twenty-two million dollars. Investigations revealed an intricate network of organisations, which led from senior ministers and the president to accounts and trusts in Jersey and in Luxembourg. The findings were that senior members of the French government were fraudulently authorising the borrowing of money on behalf of the state and shifting it into their own offshore accounts. They had infringed numerous financial standards and defrauded their own population. To this day, no official complaint has been made or legal action taken in France. (*Source: Der Spiegel*)

François Mitterrand was subsequently re-elected president for a second term.

In 1988, the socialist deputy mayor of Angouleme, Jean-Michel Boucheron, was under acute pressure to meet an increased budget for the socialist party's election campaign, which had a target of one hundred million francs. The method adopted was to take a 3 per cent slice of all municipal contracts and channel it through service companies set up by the government for this purpose. Boucheron outsourced more and more, thus providing new contracts from which to skim a margin. However, Boucheron got greedy; he took an increasing cut for himself. In 1992, when he was found guilty of corruption, money laundering, abuse of public finance, and disrupting the course of investigations, Boucheron took flight to Argentina. Sentenced in his absence to four years in prison plus a five-year ban from any civic post, he issued the most bizarre statement:

'My wish,' he said from the safety of Buenos Aires, 'is that this story should serve as an example to today's politicians and will remind them that nobody is above the law, and that corruption is something we all have to fight against.' (*Source:* Jean Montaldo)

> Urba: The Urba consultancy was established by the French Socialist Party to advise Socialist-led communes on how to extract funds from infrastructure projects and public works. The 'Urba affair' became public in 1989 when two police officers investigating the Marseille regional office of Urba discovered

details of the organisation's contracts and division of proceeds between the party and elected officials. Evidence proved a direct link between Urba and graft activity, but an edict from the office of Mitterrand, himself listed as a recipient, prevented further investigation. In 1990, Mitterrand declared an amnesty for those under investigation, thus ending the affair.

The two police officers were forced into early retirement. (*Source:* Jean Montaldo)

Paris, 1995: François Mitterrand modestly announced during an interview that because of the European Union, he would be the last of the really great French presidents, in the tradition of De Gaulle. Those who followed him, he said, would be accountants and financial managers.

I have heard and understood your call: that the Republic should live, that the nation should reunite, that politics should change.

(President Jacques Chirac, Paris, 2002)

In December 2011, a French court gave former President Jacques Chirac a two-year suspended prison sentence for diverting public funds and abusing public trust.

President from 1995 to 2007, he was put on trial on charges that dated back to his time as mayor of Paris. He was accused of paying members of his Rally for the Republic (RPR) party for municipal jobs that did not exist.

Have French male attitudes to women changed under pressure of new legislation?

In July 2012, the wife of Dominic Strauss-Kahn (known in France as DSK) finally abandoned him after months of loyal support in the face of vice allegations, and the former International Monetary Fund (IMF) president left their Paris home.

Mr Strauss-Kahn's career at the IMF was ruined when, in May 2011, a New York chambermaid accused him of attempted rape. He was cleared but admitted that a sex act had taken place. A female French writer alleged that Mr Strauss-Kahn had tried to rape her in a Paris flat, but a police investigation did not find enough evidence to support the claim, and there were no charges. Then prosecutors opened an investigation into a vice ring based in Lille in northern France in which Mr Strauss-Kahn was implicated. Young prostitutes were said to have travelled to cities including Paris to take part in sex parties with Mr Strauss-Kahn and other men. A prosecutor has also opened an investigation into a claim that Mr Strauss-Kahn was involved in the rape of a Belgian prostitute in a hotel in Washington DC.

Mr Strauss-Kahn says there was 'no brutality' involved in any of the orgies, and that he did not even know the women were vice girls. (*Source: Daily Mail*)

In a September 2012 radio interview, a humble DSK admitted serious moral faults but suggested that he would still be interested in high office, should he be invited.

Paris, June 30, 2012: France elected François Hollande as its first Socialist president since François Mitterrand's retirement in 1995 and gave the Socialist Party and its closest allies a huge majority in parliament.

History repeats itself, first as tragedy, then as farce.

(Karl Marx)

In July 2012, Valerie Trierweiler, the television journalist girlfriend of French President François Hollande, caused outrage when she used her Twitter account to publicly back a political opponent of Ségolène Royal, Mr Hollande's ex-partner and mother of his four children. Ms Royal, fifty-eight, went on to lose her bid to become the deputy for La Rochelle, later blaming the hated Ms Trierweiler for a vicious stab-in-the-back which effectively ended her political career. Mr Hollande later said he would probably find an unelected post for Ms Royal.

In February 2013, Ségolène Royal was appointed Vice President of the newly created Banque Publique d'Investissement (BPS).
The newspaper *Le Canard Enchainé* commented in a cartoon, That will cause trouble with the vice president of the Republic' (Meaning Valerie Trierweiler)
In a further discussion about the appointment, a commentator said, '. . . we must remember that (in BPS) the "P" stands for Public and there is also a "B" as in Brothel, but it may be premature to say that.' (*Source: Le Canard Enchainé*)

In March 2013, Ségolène Royal said publicly, that no woman should depend on her ex to find her a job.

Paris, October 2012: In a radio interview, the French Minister for Women's Rights claimed she had turned her attention to the state of prostitution in France. She explained that for decades, going back over several governments, France has signed up to conventions and agreements to ban prostitution, but hundreds of thousands of young women are pouring into France from Africa, Asia, the Balkans, and Eastern Europe. Very few are legal, and even fewer have actually volunteered to become sex slaves, though that is what they are. They are in the hands of violent pimps and gangs, and the big question, according to Mme Vallaud-Belkacem, is, 'How do we deal with that?' (*Source:* French Minister for Women's Rights, Najat Vallaud-Belkacem)

Is the French justice system more active in its corruption investigations and prosecutions since the Mitterrand and Chirac eras, and is the press more investigative?

In February 2013, it was reported that police from the National Financial Investigation Division raided the offices of a subsidiary of the Bouygues Group involved in tendering for the €35 billion new Ministry of Defence building in Paris. This was the eighth raid carried out on behalf of investigating judges in the last two months of their enquiry triggered by a report that confidential USBs and computer discs containing information about competitive bids had been circulating before the contract was awarded.

According to an inside spokesman, everybody thinks that this affair hides a vast network of corruption in public sector contracting. (*Source: Le Canard Enchainé*)

In December 2012, the French Budget Minister, Jérôme Cahuzac, was accused of having a bank account in Switzerland when he was responsible for waging war on the super-rich and their bank accounts in tax havens. He solemnly swore to the French National Assembly that he had never had such an account and did not have one now.

By March 2013, after he had resigned as Budget Minister in order to clear his name, more damning evidence filtered into the press, and M. Cahuzac's lawyer advised the investigating judge that his client wished to divulge the truth. It seems that M. Cahuzac did have two Swiss bank accounts during the 1990s but had since transferred them to another offshore account in Singapore. The question remained as to where the money came from. One hypothesis is that before becoming the boss of France's fiscal administration, Cahuzac owed his own financial well-being to the generosity of a few Swiss pharmaceutical companies who were paying him as a technical consultant when he was a member of the Cabinet for Social Affairs advising the Health Ministry. M Cahuzac has demanded that he should retain his elected position as a deputy, but whatever the judicial findings, it seems that his political career is over. That is unless the president finds him an unelected post.

> You must not lose faith in humanity. Humanity is an ocean; if a few drops of the ocean are dirty, the ocean does not become dirty.

(Mahatma Ghandi)

The End

ACKNOWLEDGEMENTS

Albert Camus
Ambrose Bierce
Anne-Marie Carrière
Denis Diderot
Der Spiegel
Ernst Fehr
François Mitterrand
Jacques Chirac
Jacques Dutronc
Jean Montaldo
Karl Marx
Le Canard Enchaîné
Mahatma Ghandi
Najat Vallaud-Belkacem
Napoleon Bonaparte
Oliver Goldsmith
Radio France Culture
Sigmund Freud
The Daily Mail
Thomas Jefferson
Transparency International
US Embassy, Port-au-Prince, Haiti
Wikipedia